He stared deep into her eyes as if he was searching for something there.

"You're going all sappy on me again, Nora," he said. "Don't try to fix me. You'd be wasting your time. I gotta go..."

"Asher."

"No, Nora. I have to go."

But he didn't open the door. Instead, he turned toward her. She didn't wait for an invitation, stepping in and leaning against his strong, hard chest. He hesitated, then folded his arms around her, and it felt so...right. She tipped her head back. His gaze fell to her lips and she silently begged him to finish the job this time and kiss her. Her whole body vibrated with the need of it. But he just rested his forehead on hers, shaking it back and forth.

"No, no, no." Was he talking to her or himself? "I am *not* going to kiss the mother of my son's girlfriend, no matter how much I want to."

Dear Reader,

When my husband and I met twenty-some years ago, neither of us had *any* interest in getting involved with someone new, because we were both coming off difficult relationships. But there was simply no denying the chemistry between us. Sometimes we'll say we wish we'd met earlier in our lives, but honestly? We would have been different people then, and we could have easily just passed each other by. We were meant to meet exactly when we did.

I wanted to write a story about how love brings us the people we need when we need them the most, and the result was *Nora's Guy Next Door*. This book is the newest addition to what is now the Lowery Women series, about four smart, sassy women who are cousins as well as best friends. Each has a strong will, a quick wit and a loving heart.

Loving thanks to my husband, friends and family, who encourage me every day. And a special thank-you to my amazing agent, Veronica Park of the Corvisiero Literary Agency.

Wishing you forever love,

Jo McNally

PS: My hero is stuck in the anger phase of grieving for a lost child. If you've suffered the loss of a loved one and feel you might be "stuck," please reach out to someone. Many community centers and houses of worship have grief support groups, or you can find one online. You're not alone.

JO McNALLY

—

Nora's Guy Next Door

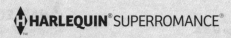
HARLEQUIN®SUPERROMANCE®

Recycling programs
for this product may
not exist in your area.

ISBN-13: 978-0-373-64046-1

Nora's Guy Next Door

Printed in U.S.A.

Jo McNally lives in coastal North Carolina with one hundred pounds of dog and two hundred pounds of husband—her slice of the bed is very small. When she's not writing or reading romance novels (or clinging to the edge of the bed), she can often be found on the back porch sipping wine with friends while listening to great music. If the weather is absolutely perfect, Jo might join her husband on the golf course, where she tends to feel far more competitive than her actual skill level would suggest.

She likes writing stories about strong women and the men who love them. She's a true believer that love can conquer all if given just half a chance.

You can follow Jo pretty much anywhere on social media (and she'd love it if you did!), but you can start at her website, www.jomcnallyromance.com.

Books by Jo McNally

HARLEQUIN SUPERROMANCE

She's Far From Hollywood

Other titles by this author available in ebook format.

It's only fitting that a book about a strong mom should be dedicated to a strong mom. My mom is an independent, jet-setting fashionista who makes ninety look like the new sixty.

To Mom, with love and gratitude.

CHAPTER ONE

NORA LOWERY BRADFORD didn't come close to losing her good Southern manners until the third time someone smacked their grocery cart into hers, nearly toppling a package of fancily frosted cupcakes. She spun on her heel, but the angry words died on her lips. The offender was an elderly lady, even shorter than Nora, pushing a cart loaded to the brim with Thanksgiving fixings.

Bless her heart.

Nora smiled and was about to wish her a happy holiday, but before she could speak, the woman rammed her cart into Nora's again—on purpose!

"What're you doin', sightseeing or something? Move over! Other people got things to do." With that, the woman pushed on by, scraping her cart along Nora's to drive home her point.

Nora stood there for a moment with her mouth open, then rolled her eyes and pushed on. With Thanksgiving just two days away, the grocery store in Gallant Lake, New York, was mobbed with people. And the mob was cranky. Maybe she was biased, but people seemed just a bit more *genteel* back home in Atlanta. Unless, of course, you went grocery shopping on senior discount day—then all bets were off, Southern or not.

The miserable weather wasn't helping anyone's attitude. Three inches of snow were on the ground when she arrived in the Catskills yesterday, and she was not happy about it. Oh, sure, the stuff looked like sugar frosting on the rooftops and tree branches, but the air was cold and raw.

The forecast for the week was snow, rain, wind, more rain, then snow again. Her cousin Amanda assured her that was typical for November, which was little comfort. No wonder people were so grumpy here in the North! She'd tried to convince Amanda and her husband, Blake Randall, to fly south for Thanksgiving with their kids, but they owned a large lakeside resort here and couldn't be gone during a busy tourist weekend. So the family was gathering at their historic castle-turned-home, Halcyon, located right next door to the resort.

Nora unfolded the store flyer she'd picked up at the door, trying to remember where the produce section was. The only good thing about being in Gallant Lake this week was that her favorite person in the whole world, her daughter, Becky, would be arriving later today. Somewhere along the line, Nora had failed as a proper Atlanta mother, because her debutante daughter had inexplicably fallen in love with the Catskills the first time she came here after Amanda and Blake's wedding. It was disappointing, but not surprising, when Becky hopped the first plane out of Georgia when Vassar offered her a scholarship.

The produce section was even more crowded than the aisles, and Nora slowly worked her way through the veggies, taking in the dramas unfolding around her.

A woman threw a round head of pale lettuce into her cart, glaring at the balding man by her side. "Of *course* your mother thinks iceberg lettuce is the best. Your mother wouldn't know a romaine leaf if it bit her in the ass!"

Two men leaned intently over a tomato display nearby. "Derrick, trust me. Vine-ripened tomatoes are better for salad than that monstrosity you picked up." He gave his partner a wink. "I know you love the word *beefsteak*, honey, but bigger isn't always better."

A young woman pushed a cart past Nora with a toddler in the seat and a little boy and girl in tow, all three complaining loudly. The girl stomped her feet.

"I don't *wanna* eat turkey! I wanna eat ice cream!"

"You gotta eat turkey on turkey day, dummy." Her older brother gave her a shove. "And you can't have ice cream. You gotta eat pie!"

The littlest one, sitting in the cart, started to scream, "No pie! No pie, Mommy! No pie!"

The mother's face was pinched and tired. Nora reached out, resting her hand on the woman's arm. "Don't worry, darlin', these days will pass. Enjoy these babies while they're young. Before you know it, they'll be off to college like mine."

She got a tight smile in return. "Right now, it feels like that can't happen soon enough, but thank you."

The family moved on and Nora headed for the fruit. Her empty nest in Atlanta was growing more lonely with every week that passed, and she spent far too much time just rambling around the Ansley Park home. She set a bag of oranges in the cart and tried to shake off her melancholy. No more pity party—she and Becky had big plans for the next few years.

Becky always teased Nora about her penchant for planning and list making, but how else did things get done? Becky wouldn't be laughing once Nora surprised her with the news that they would be spending three weeks in England next summer. Becky had always been a book lover, and finally she would get to visit all the places she'd dreamed of after reading about Narnia and Camelot and Hogwarts.

It hadn't been easy squirreling away that money, and without a careful plan and *lots* of lists, Nora never would have been able to make it happen. But she had enough saved now to give Becky her dream trip. Hopefully it would be the first of many mother-daughter adventures they'd share before Becky settled down and started her own family.

Nora gave the lime in her hand a tight squeeze, trying to quell the whispers of doubt in the back of her mind. She and her daughter hadn't spoken much lately, just a few texts and emails and the very rare call. Becky kept insisting everything was okay—she was just busy with freshman year. Nora dropped the lime into a bag with five others. She couldn't shake the suspicion that her daughter was hiding something from her.

A deep voice started cursing behind her as she reached for a bag of lemons. She glanced over her shoulder and spotted a tall, lean man in jeans and a faded flannel shirt. His gray-blue eyes were frosty with anger, but she couldn't tell where it was directed, since he seemed to be alone.

"Damned idiots. They're nothing but stupid-ass idiots." He roughly tossed a bag of apples into his cart, making it rattle, causing a few heads to turn. "Stupid, stupid, *stupid*…" Another bag of fruit landed in his cart with a bang, and he pushed it closer to hers.

She couldn't see a Bluetooth device in his ear, so he seemed to be having this conversation with himself. Flat out *raging* at himself, from the sounds of it. His face was sharp and angled, but the dark stubble along his jaw softened those lines just enough to make him strikingly attractive in a rough-hewn way. Layers of dark brown hair brushed his shoulders, and he reminded her of an aging rock star getting ready to smash a guitar somewhere.

Nora gave herself a mental shake. She hadn't looked twice at anyone since Paul's death, much less ogled someone in a small-town grocery store. And this bad-tempered stranger was very much *not* her type. But still, she couldn't take her eyes off Hot Produce Guy.

"Can't believe this stupid bullshit!" He reached for a pint of blueberries, and Nora knew the loose netting over the top of the box wouldn't be enough to hold them if they were handled roughly. Blueberries were going to fly everywhere if he…

The box hit the bottom of his cart and big, fat berries exploded up out of it, rolling in a hundred directions across the tile floor. People started shouting and dancing around. The little girl who'd been screaming for ice cream a few minutes ago was now gleefully jumping up and down, popping blueberries with her feet like she was making wine. A grumbling murmur rolled through the produce section as people tried to figure out where the berries were coming from.

Hot Produce Guy, oblivious to the chaos he'd created, was clearly having a very bad day, and Nora quickly devised a plan to help him. After all, she was a planner. That was what she did. She tossed her store flyer into his cart, covering the incriminating half-empty container. He looked up sharply, but she lifted a finger to her lips before he spoke. He followed her eyes toward the angry mob looking for a culprit and winced when the little girl leaped on a fat rolling berry.

Nora gave him a wink and gestured with her head. He followed her without a word. They didn't stop their carts until they were safely in the bakery section. When he turned to face her, she had to tip her head back to meet his eyes, but she was used to that. Some days it seemed everyone on the planet was taller than she was.

"So what was the problem with the angry holiday zombies back there?"

That voice. Gravelly, deep and seriously sexy. Forget his looks, it had been that rough voice spitting out swear words a minute ago that made her breath hitch. *That* was why she'd rescued him. She shook off her rare case of insta-lust and did her best to look unaffected.

"Someone's blueberries were causing pandemonium. And you seemed to be having a bad enough day without facing a zombie attack right before Thanksgiving."

His face reddened. "Calling this a bad day is an understatement."

"The holidays can be tough. Is there anything I can help with?"

He looked at her in surprise, then shook his head. "My son just told me…" He rubbed the back of his neck. "He did something so stupid I can't even think straight." He looked up at the ceiling and heaved a sigh, blinking a few times before looking back at her. His blue eyes softened for a moment so brief she thought she might have imagined it.

"How old is your son?"

"Old enough to know better."

"I have a teenage daughter, so I can relate. Sometimes we just have to let them learn from their own mistakes. Even when it drives us crazy."

She thought about how furious she'd been when Becky came home a year ago with that dreadful tattoo on her forearm after spending the summer in Gallant Lake. Nora had nearly had a stroke right there in the airport. It was just a tiny heart-shaped padlock, but still. A tattoo! On her daughter's perfect alabaster skin! What would people think if they saw it? What if it affected her career? And why a padlock of all things?

"Yeah, well, that sentiment might look nice on a greeting card, but here in the real world that's not how it works." The vulnerability was definitely gone from his eyes now. He was angry. With her. "It's my job to make sure my kids are…" He stuttered and took a breath. "I mean, my *kid*. I have to make him understand what needs to be done. Whether he likes it or not."

He gripped the cart so tightly his knuckles were white. Nora prided herself on being able to solve problems, but she was out of her depth dealing with rage this intense. It was time to extricate herself from this conversation with a complete stranger.

"Well…I…I should be going." She couldn't help making one last attempt to cheer him up. Becky always called her Little Suzy Sunshine. Nora was never sure if it was a compliment or not. "You know, someday you and your son will look back at this and laugh." He started to disagree, but she held up her hand. "Our children will always be our children, no matter how old they get."

"Really? More greeting-card platitudes? I hope you didn't raise your daughter to believe all that 'the sun will come out tomorrow' nonsense. News flash—some children *aren't* always our children. Sometimes they…" His mouth was set in a hard line. "Never mind. I don't know why I'm still standing here talking to you."

People didn't usually get under her skin so easily, but this guy had Nora's temper up in mere minutes. "I'm pretty sure you were going to thank me for helping you."

He stared at her long enough to make her skin warm.

"I know your type. You're a fixer. You could have minded your own business and everything would have been just fine. But you're one of those that can't help butting in. Well, now you can butt *out*. I sure as hell don't need your sugar-coated advice today."

He gave his cart a hard shove, sending more blueberries bouncing out of the container in his wake. Nora's hand fluttered up to rest over her heart as he left. She tried never to curse, even to herself, but there was no other way to say it— Hot Produce Guy was an asshole. She glanced around in guilt, as if someone might have heard her unkind thoughts. Then she regrouped. Becky would be in Gallant Lake tonight. And they were going to have another talk about removing that horrid tattoo.

THREE HOURS LATER, Nora was stomping down the sidewalks of Gallant Lake. Alone. While she'd been shopping and dealing with Grumpy Hot Produce Guy, plans had changed. Becky wouldn't be arriving until Thanksgiving Day now, instead of tonight. And she'd informed Nora by *text*. This day was not going at all the way she'd planned it.

Amanda finally chased her out of the house. "Your pacing and muttering is driving me crazy, Nora. Take my car and go into the village so you can do your pacing where I can't see you. Have you ever been to Caffeine Cathy's Coffee Café? Go check it out and keep yourself busy."

Nora came to a halt in front of the ugliest building in the village. Painted in garish orange, pink and blue, Caffeine Cathy's was a sharp contrast to the more conservatively decorated shops along Main Street. The harsh colors were out of place in postcard-pretty Gallant Lake. As if confirming her thoughts, she noticed a large For Sale by Owner sign in the window. The café might be ugly, but the aroma was heavenly, and there seemed to be steady traffic in and out the door.

The interior of the coffee shop was just as eclectic as the exterior. Wide, unfinished planks covered the floor, and the walls were original red brick, covered with artwork for sale. Mismatched tables and chairs, painted in a kaleidoscope of colors, were scattered around the long, narrow space. The counter was across the back, and Nora joined the line of customers.

One painting caught her eye as she waited. It was a beautiful image of a tall galleon sailing calm waters at night, with stars twinkling above. But the ship was heading straight for a high waterfall that led to a waiting sea monster wrapped in flames. Disaster loomed, and no one on that ship had a clue. What an odd thing to paint. Why didn't the ship have a lookout? How could the serene sea be leading to such a violent end? She turned away, feeling uncomfortable and knowing that was probably exactly what the artist intended.

"Come on, Helen, this place is a joke." An older couple was standing behind her. The man ignored his wife's shushing, and if anything, he got even louder. His accent said New Jersey. "We could have gone to Ma's for Thanksgiving, but no, you insisted we come to this godforsaken place in the boondocks. And they call this a coffee shop? I'd give my left arm for a Dunkin' right now."

"Herbie, be quiet!" Helen, wrapped in an aging fur coat that had seen better days, smacked her husband's ribs hard enough to make Nora wince. "The grandkids woulda' been bored outta' their minds at your mother's. The resort has an indoor pool, and the ski slopes at Hunter are open this weekend, which is the only reason Joey and Mary agreed to come here with their families. So shut up and enjoy yourself."

Trying to save poor Herbie from any more spousal abuse, Nora chimed in. "You're staying at the Gallant Lake Resort? I know the owners, and I'm sure you'll have a wonderful weekend there with your family. But if you get restless,

there's a casino a little over an hour from here."
That news made Herbie smile, but not Helen.

"Don't you even *think* about going to a casino,
Herbert Comisky!" The large woman rounded on
Nora. "Thanks a lot. Now we'll be fighting over
that damn casino business all weekend long."

Nora stepped back, mumbling an apology. She
was definitely losing her Suzy Sunshine mojo.
What else could go wrong today?

"Hiya, honey, what can I get you?" Nora looked
at the tall, willowy woman behind the chipped
and coffee-stained counter. Her salt-and-pepper
hair was pulled back into a thick braid that hung
down her back, and she was wearing a shapeless
tie-dyed dress that swept the floor. Literally. The
hem was filthy from where it had removed dust
and dirt from the old boards. But her dark brown
eyes were kind and friendly, and Nora returned
her smile, trying not to stare at the woman's yel-
lowing teeth.

"I'll have a cappuccino with a shot of hazel-
nut, please." She looked at the dusty glass case
sitting on top of the counter. "And I'll take that
last scone, too."

"You got it, honey. Give me just a minute."

Herbie spoke up again behind Nora. "Gawd,
give me strength. That must be Caffeine Cathy
herself. Did you see those teeth? She either drinks
fifty cups of coffee a day or smokes five packs

of cigarettes. And that outfit. She's a freakin' hippy…"

Nora moved toward the register, determined not to let poor Cathy think she was with the obnoxious couple. A large poster was framed prominently on the wall behind the register.

Life is about the journey, not the destination.

Two thoughts ran through her mind at the same time. One was that it was the most ridiculous thing she'd ever heard. What was the point of a journey without a destination in mind? And the second thought was that this was exactly the kind of "greeting-card sentiment" Hot Produce Guy had accused her of that morning. She rolled her eyes at the memory, then saw Cathy dropping her scone on the floor. The woman shrugged when their eyes met, then she laughed as she quickly retrieved the scone and dropped it into a bag.

"Three-second rule, right? That'll be four-fifty."

The amount of grime on these floors wouldn't qualify for a *one*-second rule, much less three. Nora opened her mouth to protest and heard Herbie snickering behind her. It wasn't worth making a scene over, especially with those two as an audience. She'd just toss the scone and get back to Amanda's before anything else could go wrong. She set a five-dollar bill on the counter. Apparently Herbie didn't think she was moving fast enough, and he gave her arm a nudge. It was the arm that held the coffee she was raising to her lips. The coffee that didn't have a tight lid. The lid that splattered coffee down the front of Nora's light pink jacket.

"You should be more careful, dear." Helen was biting back laughter, and it took all of Nora's strength to head to the door without responding. Random swear words were threatening to break free in her head, but she shoved them back in the corner where they belonged. Get back to Halcyon and hide for the rest of the day. That was the only plan that made sense at this point. Until she stepped outside.

Never a champion at parallel parking, she knew she'd been lucky to find a double spot open near the shop that she could drive straight into. Except it wasn't a double spot anymore. There was a truck parked behind the car and an enormous Cadillac sedan wedged into the space in front of it, leaving her about five inches to maneuver onto the street. Perfect.

She did her best, going back and forth, back and forth, back and forth between the Cadillac, the truck and the sidewalk. Finally those curse words broke free in her head, and she was mentally pulling a Hot Produce Guy routine, silently swearing up a blue streak. But she carefully kept the words to herself, even when her bumper nudged the Caddy just enough to set off the blaring car alarm.

And who came running out of Caffeine Cathy's? None other than Herbie and Helen, both yelling and waving their arms. She dropped her forehead to the steering wheel, closed her eyes tightly and tried to summon all of her Southern breeding. She always said there wasn't a problem that couldn't be solved with a smile and a plan.

She just happened to be running low on both at the moment.

CHAPTER TWO

ASHER PEYTON WAS lost in the process of staining the cherry sideboard in the work area of his shop, rubbing the finish to a satin sheen. Back and forth he went with the ball of cheesecloth, working in long strokes with firm pressure. It was a task that took a lot of time and very little thought. Clapton's bluesy guitar was coming through the speakers mounted on the wall, and Asher was totally in The Zone, focused only on the fine grain of the wood coming to life under his fingers. Until a car alarm went off outside.

At first he figured someone set off their alarm by mistake, but when it kept going, he tossed the finishing cloth onto the workbench in disgust and grabbed his lukewarm cup of coffee. He walked to the plate glass window at the front of his shop to see what was going on.

There was a tiny red Mini Cooper nudged up against a big Cadillac right in front of his shop. Whoever owned the Caddy had to know they'd blocked that little car in completely, since their car was halfway into the street. An older couple came running out of Cathy's shop, waving their arms all over the place like idiots.

Asher took a sip of coffee and watched in amusement as it took three tries for the guy to silence the alarm with his key fob. From all the yelling, you'd think the red car just totaled their gas hog instead of barely bumping it. The door of the red car opened slowly, and he caught a glimpse of pink.

Of all the rotten luck. It was that nosy little brunette from the grocery store. The one with the sweet accent and the compulsion to save people. The Fixer.

She got out of the car and faced Mr. and Mrs. Cadillac with a tight smile. Her chin-length hair was tucked behind her ears, revealing bright spots of rosy red high on her cheeks. A small crowd was gathering—the joy of small-town life. Asher drained his coffee. The Fixer was having one hell of a day. First he'd barked at her in the store, and now this. He started to turn away. Her little parking drama was none of his business, and he had work to do. Then he heard Cadillac Man yelling.

"Did you not see my car sitting right there? That must be a dye job on your hair, 'cuz you'd have to be a blonde to be this stupid…"

His wife tugged at his coat sleeve, cell phone in hand. "Should I call the cops, Herbie?"

Oh, hell, the last thing Deputy Sheriff Dan

Adams needed was to get called to Main Street to deal with this nonsense. Before he could stop himself, Asher was outside. He glanced at the bumpers to confirm there wasn't so much as a scratch on either car. The Fixer had rocked the Caddy just enough to set off the alarm, but not enough to do any damage.

"Okay, folks, let's all calm down, okay?" He stepped forward and faced the older man, forcing him to look up to meet Asher's eyes. The considerable difference in their size and age wasn't lost on the guy. Good. "Sir, there's no harm done to your car. Your parking job didn't leave the lady much room to maneuver. Why don't you just pull out, and then she'll be able to leave, too?" And Asher could get back inside his quiet shop, away from all these curious faces.

The Fixer was handing her insurance card to the fur-clad wife while babbling at the speed of light.

"I'm terribly sorry, but really, there appears to be no damage, except to my pride, of course." She forced a laugh, but it fell flat. "Feel free to write down my insurance information, though I'm sure you won't need…"

The old guy snatched the card from her hand before she could finish, and Asher's fingers curled into a fist. He didn't have a lot of patience on a good day, and today was not a good day. He thought about Sheriff Dan and forced himself to relax again as Cadillac Man spoke.

"Your name's Randall?"

"What? Oh, no. The car belongs to my cousin Amanda Randall."

"So you don't even *own* this car? Maybe we *should* call the cops."

She put on a bright, tight smile. "I really don't think that's necessary…"

Asher sighed. Miss Fixer was connected to the resort, which meant this jerk was wasting his time trying to cause trouble. He pulled the guy aside as if he was doing him a favor, going so far as to drape his arm casually across the man's shoulders before digging in firmly with his fingers.

"Here's the deal. The Randalls own the Gallant Lake Resort. They also own half the waterfront. You're not winning this one, pal. Just drive away and let it go, okay?" The words were spoken calmly and quietly. It was a technique he'd seen Dan use many times on hotheads, including during their first meeting, when he'd used it on Asher. To the casual observer, everything looked friendly, but Cadillac Man flinched under the pressure of Asher's grip.

The man nodded and shrugged away from him. "Get in the car, Helen. Maybe if we move, she'll be able to figure out how to drive." Helen harrumphed but obeyed, slamming the passenger door shut. The big car pulled away. People were dispersing when he looked to the Fixer. Why hadn't he noticed how unusual her golden-brown eyes were before now?

"I had that handled, you know."

Okay. That wasn't exactly the thanks he'd expected.

"You could have handled two people screaming in your face and calling the cops about driving a car you don't own? Yeah, I could tell. Great job."

She squared her shoulders, tipping her chin up. "I had it *handled*. I was being nice, I was cooperating and I was working on getting them to like me. I didn't need you to swoop in and save me."

"The only thing you were handling was getting the sheriff's office called. And the sheriff's deputy would have called Blake Randall, and Randall would have rushed down to resolve your little mess. With an audience. In the middle of town. Was that the plan you had in mind?"

The red dots on her cheeks got brighter.

They glared at each other for a heartbeat before something in her seemed to snap. "You know what? I tried to be nice to you in the store, and instead of thanking me, you insulted me and questioned my parenting skills. And now you show up here… Where did you swoop in from, anyway?"

The corner of his mouth twitched. Every time

she said that word—*swoop*—her mouth formed a perfect little kiss. Her eyes narrowed and he noticed the hazel sparks for the first time. She had the eyes of a cat, and she was ready to hiss and spit at him.

"You didn't need my help this morning, and I certainly didn't need yours now. I had it handled. I've got this whole damned day *handled*." Her hands gestured wildly. He had a feeling she didn't get worked up like this often. "Now crawl back to whatever cave you live in and let me get on with my perfectly handled afternoon."

Sarcasm dripped from her words, and he realized he was smirking at her. A smirk was just one step away from a smile, which meant he was in dangerous territory. But who would have guessed the sweet, Southern Fixer had a backbone?

He reached up to touch the imaginary brim of the hat he wasn't wearing and backed away, giving his best Clark Gable impression. "Whatever you say, ma'am. Because frankly, my dear, I don't give a damn about your day."

He turned away, pretty sure he heard her call him an "arrogant jackass" as he walked off. He was glad she couldn't see the rare smile that brought to his face.

THE FOLLOWING NIGHT, a smile wasn't even a glimmer of a possibility for Asher. He stared at his son in disbelief.

"*Marry* her? Are you out of your freakin' mind?"

He'd known for a few days that Michael had gotten some girl pregnant, and that was bad enough. But *marriage*? Michael had been dating this girl, whom he'd met snowboarding, but he'd never brought her by. And now that Asher knew she'd just turned eighteen in April, he understood why.

He turned to face Michael and wondered for the hundredth time when his son had become this tall, bearded adult. Wasn't it just yesterday Asher had been watching him play in the yard? The memory of two laughing little boys caused its usual slicing pain, and he clenched his jaw tightly to maintain some semblance of control.

"You are *not* going to marry this girl."

Michael leaned back against the unfinished sideboard and shook his head with a pitying smile.

"Oh, I'm definitely marrying this girl, Dad. And you are *definitely* going to become a grandfather in six months. Nothing's changing those two facts. You just need to decide how much of an ass you're going to be about it. Or not."

Michael's eyes were calm and steady, but Asher could see the tightness in his son's shoulders and the pulse pounding rapidly on the side of his neck. His own stance probably reflected the same. The tension had been part of every conversation they'd had over the past few years. But there was a difference today. There was something in Michael's eyes that exuded a confidence he hadn't shown since his brother's death.

Too bad Asher would have to squash it.

"Oh, trust me, boy, I'm going to be a major ass about this. This wedding is *not* happening. You got some girl pregnant—that's on you. If she insists on having it, you'll have to support it, which I'm sure was her plan all along. But she is *not* marrying you." Asher turned away, staring through the window of his furniture shop to the dark and silent street outside. "You need to finish your degree and start the career you planned." He looked back and narrowed his eyes. "Have you even *told* your mother about this? Does your grandfather know?"

Michael rolled his eyes. It was something he'd done since he was a kid. His baby brother always made fun of it, telling Michael he rolled his eyes so much that one day they'd just roll right out of his head. Asher's teeth gnashed together again, this time sharply enough to make his jaw ache. His eyes landed on the bottle of bourbon on the workbench, and he headed for a shot of painkiller.

"I called Mom this morning. She said she's too young to have grandchildren." Michael's foot kicked softly at a pile of wood shavings on the floor. "She said Grandfather would pay for 'any-

thing necessary' to make this 'problem' go away."
His fingers made sharp air quotes. "But here's the
thing none of you get." Michael stood straight,
and Asher had to look up just a bit to meet his
son's eyes. It was another unsettling reminder that
his son was a man now. "This isn't a problem to
be solved. I *love* Becky. She's *it* for me."

Asher scrubbed his hand over his face, then
took a drink, letting the familiar burn steady him.
"I thought marriage was out of style these days—
why the big hurry to tie yourself to this girl in
some ceremony?" He drained the glass and re-
filled it.

"What can I say, Dad? I'm in love with an old-
fashioned girl."

Asher snorted. "An old-fashioned girl wouldn't
be pregnant at eighteen. But a clever one would.
Can't you see she's just using it to get her hooks
into…"

"Careful, Dad." Michael's expression hardened. "This baby is not an 'it' or a 'problem' or
a scam or anything else but a child. *My* child."

Michael, more than anyone, had to know the
thought of a child was no comfort to Asher.

"What does *her* family think of this mess?"

"You'll find out this weekend. Her mom is in
town, and Becky wants to set up a meet-the-parents
brunch after I get back from spending turkey day

with Mom in LA. I'll meet her mother and you get to meet Becky."

"Where's her father in all this?"

"Killed in a plane crash. The year before Dylan died."

The furniture shop was usually Asher's sanctuary from his youngest son's ghost, but Dylan's memory was so sharp in here tonight he could almost feel it brushing against his skin. He turned away to hide his grimace, taking another drink.

How could he explain to Michael that parenthood simply wasn't worth it? How could he explain that putting all your hopes and dreams onto a child meant the risk of *losing* all those hopes and dreams? What was it the golden-eyed brunette had said in the grocery store that morning? *Our children will always be our children...* She was wrong. Children *weren't* always your children. Sometimes children died. He took one more gulp of liquor to bolster his resolve.

"Count me out."

"Dad..."

"No." His voice hardened, and the walls went up around him so solidly he could almost see the bricks stacking. "I won't be a part of it. You're too young, and she's *definitely* too young. You're being reckless with your life and with hers."

"That's rich coming from someone who had me at twenty-one."

"But your mother was twenty-*three*, not a freakin' teenager. And we didn't get married for another two years, after I was out of college and had a job."

Asher could see his younger self standing in the hospital, holding another baby boy in his arms, dreaming all those golden dreams for the boy's future. Twelve years later he was back in that same hospital, holding his son's lifeless body, cursing the universe and everyone in it. He drew in a deep breath and forced the words out.

"And look at me now, Michael. The marriage is over and your brother is gone. *Gone.* Are you ready for that to happen to *your* baby? Because I don't think you are."

Michael's face paled and his lips pressed thinly together for a moment. He stared long and hard at the glass in Asher's hand, as if trying to convince himself it was just the booze talking. His son had no idea how deep Asher's fears ran—right to the marrow of his soul.

Michael ended the conversation by walking away, looking over his shoulder at Asher when he reached the door. "I'll text you the time for the brunch. If you don't care about meeting Becky, at least show up for me. I don't imagine her mom will be too crazy about me considering the circumstances. But I guess you aren't, either."

"Michael…" A shot of regret hit Asher's heart,

but his son was gone, the door closing softly behind him. The tinkling of the bell over the door,
there to alert him to customers during the day,
seemed cruel and mocking in the middle of the
night. He turned the lock, then leaned against
the door.

For some reason, the Fixer was in his head
again, suggesting he and Michael would look
back on this time and laugh. He'd liked the ca-
dence of her soft Southern accent and the glimpse
of fire she'd shown out in front of his shop, but
she couldn't be more wrong.

This mess would never be a laughing matter.

CHAPTER THREE

"I'M SORRY...YOU'RE *WHAT*?"

Nora brought a shaking hand to her forehead, wondering if she was losing her mind. She had to be hearing things. Or hallucinating. That was it—she was hallucinating. Maybe she'd bought the wrong kind of mushrooms at the store the other day. Hot Produce Guy had distracted her, and she'd bought hallucinogenic mushrooms. That would explain why she'd just imagined her daughter saying something that couldn't possibly be true.

The Thanksgiving table was eerily silent. Amanda held her wineglass suspended in midair, not quite reaching her lips. Blake's mouth kept opening and closing, with no sound coming out. Their twelve-year-old son, Zachary, muttered a quiet "Uh-oh." But it was the youngest child, Maddie, who broke through the quiet, clapping her hands together.

"Annie Becca have *baby*!" Unable to pronounce *T*s yet, all of Maddie's aunties were *annies* at this point.

Becky sat directly across from Nora, eyes wide but steady. The only hint of emotion was the rapid tapping of her fingers on the edge of the table, like she was playing an invisible piano. Her light brown hair was pulled up into a high ponytail tied with a ribbon, making her look even younger than her eighteen years.

Eighteen!

"I'm sorry, Mama." Becky's hands fell to her lap. "I didn't mean to blurt it out over dinner like that, but you kept insisting it was okay to drink wine with dinner and I can't, and I had to tell you anyway, so it just came out. I'm sorry."

Nora shook her head. The news simply wasn't computing. Amanda reached for her, but Nora jerked away. If anyone touched her right now, she'd shatter. Her eyes narrowed as she looked at her *pregnant* teenage daughter.

"Rebecca Scarlett Bradford, did you just apologize for the bad *timing* of the announcement? Yet you're not apologizing for being *pregnant*? At *eighteen*?" Every word grew louder and louder, which was a new experience for Nora. She prided herself on maintaining her composure at all times.

Her late husband's shenanigans had tested that composure on a regular basis, but she'd rarely cracked. She rose to her feet in a flash of hot temper. She was definitely cracking now. In fact, she felt like she was about to burst into a thousand shards of fury.

"How could you be so careless? So stupid? Your life is just beginning, and now you're telling me you're *pregnant*? My God, Becky, I raised you to be smarter than that!" Her pulse was pounding in her ears. Rage? Panic? Was there a difference? "You have a scholarship at Vassar, for God's sake! And you're throwing it all away because you couldn't keep your legs…"

"Nora!" Amanda's voice was sharp. Her two children were at the table. Nora's face burned. All she could do was glare at her daughter and wonder what the hell they were going to do. How was she going to fix *this*?

Blake cleared his throat as awkward silence returned. Nora was still standing, leaning over the table as if she wanted to leap across it and pummel her daughter. And, right now, the idea had a shocking amount of appeal.

"I think it's safe to say dinner is officially over." Blake gave his wife a pointed look. "Let's take a little break before dessert, okay? The kids and I will go down to the resort, and you ladies can talk." It was obvious he intended for Amanda to be the referee. Amanda. Her cousin who'd spent more time with Becky than *she* had over the past few months. Nora looked down, her own voice sounding like cracking ice.

"Did you know about this?"

Her cousin threw her hands up in defense. "No! I knew she had a boyfriend, but…"

A heart attack. That was what this was. Nora was having a heart attack and this was all a crazy dream. They'd take her to the hospital, and when she woke up, no one would be pregnant. No one would have a boyfriend they hadn't mentioned to their mother. Because Becky told her mother *everything*.

"You told *Amanda* about having a boyfriend and not me?"

Becky shifted in her chair, then raised her chin defiantly. "If you knew I was seeing someone here, there's no way you would've let me come to Gallant Lake so often…"

"He's *here*? In Gallant Lake? How long has this…"

"Two years."

Amanda sucked in a sharp breath, which somehow made Nora feel better. At least her cousin didn't know *everything*. Nora knew Becky had made friends here, of course. She visited often, and they all went snowboarding and rock climbing together. Even when she was home in Atlanta, Becky was always texting or video chatting with someone in Gallant Lake. It just hadn't occurred to Nora that there was a boyfriend in the picture. She was such an idiot.

Two years. Becky would have been sixteen. Nora settled down into her seat like a balloon slowly losing air. Sixteen. Someone had taken advantage of her innocent child and now she was pregnant. Okay. They could fix this. First, Nora would make sure this monster was prosecuted for…something. Anything. A stranger had come into her happy family and tried to destroy it, but Nora wouldn't allow that to happen.

"How old was this…this man?"

"When we met? Eighteen."

There was an odd bit of relief in that. At least it wasn't some forty-year-old cyber-stalker who'd victimized her daughter. It was a horny teenage boy. Who, at eighteen, had still been old enough to know better and could still be held responsible.

"So this young man pressured you into having unprotected s…"

"Blake is right," Amanda interrupted, standing quickly and reminding Nora once again there were children present at this train wreck of a holiday meal. "He and Zach can clear the table and go for a walk with Maddie. The three of us can take a minute to collect our thoughts, then we'll sit in the solarium and figure this out over tea."

Everyone stood, and Nora stared at her daughter, trying to understand how this had happened. Becky was an intelligent young woman with big plans. She was going to work to protect the environment and make a difference in the world. Was that a baby bump? How far along was she? Was it too late for options? Would Nora support that choice if Becky made it? Her pulse amped up another notch.

"There's nothing to figure out, Amanda." Becky looked at Nora for a long moment, then her hand moved across her belly. "I know you're disappointed, Mom. This wasn't part of your precious plans. Michael and I didn't plan it, either, but we're happy to be having a baby together. We love each other, and Michael asked me to marry him. I said yes."

As *that* bombshell sent shock waves through the room so forceful that Nora physically felt their impact, her daughter walked away from the table.

NORA GLARED SO hard at the back of the bearded man holding her daughter's hand that she was surprised she didn't bore a hole right between his shoulders. His sweater sleeves were pushed up to expose a small tattoo of a key on his right forearm. It now rested right next to the padlock on Becky's arm as they walked down the sidewalk in Gallant Lake.

Well. That explained that.

She wanted to hate this horrible young man who'd gotten her daughter pregnant and ruined all the plans Nora had for Becky's future. This…

this…*Michael* person had made a mess of everything. She narrowed her eyes on the back of his head.

He nudged against her daughter's shoulder in what appeared to be some affectionate ritual between them, and Becky nudged back without looking at him. Nora wanted to hate him. But she couldn't.

Michael Peyton had been mature and charming over brunch. He clearly worshipped the ground Becky walked on and was constantly attentive to her every need. They seemed to be truly in love with each other. Of course, it was *young* love, and who knew if it would last, but still, it seemed real for the moment. It was honestly the kind of love she'd dreamed Becky would find, but she'd wanted her to find it ten years from now. Without being pregnant. Her eyes narrowed again.

While Nora had been making plans to take a tour of England with her daughter, Becky had been making plans of her own. She was at the end of her first trimester, and she'd already made arrangements to leave Vassar. Michael was transferring to the law program at Albany, which was closer to Gallant Lake than Columbia was. Becky said she was looking at "other options" for school, but she vowed the baby wouldn't stop her from getting her political science degree. Michael was already renting a two-bedroom bungalow in Gallant Lake, and they wanted to stay in this town, where they'd met and where they had friends.

There were some major gaps in their plan, such as the loss of scholarships and a source of steady income, but Nora had to admit they were approaching this in a fairly mature manner, so far. Nora had told Becky yesterday she could move north to help, but her daughter was adamant about not needing Nora there. She was just like her father that way—always so sure everything would turn out rosy. So quick to dismiss Nora's concerns. When she tried to point out that having a baby was hard work and they would need help, Becky just laughed.

"It's time to start living your own life, Mom, and stop running mine."

Her daughter didn't want her here. And that hurt.

Michael glanced over his shoulder at Nora, his blue eyes clouded with worry.

"Mrs. B., are you sure you want to do this?" It took her a moment to realize what he was referring to. "I have no idea how Dad will react to us just showing up..."

Nora smiled before she could catch herself. Darn it all, she kept forgetting she wanted to hate this kid! His mom lived in LA, but his father lived right here in town. The man hadn't bothered showing up for brunch, leaving Michael so embarrassed she couldn't help but feel sorry for him.

"Of course I'm sure, Michael. In the South, there isn't a problem in the world that can't be fixed over blueberry cobbler and strong coffee."

Becky turned with a laugh. "Don't you mean a smile and a plan, Mom? Isn't that how you solve everything?"

Nora nodded. "The *plan* is to make him *smile* over cobbler, then we'll get him talking and win him over."

Becky pulled up short, forcing Michael to stop with her. Nora bobbled the white box of cobbler in her arms to keep it upright. "Mom, what exactly are you winning him over to? Are you saying you're on our side now?"

The smell of freshly ground coffee was a welcome distraction from answering that heavily loaded question. They were standing in front of Caffeine Cathy's Coffee Café. The place didn't exactly hold happy memories for her—she still hadn't managed to get the coffee stain out of her jacket. But maybe they should pick up coffee here instead of expecting Michael's father to provide it unannounced.

"Mom?"

Nora looked back to her daughter—her pregnant daughter with a plan—and the tall man at her side, arm now draped affectionately over her shoulders. The young man who loved her daughter. The father of her daughter's child. There was a tightness in her chest that was something other than pain. It was a flood of emotion so strong she almost couldn't breathe.

"Rebecca," she said, ignoring the wince on her daughter's face at the use of her full name, "there are no *sides* here. There's just a baby. And two very young people who are obviously going to love that baby. I'm not a fan of you getting married…" She shook her head when Becky started to protest. "I *really* want you to wait before having a wedding. Your plans sound very nice and tidy, but life isn't tidy. And you're going to need family. For you, that's me. For Michael, that's his mom and dad. So let's bring his dad some cobbler and coffee—" she tipped her head toward the coffee shop with a smile "—and see if we can help him accept his impending grand-fatherhood."

Michael placed a soft kiss on the top of Becky's head, and Nora blinked, then stared out at the blue lake across the road, surrounded by russet-colored mountains. She took a deep breath, closing her eyes, and felt her daughter's arms surround her.

"Thanks, Mom. I didn't expect you to be so… cool about this."

Nora laughed. "I wouldn't go so far as saying I'm *cool* with it, but you're *my* baby and I love you." Michael headed into the coffee shop. Nora looked at the For Sale sign in the window and winked at Becky to lighten the moment.

"I could always buy a coffee shop in Gallant Lake so I could be closer to you."

Becky started to laugh. "Oh, God, Mom, that would be a *disaster*! You don't know anything about business, much less running the world's ugliest coffee shop. Besides, I already told you it's time to live your own life. I don't need you running mine anymore."

Nora couldn't decide which emotion to go with. Pain that her daughter thought she was incapable of running a business or panic at the realization that she had no idea what living her own life might look like. She pulled her jacket more tightly around her as a cold breeze blew off the lake. She lifted her chin and gave Becky a bright smile to hide her roiling emotions.

"Maybe I've always wanted to run a place like this. Well, not looking like *this*, but an artsy little coffeehouse…"

"You've always wanted to own a coffee shop? For real?"

Nora had never in her life thought about *owning* a coffee shop. But she did enjoy sitting with a good book in the one near Peachtree Mall.

"Whatever, Mom." Becky took the box of cobbler from Nora's arms. "Buy a coffee shop somewhere. Toss away that stupid planner of yours and start living."

Michael returned with coffee, and they headed next door to the plain brick building with a carved sign reading Peyton Custom Woodworking. A beautiful arts and crafts chair and side table sat in the window. On the table were two dark bowls made of polished burled wood. If Michael's father had built this, then the man truly was an artist. A bell jingled above the door when they walked in.

Furniture and carved pieces were displayed in the front of the shop, creating a showroom of sorts, anchored by a large oriental rug. In back was a work area. Workbenches full of tiny drawers lined the walls, and in the center sat a half-finished cherry sideboard and an oak dining table with a pile of steel wool sitting in the middle of it. The whole place smelled of sawdust and varnish. Guitar music was coming out of speakers on the wall, bluesy and mellow.

The masculine presence in the room was so strong she could breathe it in and taste it. This was a man's space, through and through. Exposed brick walls, light bulbs hanging from the ceiling with round metal shades above them. It was orderly, but raw somehow. As raw as the board lumber stacked high against the back wall.

She ran her hand across the silky-smooth top of the sideboard and heard footsteps approaching. A side door opened and a man walked in, wiping his hands on a rag. When he looked up, she took in a sharp breath and stepped back. It was Hot Produce Guy. The man who'd been so rude in the grocery store. The man she'd yelled at on the sidewalk…she cringed inwardly…the sidewalk right outside his business.

He froze, still holding the rag, but not moving a muscle. His icy blue eyes looked first to Michael, who was setting the coffee and pastries on a workbench, and he frowned. His frown deepened when he saw Becky nervously twisting her fingers together in front of her stomach. Then he turned to Nora and the frown faded into confusion.

"What are *you* doing here, Miss Fixer?"

The name hung in the air for a moment before Becky found her voice.

"Wait—you two *know* each other? How the hell does he know you, Mom?"

"Mom?" He set the rag down, shook his head and gave a humorless laugh. "Of course. You're the mom of the little mom-to-be." He took a long look at Becky, and there wasn't an ounce of warmth in his gaze. He turned back to Nora. "So, was our chance meeting in the store Tuesday just as orchestrated as the rest of this farce? And I suppose you just happened to be parked right in front of my shop that afternoon?"

"I didn't orchestrate anything." His brow rose in obvious skepticism, and she bristled. "Listen, I'm just as surprised as you. It looks like we're going to have to get to know each other, whether we want to or not." She held out her hand, but he didn't take it. She remembered his rage in the grocery store over his son doing something stupid, and understood it a lot better now. "The circumstances may not be the best, but we can still make the best of them…" Becky groaned behind her and Michael's father shook his head in amusement. Or perhaps derision.

"There you go with the greeting-card platitudes again. Do you work for Hallmark or something?"

Becky snorted at that and Nora glared at her. Why didn't people understand she was trying to bring everyone onto the same page here?

Michael stepped into the silence that followed. "Dad, this is Nora Bradford, and yes, she's Becky's mom. She lives in Atlanta but came here for the holiday. She's related to…"

"The Randalls. Yeah, she made sure to mention that the other day."

Nora took a sharp breath, but Michael kept talking.

"Nora, this is my father, Asher Peyton. This is his furniture studio. And, Dad, this is Becky. The girl I'm going to…"

Asher looked straight at Nora, ignoring his son.

"Look, this little ambush of yours isn't going to work. I know you're trying to make nice, but you can forget it. I won't let you and your daughter rope my son into a marriage with your little baby scam."

With that, everyone started speaking, each more furious than the last.

"You think I masterminded some scheme that included my eighteen-year-old daughter getting *pregnant*?"

"You think my pregnancy is a *scam*?"

"Dad, if you don't shut up, I swear to God, I'll shut you up myself!"

Michael grabbed his father's shirt in his fist and pushed him hard against the wall. The tools hanging there rattled, and a few tumbled off shelves. Becky burst into tears, covering her face with her hands.

Nora stomped her foot hard on the wooden floor. "That's *enough*!"

She rarely used her angry voice, and people tended to be shocked into silence when such a big voice came from such a tiny woman.

"Michael, you let your father go this instant! And you." Her finger pointed straight at Asher Peyton and her accent grew thick. "Sugar, you should follow your son's advice and remain silent for the time being." She didn't take her eyes from him, and he didn't move or speak as his son took a step back. She nodded in approval. "Bless your heart, Mr. Peyton, you might just have a brain somewhere in that hard head of yours, after all. Now, there will be no more shouting in front of my pregnant daughter, and there will definitely be no more violence, is that clear?" She arched a brow in Michael's direction and the young man gulped.

"Yes, ma'am."

"Why don't you take Becky somewhere where she can wash her face and calm down while your father and I have a chat?"

Becky chewed her lip, her face tear soaked, looking painfully like the teenager she was. She silently preceded Michael through the side exit. Michael sent a hard warning glance at his father before closing the door behind them.

Nora turned back to Asher, who was still against the wall, his gaze moving from her face to her pointing finger and back again. Storms raged behind those blue eyes. He was like a wounded animal looking for an escape. Her stance softened automatically and she lowered her hand, reminding herself that cornered animals were dangerous.

Asher's brooding silence was a physical presence in the room. Was the man capable of violence? Did father and son often resort to physical blows? What kind of family was her daughter getting tangled up with? He glared at her for another long moment, then brushed past her, heading for the workbench. He opened a cupboard door and pulled out an almost empty bottle of whiskey and two glasses. He drained the bottle into the glasses and handed her one. Violent *and* a drinker? Perfect. But she took the glass, figuring she could use a little liquid courage.

"Your son seems like a fine young man, Asher. If you give her a chance, I think you'll find my daughter is an equally fine young woman, incapable of whatever you suspect her of." She had to find a way to bring him into this forced family dynamic, to make him see that these young people needed him.

He took a sip of liquor, and she did the same. "I understand your shock at our children's predicament. I'm still in shock myself. Michael was so disappointed when you weren't able to join us this morning…" Her voice faded as she looked from the drink in his hand to the dark circles under his eyes. The pieces started falling into place. That bottle had probably been full at some point last night and may have been part of the reason he didn't make it to brunch this morning.

Okay, so this guy had some serious issues. But their kids needed them. She gave him her brightest smile, but his scowl just deepened. "So we decided to bring the brunch to you. There's homemade blueberry cobbler in the box, and we picked up some coffee from next door. I thought we should get to know each other, since we have a mutual grandchild on the way."

Blue eyes stared hard at her, as if trying to decipher her words.

"That's not going to happen. Not today. Not any day. You're trying to play me, and it won't work. You're trying to fix a problem that can't be fixed." He started to step away. Without thinking, she put her hand on his arm to stop him.

"I understand you're angry, but we're their *parents*, and those two kids need us. That baby needs us. And you're the one who lives here in the same town."

He spoke to her hand on his arm instead of looking her in the eye.

"This isn't some damned Norman Rockwell painting, Nora. I'm not that guy. You may be the ride-in-and-save-everyone type, but don't bother trying to save me, okay?" He looked her right in the eye. "I'm going to do everything in my power to stop this pregnancy, and if I can't do that, I'll make sure they don't get married."

"Stop the pregnancy?" Her stomach rolled and soured.

"Doctors can be called. Appointments made. Then both our children get on with their lives."

A chill swept across her skin. He couldn't be this calculating and cruel.

"They're in love with each other. Doesn't that mean anything to you?"

"Don't give me your rosy fairy tales. They're young and resilient. They'll move on from this."

Before she could answer, Michael and Becky came back into the shop. Becky's face was red and blotchy from crying, but she'd regained her composure. Michael purposefully moved her well past his father, but his eyes fell to Nora's hand, still on Asher's arm. Apparently people didn't touch him a lot. Small wonder. She yanked it away.

Asher looked at her with eyes devoid of any emotion, as if he'd pulled the shutters down from the inside. He glanced at his son and her daughter, and she saw the briefest glimmer of regret when he looked back and met her eyes.

"Look, you seem like a nice woman. Your daughter's probably a nice girl. But I'll have no part of this."

"This?"

"Them." He lifted his chin to where Becky stood in front of Michael, his arms wrapped protectively around her. "The baby. The wedding. All of it. None of it. I won't be involved. Just… just leave me out of it, okay? I'm out."

"Dad, please…"

Michael's plea went unheard. Asher was through the side door and gone before anyone could react.

CHAPTER FOUR

NORA WRAPPED THE last Christmas ornament with care, tucking it into the single remaining open square in the plastic storage bin designed specifically for that purpose. She glanced at her cousin Bree, then frowned.

"Oh, no, honey, don't put the garland in with the ornaments. The garland goes in the box with the lights. There should be a labeled bag in there to keep it separate."

Bree Caldwell, former reality star turned farmer's wife, arched a perfectly manicured brow. "You have a labeled bag for your Christmas garland?" She rolled her eyes. "Of course you do. You have labels for everything. You're the most label-y person I know."

Nora straightened. "Why does everyone make fun of my labels? I know exactly where everything is, and if I don't, the labels tell me. It's called being organized. It's a *skill*, not a disease."

They'd filled all three bins according to their labels, and tomorrow Nora would store them in the back of the closet, where they wouldn't get too hot during the long Atlanta summer. Everyone in the South knew a hot attic was out of the question for storing anything of value.

She really didn't need her cousin's help, but Bree had driven from North Carolina as part of an informal family mercy mission. Next week, another cousin, Melanie, was flying in from Miami for a visit. And Amanda called at least once a day from Gallant Lake. Her cousins were worried about her being alone in Georgia after a disastrous holiday. She'd like to say their worry was unfounded, but the truth was that she appreciated their support.

Bree held her hands up. "Hey, it's your house. We'll do it your way. But when I packed up Christmas at home last week, I just wrapped the stuff in paper towels and stuffed them in old liquor boxes from the bar. Not a label in sight, other than writing *Xmas* on top of the boxes."

"You wrapped your ornaments in paper towels?" Nora shuddered. "But how will you ever find…" She stopped, doing her best to keep from imposing her planning skills on her cousin. Bree brushed her long red hair over her shoulder and laughed.

"How will I find things? Well, in December I'll unpack everything onto the dining table and decorate the tree from there. It's really not a big deal. Besides, I was too tired from my honeymoon to care." Bree became Mrs. Cole Caldwell on New Year's Eve. The wedding was held at Halcyon in Gallant Lake, creating a travel-filled holiday for everyone, which was why they were packing up Christmas in mid-January. Cole and Bree had honeymooned in Barbados for a week, while Nora stayed in Gallant Lake just long enough to live through the biggest argument with Becky she'd ever had.

"Has she called yet?" Bree's voice softened. "You've got that look. You know, the I-have-to-replay-that-fight-in-my-head-for-the-fiftieth-time look."

Nora just shook her head and sat on the sofa. Becky hadn't called. Nor had she answered Nora's calls. Or her emails. Or her texts.

"She'll come around, honey. She's stubborn, like her momma, but she'll come around." Bree sighed. "I'm sorry if it was my wedding that started this whole mess."

"It wasn't the wedding. She always misses her dad the most at Christmas, and I said the wrong thing."

"What did you say?"

Nora picked at a thread on her sweater sleeve. "It started with Michael's father, Asher." Nora felt an odd shot of energy just saying his name. Probably because he was causing so much trouble for everyone. "He's determined to stop the wedding at all costs, and even resorted to 'forbidding' Michael from being with Becky." Nora made air quotes with her fingers.

"I laughed when Becky told me, and she flipped out. And then I made the mistake of saying it sounded like something *her* father would have said. As if by pronouncing something, he'd make it so. Comparing Asher to her perfect father was a mistake. And then I said I *agreed* with him on delaying the wedding, and kaboom." Nora made an explosion motion with her hands. "We started fighting about the pregnancy and the wedding and what an awful control freak I am and how she doesn't want my negative, uptight attitude around her baby, and on and on and on."

"So Asher is the guy you flirted with in the grocery store, right? Before you knew you were both about to become grandparents together? Amanda says he's a handsome devil."

Nora nodded. She'd thought about those angry, ice-blue eyes more than once since their confrontation in November.

"*Devil* being the operative word." She hadn't spoken to him while in Gallant Lake for Bree's wedding, but she did walk past his studio one afternoon after buying coffee at that weird coffee shop next door. Through the glass, she'd watched him working on a large dining table, making smooth, measured movements while rubbing the top with something. His too-long hair covered his face, but with his sleeves rolled up, his strong, sinewed arms were on full display.

She'd stood there, transfixed, until he straightened and looked out the window at her. He'd just stared at her for the longest, most electric moment she'd ever experienced, then he turned away. It was several moments before she could convince her feet to move in the proper direction, away from the door to his shop—away from him.

"Are you *blushing*?" Bree asked. "You're thinking about him right now, aren't you?" She chuckled and moved back to stacking the boxes. "And just thinking about him makes you hot and bothered. Very interesting."

"Seriously, Bree? What are we—twelve? I'm not hot and bothered about anyone." Nora turned away, feeling the heat in her cheeks increasing.

Bree scrutinized her. "I don't know. You definitely seem to be blushing over this guy."

Nora turned back to argue, then saw how Bree was stacking the holiday boxes.

"No, don't put that box on top. See the numbers on the side? That's the order I stack them in. Turn them so the labels are all facing front. And be careful with the treetop angel—if you tip that box, her wings will be damaged. That's why it's important to…" Nora stopped midsentence. "Oh, my God, I *am* uptight and negative, aren't I?"

"Well, yes on the uptight part, but no on the negative." Bree restacked the bins, then came to sit next to Nora on the sofa. When Bree draped her arm around Nora's shoulders, Nora was horrified to feel tears welling in her eyes.

"Becky always said I was too controlling, and she's always hated my lists and my planners." She looked to Bree. "And my labels. Do you think I drove her into this boy's arms? Was she trying to escape *me*?"

"Whoa! Slow down, cuz. It's a big leap from your teenage daughter thinking her mom's too controlling—hello, doesn't every teenage girl think that?—to blaming yourself for her current situation." Bree looked her straight in the eye.

"Nora, you are *not* a negative person. Wasn't it Becky who christened you Suzy Sunshine? You've been the wise mother hen for your three crazy cousins. And you've provided a beautiful home for Becky here." She leaned over and gave Nora's shoulder a gentle nudge with hers. "Can you be uptight? Maybe a little. You do like to contr…um…organize things."

Nora winced, and Bree squeezed her shoulder.

"Stop. Control isn't always a bad thing. You did what you had to do to raise Becky as a single mom, especially under the circumstances. But you can't control *everything*, sweetie. When things don't go according to your detailed plans, you…um…" Bree's face scrunched in concentration. "You don't always… You can't…"

"I freak out."

Bree laughed and snapped her fingers. "Yes! That's it! You freak out." Bree sat back and smiled. "But, honey, plans change all the time. Do you think I planned on falling in love with a Carolina farmer and leaving Hollywood for him? Of course not! Cole was the most unexpected thing to ever happen to me, but he's also the best."

Bree's green eyes softened, then she winked. "For heaven's sake, Nora, I know it wasn't in your plans, but you're going to have a little grandbaby! And you're going to be the best grandma ever." Bree nudged her shoulder. "Hey, how did your former mother-in-law take the news that she's going to be a great-grandmother? That couldn't have gone over well with the ice queen."

Nora wiped her tears, but she couldn't hold back a little smile. "It made for an interesting Christmas Eve dinner at Mother Bradford's when Becky announced her pregnancy and engagement in one breath. Meredith's eyebrows shot upward almost as much as her jaw dropped, which is pretty impressive considering how many Botox shots that forehead has seen."

"I would have paid to see that!"

Nora had stood behind her daughter in Meredith Bradford's lavish home on Christmas Eve, silently daring any of Becky's relatives to utter a negative word. No one did, at least, not to her face. But Nora had burned at all the private looks going around the table during dinner.

Her late husband's family would get loads of mileage out of this little scandal, even though it was peanuts compared to the antics of Paul and his two brothers. "Meredith was only annoyed because Becky's news stole the thunder from the other big announcement of the night. Paul's little brother, Geoff, is running for governor."

Bree started to laugh again. "Seriously? Isn't Geoff the one that cooked up that phony charity to fund Paul's campaign? And wasn't it his secretary that Paul was..." Her laughter faded.

"That my husband was sleeping with? She was one of many, yes." Nora shook her head. Paul's betrayals still stung, but the years since his death had dulled the pain. "But it was the older brother who got in trouble over the campaign funding. His political days are over. However, Meredith thinks Geoff's hands are clean enough for him to take Paul's place as the anointed candidate for governor."

Bree shrugged. "At least you won't have to be involved with the campaign."

"No, but I'm worried about what kind of dirt the campaign might bring up." There had been whispers about Paul's philandering ways during his campaign, and even about his gambling, but people lost interest after his death.

"The Bradfords are not your problem anymore." Bree stood and waved her hand dismissively, as if making a decree. "Let them drown in their own lies. It's time for lunch. And wine. Definitely time for a glass of wine."

"My daughter is still a Bradford." Nora followed Bree toward the kitchen. "And she has no idea what kind of man her father really was, or the things his family did. I'd like to keep it that way."

Bree opened the refrigerator and pulled out a bottle of chardonnay. "Maybe it's time she learned the truth about her dad, warts and all. Isn't it exhausting keeping his myth alive?"

Yes. Of course it was.

"No. She was only thirteen when he died. She worshipped him, the way every little girl should worship their daddy. I made a vow to myself that she would always know her father as the man she believed him to be—charming, successful and honorable."

"As opposed to the truth of him being a lying, cheating SOB who gambled away her inheritance?"

Nora took the glass Bree handed her. "He was a lousy husband, but he wasn't a bad father. Paul was the ultimate live-in-the-moment kind of guy, with never a thought to consequences. She was the daughter of a popular politician who people liked a lot. I don't want to take that away."

"Okay, well, here's my next question. Becky's not in Atlanta anymore, and you've done enough for the Bradfords. When do you start living for yourself, Nora? There's nothing holding you here, right?"

Nora frowned. After spending all of her energy protecting Paul's legacy and raising her daughter, if felt as if her entire life's purpose had simply vanished the day Becky went to college, leaving her adrift. The truth was, she had no idea what to do next with her life.

Bree gave her a mischievous grin. "Hey, Amanda said that coffee shop in Gallant Lake is still for sale."

"Oh, God, don't remind me!" Nora shook her head and took a sip of wine. "She actually put a sales flyer for it in the Christmas card she sent me. That idea is a nonstarter."

"Why? You keep saying how bored you are now that Becky's gone. A coffee shop would keep you busy. You'd be close to Amanda and Blake and the kids. And it would give you an excuse to be in Gallant Lake near Becky." Bree ticked off each point on her long fingers. "It's a win-win-win!"

Nora thought about steely blue eyes and strong

arms. "Asher Peyton's furniture studio would be right next door. Remember him? The man who accused Becky and me of some evil plot to trap his son in marriage? No, thanks."

"So you think it would be a bad idea to be neighbors with the guy who makes you blush from head to toe, like you're doing again right now?" Bree leaned against the kitchen island and grinned. "Not all hot, grumpy neighbors are bad, you know. That's how Cole and I started out."

"Read. My. Lips." Nora pointed to her face. "Not. Going. To. Happen."

The doorbell rang before Bree could come back with a sarcastic response. Nora set her glass down and went to the door.

Her first thought when she opened it was that maybe she'd been wrong to say people couldn't make things happen just by saying them. After all, Bree had just mentioned Paul's affair with his brother's assistant, and here she was—the woman he'd slept with.

Daphne Tomlin was one of several women Paul had cheated on Nora with, actually, and not the one he eventually fell in love with. But she was the one standing on Nora's doorstep, all tall and beautiful with her long blond hair. Her clothes were tailored and expensive, and gold chains filled the opening at the top of her silk blouse. She'd matured well over the past five years, and

Nora was suddenly self-conscious about her tired old sweater and brightly striped leggings. Knowing her shock must be plainly visible on her face, she took a deep breath to compose herself.

"Hello, Nora. I'm not sure you remember me, but…"

"Oh, I tend to remember *all* the women who slept with my late husband, Daphne. So whatever you're selling, I'm not…" Nora took a step back and started to close the door, but Daphne put her foot out and stopped it.

"I'm not selling anything, Nora, but you might be."

"What on earth are you talking about?"

"I've moved up the ladder in the political world over the past few years." Nora wondered uncharitably how one climbed a ladder while lying on her back. "I'm the managing director for a conservative website. We have a major internet and social media presence, focusing on issues specific to Georgia."

"How nice for you," Nora said. "But I don't care."

"I want to give you a chance to be on the right side of the story we're working on."

"What story? And what do you mean by the *right* side?"

Daphne smiled, probably intending to look reassuring, but her tight, predatorial grin was anything but.

"Our organization is working closely with Tom Wilson's campaign in the primary, since he's the most conservative candidate in the governor's race right now." She paused, as if expecting Nora to react to this news, but Nora was still trying to figure out why Daphne was on her doorstep. What could she possibly be after?

"I'll get right to the point, Nora." She put an emphasis on Nora's name, as if using it suddenly made them friends. "Considering your apparent lack of involvement with Geoff Bradford's campaign, we were wondering if you might be interested in publicly endorsing Tom Wilson. You know, before any rumors about the Bradford men become public knowledge."

Bree coughed behind Nora, and she heard the derisive curse cloaked inside that cough. Nora squared her shoulders and looked Daphne right in the eye.

"First, you are *not* my friend, so please address me as Mrs. Bradford. Second, are you threatening me?" She stepped forward, her fury just slightly ahead of her panic. "Are you actually standing on my doorstep attempting to blackmail me into supporting your candidate over my own brother-in-law?"

Daphne's eyes widened fractionally. "Are you

saying you're endorsing Geoff Bradford for governor? May I quote you on that? Because, *Mrs. Bradford*, there's evidence your late husband, much like his brother, had a serious gambling problem. Isn't that why you sold your country estate after his death and moved to this much smaller home? And, of course, the women…"

"Women like *you*, Daphne? You'll be implicating yourself."

Daphne shrugged. "It's a website, Mrs. Bradford. In the Wild West of the new political world, the fact that I was one of many women your late husband took advantage of will just make the story more scintillating. It's all about the spin."

Nora gave her a look from head to toe. "Looks like you've done pretty well for yourself for someone so terribly victimized."

Daphne stiffened, her bright red lips thinning. "Careful, Mrs. Bradford. Slut-shaming isn't as popular as it used to be, so you won't win a lot of points with that approach." Nora looked down at her feet, chagrined. Daphne was right. "And, so you know, I've worked my ass off to get to where I am. Getting Tom Wilson elected will be a lot easier once the truth is out about Geoff Bradford. But that truth can't come out without disclosing Paul's involvement."

Daphne's eyes softened fractionally. "I know I shouldn't have gotten involved with your husband. I'm offering you a chance to tell your story from a sympathetic point of view before the news cycle picks it up."

"Don't pretend you're here on some charity case. That I should be *thanking* you. If I do what you suggest, it will destroy Geoff's candidacy, which hands you your goal on a silver platter."

Daphne nodded. "That's true. But it doesn't hurt you, either. It's not like you knew what they were up to, did you?" Nora ignored the veiled accusation.

"You're talking about my daughter's *father*. I don't know what you expected to accomplish by coming here, but we're done. And if you stick your foot out again, you'll lose some toes when I slam this door on it."

"Mrs. Bradford, as long as you live here in Atlanta you won't be able to hide from this. You'll have to take a stand once the story comes out. Don't think you can avoid… Ouch…damn it!" The last two words were muffled, coming from the other side of the now-locked front door. After a beat of silence, Daphne called out, "You had your chance, Nora. Remember that."

Nora turned and leaned against the door, staring at a stunned Bree.

"This is exactly what I was afraid of. What am I going to do?"

Bree was thoughtful for a moment. "She was

right about one thing. If the person at the heart of the story isn't around, the story loses steam. It doesn't mean the Bradfords won't get roasted, but this is a state story, not a national one." Then Bree brightened. "I bet that coffee shop idea is starting to look pretty good now, isn't it?"

Nora's head went back and forth in denial, but in her mind she smelled freshly sanded wood and saw blue eyes full of tangled emotions. "Not happening, Bree. I just need to talk to Meredith. If I can make her see that the campaign is hopeless, maybe Geoff will drop out and the story will be dead."

Bree gave her a pointed look. "And when exactly has Mother Bradford ever believed her precious boys were anything but perfect and invincible?"

Never. The answer was *never*.

And, sure enough, Meredith refused to take the threat seriously when Nora called her that night and relayed her encounter with Daphne.

"They're just on a fishing expedition. As long as you didn't give her anything, they have no story." Nora looked at her phone in consternation.

"Meredith, I didn't *have* to give her anything. Daphne was one of Paul's…women." The word *mistress* was too old-fashioned and, frankly, humiliating. "And probably one of Geoff's, too. She had a ringside seat to everything they did."

"Don't be ridiculous. Geoff has a lovely, supportive wife, and he would never cheat on her." Nora bit her tongue to keep from taking the bait. Meredith's inference was clear—if Paul cheated, it must have been Nora's fault. "I'm telling you," her former mother-in-law continued, "she's bluffing. And if she's not, just deny, deny, deny."

After that phone call, Nora and Bree called Amanda and they talked into the wee hours of the morning, trying to come up with a plan. Nora wrote lists of pros and cons and things she might do. But it always came back to leaving Atlanta.

At the top of one list, she'd sketched a steaming mug of coffee, thinking of a particular coffee shop. She also thought about the complex man who lived next door to that shop. About her angry, pregnant daughter. About the serious, bearded young man who was going to be the father of her grandchild. Did she really think living in the midst of all that drama was a good idea? Surely it would be easier to stay in Atlanta and deal with a little story on some obscure website.

As they finally headed to bed, Nora turned to Bree, holding up both hands, with fingers crossed on each. "Maybe Meredith was right. Maybe Daphne was bluffing. Maybe I'm worrying for nothing. Let's get some sleep and see what tomorrow brings."

CHAPTER FIVE

"Um…Nora?" Bree's voice was muffled through the bedroom door, but Nora could hear the tension in it. "You might want to come down and take a look outside. And make sure you're dressed."

Nora tossed her blankets aside. Had there been a storm overnight? Had a tree fallen? She obediently put on a pair of pants and a sweater, pulling her hair back with a headband. She glanced at the alarm clock—good Lord, it was after nine o'clock. Apparently that wine had gone to her head more than she'd thought.

Bree was waiting for her right outside the bedroom door. She silently handed Nora the editorial page of the newspaper. The headline read "The Bradford Dynasty?" It was written by guest editor Daphne Tomlin.

Nora couldn't keep the curse words silent this time. "Son of a bitch."

"That's not all," Bree said.

"It gets worse?" Nora's laugh had no humor in it at all.

"Reporters came to the door earlier. I didn't

answer, of course, but I saw the news van out front. It's still there."

In her mind, Nora pictured Daphne Tomlin roasting slowly over hot coals. Nora probably *should* have known everything Paul was up to, but she'd ignored the evidence and denied the rumors until the very end. It wasn't until after his death that she'd learned the full weight of what he'd done. There were three mortgages on their beautiful country home. Becky's college fund had been emptied. The credit cards were maxed out. She'd known he played poker too much, but she'd had no idea how *bad* he was at it until it was too late.

And now Nora's years of carefully crafting a legend around Paul for her daughter's sake may be wasted. "Have you read the whole story? How bad is it?"

"It's basically a rehash of the rumors already out there. Unfortunately, she worded your refusal to cooperate so that it looks like you're hiding something."

Nora was silent, but her mind was racing. A plan. She needed a plan. A list of priorities formed in her head, and her nerves started to calm.

"Okay, I need to call my attorney and get her working on this. I'll go downstairs and close all the blinds, and we'll just hunker down here until

Geoff announces he's dropping out of the race. Once he does that, the story should fade away."

"WHAT DO YOU *MEAN*, Geoff's not quitting? He *has* to drop out of the race!" Nora's hand clenched her cell phone so tightly she was surprised the screen didn't pop right out. She'd managed to smuggle Bree out of the house and off to North Carolina without anyone seeing her. After three days holed up in her house, she'd finally called the Bradford matriarch to see what was taking so long.

"Nora, don't raise your voice with me. It's unseemly."

"No, Meredith, what's unseemly is pretending that your son's political career isn't over. My God, think of his wife and children! Think of me and *my* child! He can't win the primary with this story out there. He has to quit."

"Bradfords aren't quitters, dear. These rumors will blow over before the primary. The fools released the story too early to affect the election."

Nora knew enough about political campaigns to know that was true. Tom Wilson should have waited until just before the primary to sabotage his opponent. Daphne had jumped the gun, but Nora wasn't prepared to deal with this for months on end. She was wasting her time appealing to Meredith's logic and sense of decency, since the woman didn't have either.

She curled up in the corner of the sofa after ending the call and looked around the darkened room. The sun was shining brightly outside, but reporters kept showing up at odd hours to try to catch her, so she was a prisoner in her own home. Past conversations were her only company and they kept rolling through her head.

A coffee shop would keep you busy. You'd be close to Amanda and Blake and the kids. And it would give you an excuse to be in Gallant Lake with Becky. It's a win-win-win.

Oh, God, Mom, that would be a disaster! *You don't know anything about business, much less running the world's ugliest coffee shop.*

So, you think it would be a bad idea to be neighbors with the guy who makes you blush from head to toe, like you're doing again right now? Not all hot, grumpy neighbors are bad, you know.

She got up and went to the kitchen for…something. Wine sounded like a great idea, but it was only two o'clock. Coffee would be a better choice. She paused. *Coffee would be a better choice.* She hadn't made a single hasty decision since Paul's death, but maybe it was time to shake things up. She pulled her phone from her pocket.

"Amanda? Is that coffee shop still for sale?"

"So, HAVE YOU welcomed your new neighbor yet?" Deputy Sheriff Dan Adams tipped the unfinished chair he was sitting in perilously close to horizontal, watching Asher sand the sides of a drawer for the side table he was building. Dan was still on duty, so he was drinking soda instead of the beer he usually had when he stopped by the shop after shift.

Asher ignored his question, the same way he was ignoring what was happening next door. People went back and forth on the sidewalk outside his window, carrying boxes in and out of the cafe, laughing and talking nonstop. Someone was hammering something inside Cathy's café.

Except it wasn't Cathy's anymore. Two weeks ago, Cathy announced it was sold, and, unfortunately, who she'd sold it to. Nora Bradford hadn't wasted any time getting here. Blake and Amanda Randall were outside. Bobby Davis, a local contractor, was hustling in and out of the café, too. And a petite brunette, her hair pulled back with a bright red headband, had just pulled up in a silver sedan, clipboard in hand.

Okay, maybe he hadn't been ignoring them as well as he'd thought.

"Eventually you're going to have to talk to her, you know." Dan was pointing out the obvious. That didn't mean Asher had to acknowledge it. "You're right next door to each other. And Blake told me she's fixing up the apartment above the café, so you'll be neighbors 24/7."

"That apartment hasn't been lived in for years. I thought she'd be living with the kids." Weren't those two idiots the reason she'd bought the café in the first place?

"Did Michael tell you that?"

"No. We haven't spoken in…a while." Since Christmas. When Michael had rejected Asher's plan to salvage his son's life.

"Hmm, you're not talking to your son, your neighbor or your future daughter-in-law. What are you doing, trying to become a hermit? Are you just going to move up onto the mountain and hibernate?" Dan shook his head and straightened his chair. "There's a wedding coming, man, whether you approve or not. You don't want to miss that."

"There's not going to be a wedding."

Dan just laughed. "You keep saying that, as if you can make it true just by uttering it out loud. But since you're not speaking to them, you really don't know anything."

"Why? What have you heard?" As soon as the words were out, he knew it was a mistake. Dan was a good cop, and he never missed a clue, even in casual conversation.

"For someone claiming to be uninterested, you're pretty curious. Talk to your son, man." Dan drained his soda. "You know they're going to be neighbors of mine, right? My new house is within a stone's throw of their rental."

Asher jumped at the chance to change the subject. "Are you really buying that crazy old Victorian?"

"Yup. I close on it next week. Chloe needs a place that feels like home, and my apartment ain't cuttin' it. Anyway, I fully expect my architect friend to help me."

Dan's divorce had been tough, but he and his ex were working hard to keep things civil for their daughter's sake. Dan bought a house right around the corner from her so Chloe could go back and forth easily and not miss her school or her friends.

"I'm not an architect anymore." That career, working for his former father-in-law's firm, had evaporated at the same time his marriage did.

"Uh-huh." Dan sat up and put the empty soda bottle on the workbench. "Says the man building a house on the side of a mountain. Michael could probably use some help babyproofing his place."

Asher had driven by his son's blue bungalow on Sunset Lane a few times recently. Nearly a hundred years old and in desperate need of a coat of paint, at least the little house was sturdy. Asher had helped him with a few projects before he'd learned about the girl.

"Why? Have you heard about any problems with the place?"

Dan laughed, sweeping his hand up and down in Asher's direction. "Again, not looking like someone who isn't interested. No, I haven't heard of any issues with the house. Though I did hear old man McGregor told Michael he could pretty much do whatever he wanted to the place. They've been working on it…"

More hammering from next door distracted Asher from Dan's words. Cathy had told him Nora was planning on changing just about everything in the café, starting with paint and continuing with adding state-of-the-art equipment. Asher liked Cathy, despite her freewheeling approach to life. He didn't like the idea of her place changing into some snooty, upscale coffeehouse. And he *really* didn't like the idea of Nora Bradford owning it.

"Earth to Asher. Are you listening to me at all?"

He set the sanding block down. "Sorry. What?"

"I said it looks like Michael and Becky are going to settle here in Gallant Lake for a while. He got a part-time job working for Judge Wilkes." Dan stood up and adjusted his belt, getting his weapon settled on his hip. He started for the door but stopped at Asher's next comment.

"No."

"No?"

"I'm trying to get Michael as far from Gallant Lake as possible."

"What? Why?"

Wasn't it obvious? Was he the only person who could see what had to happen here?

"If I get him away from that girl, he'll get focused on his career again. I've offered him a full ride at Stanford. I'll pay tuition and all expenses if he goes out there alone. No way they'll last long on opposite coasts."

Dan looked down at the floor and scratched his head, making his sandy hair stand on end. Asher knew his plan sounded devious. Maybe even cruel. But he had Michael's best interests at heart. And those interests didn't include raising a baby.

"Okay…" Dan sighed heavily. "Let me see if I have this straight. You're trying to *bribe* your son into *abandoning* his girlfriend *and* their unborn child? What the hell, Ash?"

"He can still be responsible for the child financially." His friend's obvious disapproval made Asher's temper rise, along with his voice. "He has no idea what he's getting into, Dan. What parenthood means. I'm trying to protect him, damn it!"

Dan stepped forward, and Asher recoiled. "Protect him? Ash, is this all because…" He shook his head. The two of them had shared a lot of late-night talks, but the loss of his youngest son was never up for discussion. "What does Michael's fiancée think about your plan?"

"Stop calling her that. And I have no idea."

"And Michael's future mother-in-law?" Dan nodded his head toward the window, where they could see Nora Bradford standing next to Amanda Randall, head down, staring at her clipboard as if her life depended on it. She was wearing the same pink jacket she'd worn in November, and it highlighted the rosiness of her cheeks on this raw February day. She laughed at something Amanda said and looked up, her eyes meeting his through the glass.

Her eyebrows rose in surprise, then she nodded her head at him in acknowledgment. Or dismissal. He wasn't sure, since she went right back to her conversation with her cousin. But the cousin kept a close eye on him while Nora talked. She finally smirked and looked away, studying the front of the coffee shop. The Randalls were regular clients of his, and he liked them both. He bit back a sigh. It was going to be more than a little complicated having Nora for a neighbor.

"She's not going to be his mother-in-law." Asher ignored Dan's snort of laughter. "And if she has any sense, she'll want them to avoid marriage as much as I do."

Dan headed off to finish his shift, while Asher

purposefully stayed as far to the back of his studio as possible, working hard on fitting the dovetailed drawer to the table he was finishing for a client in Albany. Word of mouth was bringing new customers every month, and the work would be enough to keep him from thinking about his pretty…scratch that…his *annoying* neighbor.

CHAPTER SIX

"HOW IN THE world did I get here?"

Nora didn't realize she'd said the words aloud until Cathy answered. They were going up the stairs behind the coffee shop to see the apartment that would soon be Nora's home. So far, she'd only seen photos of the open loft space.

"These stairs climb right over the storage room, honey."

"I didn't mean…" Nora stopped. There was no point in telling a complete stranger that she was referring to her life in general. How in the world had she ended up owning a coffee shop in Gallant Lake in February, with the temperature hovering in the single digits outside? It wasn't at all her style to make an impulsive decision, especially one that would uproot her entire life, but her former in-laws had forced her hand. Bree was right—the only way to avoid being the center of a scandal was to remove herself from Atlanta. So she had. She'd received an offer on her house right away, and even though it wouldn't close for another month, she was able to get a mortgage for the coffee shop and the building that housed it. Cathy had been more than happy to close quickly.

Cathy Meadows, otherwise known as Caffeine Cathy, unlocked the brightly painted door at the top of the stairs and pushed it open. A wave of heat rolled out into the hallway.

"I know it needs a little cleaning up, but it's homey, you know?"

Cathy proudly waved a bangle-wrapped arm toward the room. The movement only managed to stir up more dust in the stuffy air.

Nora stood at the entrance to the…well…*apartment* seemed too fancy a word. The *space* above the coffee shop. *Her* coffee shop. *Her* space. *Her* new home. This was why she didn't believe in making spontaneous decisions—you ended up living in a hot, filthy loft that smelled vaguely of sweet herbs. It had to be eighty degrees in there.

Throughout the telephone and email negotiations for the coffee shop, Cathy had given the impression that the apartment needed little more than a broom sweep. Cathy emailed her pictures that made the small space look charming, with cheerful gingham curtains over the wide windows facing the street and cute little throw rugs on the wide plank floors. She wasn't sure which decade those photos had been taken in, but they were far from recent.

A heavy layer of dirt lay on every surface,

from the floors to the faded curtains drooping sadly over grimy windows and right on up to the exposed beams crossing overhead that were draped in dusty cobwebs. One kitchen cabinet had a door that was hanging precariously from its hinges. The counter, a gold-flecked Formica relic of the sixties, was chipped and... Was that actual black *soil* scattered across it? Nora couldn't keep her nose from wrinkling in disgust, but Cathy was too busy gushing about all the "potential" to notice.

"My mom used that up there as her bedroom until the stairs got to be too much for her. I just used it for storage, but it does have a little bathroom and closet. And there's another small bedroom down here and a bathroom."

Nora pulled her eyes away from the tiny kitchen and looked up. Sure enough, there was a rather large loft there, with an open metal staircase coming down the exposed brick wall on the far side of the living room. For the first time since walking through the door, she started to see the possibilities.

Sure, she had to squint her eyes and rely heavily on her imagination, but she could envision the kitchen cabinets repaired and painted a cheery color. Once clean, those big windows would give her a pretty view of Main Street and the mountains beyond. The plank floors would clean up nicely, and the loft was a perfect place to put her bed.

She followed Cathy up the open stairs. The loft was roomy, and sure enough, there was a bathroom up there with a tiny shower in it. It wouldn't be the most private bedroom, with just a commercial-looking metal railing around the edge of the platform, but she'd be living alone, so it was fine. She looked out over the living room. Above the first row of windows, and directly across from the loft, was a large arched window in the peak of the old building. From up here, she could look out onto Gallant Lake and the surrounding mountains that were covered in a blanket of snow at this time of year. She nodded to herself in satisfaction. She was already creating multiple to-do lists in her head. A plan was taking shape, and plans made her feel calm.

Cathy was heading back down the stairs, still talking nonstop. The woman had hardly taken a breath since handing Nora the giant ring of keys down in the coffee shop.

"I know the place is a little messy." Was that sarcasm? Nope. Cathy really did seem to consider this chaos to be just a minor mess. "And sorry about the heat. I forgot to turn it down yesterday when I moved my plants out of here."

"Plants?" That explained the soil on the counters. "So you grew flowers up here? I bet the windows were great for that." Especially when combined with the tropical temperature. At least she knew the furnace worked. Cathy's cheeks flushed.

"Flowers? Oh, hell no. Honey, I grew…" The older woman's dark eyes narrowed and she stopped short. Then her lips pressed together and she made an exaggerated motion with her hands like the turning of a key in a lock. "Not that I think you're a narc or anything, but let's just say I grew…um…medicinal herbs up here."

It took Nora a minute to catch on, and when she did, her mouth dropped open.

"You were growing *pot* in this apartment?" That explained the sickly sweet smell.

"Well, hell, say it a little louder, princess! I don't think Sheriff Dan quite heard you. It's not like I was dealing or anything. It just helps me sleep at night." She gave Nora a wink and turned away, heading toward the back of the apartment beyond the kitchen with a swish of her long cotton skirt. "The thermostat's back here. The plants liked it warm, but I'll turn it down for you. Over there's the other bedroom and the bathroom, and the utility room's by the back door. The washer and dryer aren't exactly new, but I had Ash check everything and he said the plumbing and appliances were all functional."

Nora stopped short. "Ash? Asher Peyton?"

Cathy was fighting with the deadbolt on the back door. She nodded without looking back to see Nora's discomfort. "Yup. He's your neighbor to the west, with the furniture shop. He's a little crusty on the outside, but a good man underneath. If you ever need anything, just knock on the wall and he'll come right over."

"Knock on the wall?"

The deadbolt finally opened, and Cathy gave the door a hard yank to pull it open, letting in a rush of cold air. "Well, not the brick wall, of course, but you see those filled-in windows along the side of the apartment?" Nora looked back at the arched openings in the brick, filled with wide boards painted reddish brown to match.

"His place was built after this one, back in the early 1900s, and it butts up against this wall. The brick is thick enough that you can't hear anything, but those old boarded-up windows allow a little noise to seep through. Sometimes I'll hear his music if it's turned up really loud."

Cathy smiled. "Two winters ago I was working up here, trimming plants, and I tripped over that crazy old cat of mine and everything went crashing down—lights, plants, table, tools and me. What a racket! Before I was on my feet, Asher was pounding on this very door to get in, scared someone was killing me over here."

The cold air wasn't the only thing making Nora

feel chilled. Buying a business next door to a man who hated her and her daughter was one thing, but knowing he might be listening was entirely another. Cathy must have noticed her concern.

"Oh, honey, don't worry. When I say I can hear his music, I mean only if he's *cranking* it, and even then it's just low, fuzzy bass notes. He doesn't do that a lot." Cathy's smile faded. "But when he does, he doesn't want company, just so you know."

Cathy stepped outside, oblivious to the cold. "He's not the type to hold a glass up against the wall trying to hear what you're doing. He keeps to himself. More than he should." Those last four words were spoken under her breath, as if to herself.

Before Nora could respond, Cathy was pulling her outside onto a long metal fire escape overlooking a gravel parking lot behind the row of buildings. The walkway stretched across three or four buildings, with a matching one right above it. On the rear of each building a small wooden balcony jutted out over the parking lot. Narrow metal staircases led down to the ground at regular intervals. There was one right between her doorway and Asher's.

Their buildings were not only connected, they also shared a fire escape. Nora frowned.

"Well, this isn't very private, is it?"

Cathy just shrugged. "There was a big fire in town ages ago." She stepped back into the warmth of the apartment and closed the door behind Nora, turning the deadbolt. "Grandma used to talk about it. These buildings didn't burn, but some across the street did. Back then, a lot of places used these upper floors as boardinghouses. Some people were trapped in their rooms and died. After that, the town decreed that all downtown structures had to have fire escapes for each level. They're not the prettiest thing to look at, but it's nice to sit out there in the summer and watch the sun come up over the mountains. The neighbors used to get together for drinks out there in the evenings."

Nora kept her thoughts to herself. She couldn't imagine she and Asher Peyton would be sipping wine on the fire escape anytime soon. Cathy kept talking as she headed past the kitchen.

"Of course, that was back when more of them lived here, you know? I think the only places being used as homes now are Asher's and Carl Wallace's. Carl owns the liquor store a couple doors up. He's lived over that store forever, but he's been talking about retiring. His wife, Eunie, just passed away last year. And Asher's building a house up on Gallant Mountain, so he'll be out eventually." Cathy opened the door leading to the coffee shop downstairs. "You might be the only one left if you really want to live up here."

"I do." Nora followed Cathy down the narrow steps after locking the apartment door. Amanda had offered her a suite at Halcyon for as long as she needed it, but she wanted her own space. Even a ten-bedroom castle started feeling small when you were living in it with someone else's family. Besides, she was determined to show Becky that she could do this, be independent.

"Hey, look! We have customers!" Cathy walked over to greet Blake and Amanda in the center of the now-empty café. The tables and chairs were stacked in the back of the building, just as she'd written on her to-do list. She'd have to start a whole new list for the work required upstairs, of course. The artwork was off the walls. Even the old counter was gone, ripped out today and set aside. And there, by the window, stood her daughter.

Nora stopped, afraid to speak. Becky was staring outside, so she had a moment to take in her appearance. They hadn't seen each other since Christmas. Becky's hair was longer than usual. She wore a dark wool coat, but it was open and Nora could see the swell of her stomach. She was almost six months pregnant now.

She wanted to run and hug her daughter and never let go, but she was afraid to make the wrong move. Becky hadn't exactly been supportive of this move when she'd finally answered her phone so they could talk about it.

Are you for real? After I told you I didn't want you here, you went and bought that gross coffee shop? God, Mom, how desperate can you be?

And now her angry daughter was standing in that gross coffee shop. She was ignoring Nora with every ounce of stubborn energy she had, but she was here. Amanda stepped closer and whispered to Nora as Cathy wandered back to the kitchen.

"Blake told me the upstairs was pretty grungy."

Nora shrugged. "It has potential. I just need a lot of cleaning supplies."

"You don't have to live here to run the coffee shop." Amanda ran her finger across a shelf, grimacing at the dirt she lifted. "We have tons of space at Halcyon."

Nora shook her head, speaking loudly enough for Becky to hear. "I've been told I need to live my own life and find my own way. This is me doing that."

Becky finally turned to her mother, rolling her eyes with all the drama a teenage girl could muster. She gestured around the empty café. "Whatever, Mom. You bought a business for yourself. Big deal. You still have no idea how to run it, since you've never done it before."

Nora tried to measure her response, but her daughter's lack of confidence in her stung. "Well, then, I guess we're even, because I don't know how you're going to raise a child alone when you've never done *that* before."

"I'm not alone. I have Michael. Who do *you* have?"

"Becky!" Amanda was shocked, but Nora wasn't. Becky had always been fierce, unafraid to stand her ground. And she had just enough of Meredith Bradford in her to go for a scorched-earth policy with anyone who challenged her.

"I ran all of your father's campaigns, Rebecca—every detail. If I can run a gubernatorial campaign, I can certainly figure out how to manage a little coffeehouse in Gallant Lake." She took a step closer to the window. "But, unlike you, I'm more than happy to accept help when it's offered. Are you here to offer your help?"

Becky eyed her warily. "Let me guess—if I agree to help you, then you'll expect to help me, which basically means telling me what to do?"

Becky was trying to goad her, but Nora wasn't going to play into her hands. She measured her words carefully, stepping in front of Becky and looking her straight in the eye.

"Rebecca Scarlett Bradford, I love you." Becky's head snapped back in surprise. Nora took her hands. "I am not here to take over your life. If you want my help, ask for it. Until then, I'm minding my own business. Literally, *this* business, which is more than enough to keep me busy. I did this because I wanted to." And because she was trying to protect her only child. "I'm here if you need me, but it's up to you, sweetheart. Until you say the word, I won't interfere in your life. No matter how much it kills me."

Becky's mouth twitched at the joke, then she sobered. "Mom, Michael and I need to do this on our own. It's important to us."

Nora nodded, then looked around the shop. Cathy and Blake were out of sight, and Amanda was quietly sketching design ideas in the corner.

"And I need to do *this* on my own. It's important to *me*." She didn't realize the deep truth of those words until she spoke them. All her adult life she'd been Paul's wife, Paul's widow or Becky's mom. This move was her chance to be Nora. Just as soon as she figured out who Nora might be.

"Fine, Mom. But don't hate me if I don't include you in every little detail of my pregnancy or my life with Michael. Because all it's going to take is one look of disapproval or one time telling me what I *should* be doing, and I'm going to lose it."

"I can agree to that. You set the ground rules

and I'll follow." Nora opened her arms but made no other move.

Becky hesitated only a heartbeat before rushing into Nora's embrace. Nora sent up a silent prayer of thanks. Now she just needed a plan to make this family whole and strong again.

Amanda blew her nose, breaking the moment. "I'm sorry! You guys made me cry!"

Nora stepped away, being careful not to presume all was forgiven with Becky. She was going to have to prove herself to her daughter, and she may as well start by proving she wasn't an idiot for buying Caffeine Cathy's Coffee Café. Becky needed to see her succeed.

"Blake and I talked last night—" Nora turned to Amanda "—and he thinks the contractor can have everything done within ten days. I've got a list here of the priorities..."

Amanda laughed. "Of course you do. Nora Bradford *always* has a list." Becky giggled behind her. Funny how much it meant to hear her daughter's laughter again.

"Yeah, yeah, laugh all you want. But I also know how to get things done."

Blake and Cathy walked back into the room. Blake nodded in Nora's direction.

"Bobby and his crew will be back tomorrow. I told him to plan on..." He glanced toward Cathy, but she was obliviously humming to herself as she ran her hand over the antique brass espresso machine in the corner. "I told him to plan on some heavy-duty cleaning upstairs before they start painting and remodeling down here." Nora started to object, but he held up his hand, shaking his head. "I know, I know—you want to do it all yourself, because you're one of the independent Lowery women." Amanda snorted. "But let Bobby handle the first pass up there. His guys can set up scaffolding and make sure everything from floor to ceiling is clean and safe for you, then you can do what you want with it."

She frowned, but he was right. She had no desire to climb ladders and attempt to clean those windows or shovel out all that dirt. "Okay, but just the cleaning. I want to paint and decorate up there on my own."

"Hey!" Amanda, an interior designer by trade, voiced her objection.

"Don't worry, cuz, I'll be happy to listen to your advice. And I'll be more than happy to stick a paintbrush in your hand."

The plan was for Nora to stay at Halcyon for a week or so while the heavy remodeling took place in the shop, so that would provide time to get the apartment cleaned up and hopefully livable before the shop opened.

"Nora, sorry to interrupt, but I'm going to take off now, if that's okay." Cathy ran her fingers down the front of the tall brass coffee maker sadly. "I'm not sure what to do with myself when the machines are this quiet."

"Oh, Cathy, I'm sorry. This must be hard for you, listening to our plans to change things."

"Change is part of life, so don't be sorry. It was my decision to sell, and it needed to be done." Nora knew Cathy was unhappy about her plans to revamp the shop and replace her aging espresso maker with a state-of-the-art La Marzocco. The shiny new machine was sitting in its box in the back room, waiting for a place of honor behind the new counter.

"Cathy, why *did* you sell the shop?" Amanda asked.

"My granddaughter needed the money."

Blake frowned. "I've known you for five years now, and I never knew you had grandchildren."

"I didn't know, either, until last summer." Cathy looked at their surprised expressions and shrugged. "It's a long, sad story of ruined relationships between mothers and daughters, and I'm not about to depress you with it."

Nora and Becky locked eyes. Nora silently vowed that would never happen to them.

CHAPTER SEVEN

NORA'S FIRST WEEK of business with the newly re-
named Gallant Brew threatened to be the death
of her. She wasn't at all used to spending twelve
hours on her feet, and she definitely wasn't used
to setting her alarm clock for 5:30 a.m. But if she
wanted the shop open by six thirty, she had no
choice. The mysterious and complicated science
of coffee brewing made her brain even more tired
than her feet were, and Cathy's voice repeated in
her head on an endless loop.

Nora had watched hours of video tutorials online before leaving Atlanta, but nothing prepared
her for the real deal, with Cathy watching her fill
the filter, level it, then tamp the grounds, but not
too hard. But they couldn't be too loose, either.
The coffee stream had to be fine, like a mouse's
tail. If it was dripping out instead of streaming,
the grounds needed to be thicker. A proper ex-
traction should take no longer than twenty-five
to twenty-seven seconds. The milk had to be the
perfect temperature or the froth would be too
thin. Or too thick. Neither was good. It was im-

portant to use metal pitchers for the milk. When the pitcher was too hot to hold, it was done. The used grounds had to be dumped immediately, and it was important to have beans ready to grind fresh.

Nora's head had spun with all the directions, and she'd written lists as fast as she could. Cathy had insisted she learn how to brew first on the antique brass espresso maker, then on the twenty-year-old manual machine.

"This is an *art*. You'll never know if that new-fangled machine is making a good cup of espresso if you don't understand the whole process."

After three days of "art" lessons, Nora banished Cathy's old machine to the kitchen and fired up the ruby-red automated espresso machine. She still had to keep an eye on the grinder, but the measurements and temperatures for the brew and the milk were much more controlled. Even Cathy finally admitted the "newfangled" machine made excellent espresso and cappuccino, *and* made it more efficiently. She'd managed to open in time for Valentine's Day, offering a two-for-one sweetheart special that had brought a lot of traffic into the coffee shop the first week. They were off to a good start.

Nora pulled the trash bag out of the kitchen receptacle, closed it with a twist tie and set it in the hallway with the full bag from the café. The front of the shop was locked up tight with the shades pulled low.

She'd spent longer than expected working on the books tonight, trying to make sense of Cathy's records for the past few years. She didn't know how much to order of anything based on Cathy's scribbled notes in an old spiral binder. How did the woman ever manage to make money? Or had she made a fortune and just didn't have the records to show it?

Nora sighed. It would probably take her another month or so to get the paperwork in order, but she couldn't deal with it anymore tonight. One last trip to the Dumpster and she could crawl upstairs and maybe eat something before collapsing into bed. Tomorrow it would start all over again. The muscles running up the back of her legs protested at the very thought.

Too tired to grab the heavy jacket hanging by the back door, she figured she could handle the short walk to the giant green trash receptacle on the far side of the parking lot without it. She thought she was getting used to the bone-chilling dampness of winter in the Catskills, but she still gasped when she pushed the back door open. Bracing it with her hip, she tugged the heavy trash bags outside.

She checked her wrist to make sure the key fob was still there before the door closed behind her.

After having to call Amanda twice in two weeks to come unlock the door with Blake's extra key, Nora was hypervigilant about not locking herself out again.

There were many challenges in Nora's new life, but that massive metal monster in front of her was the bane of her existence. It was not designed for someone as vertically challenged as she was. The high door of the Dumpster was heavy, and she had to hold it open while tossing the trash inside. That was no easy task with short, tired arms.

The only way for her to do it was to attack it. She'd throw open the door, whip the garbage bags in, then jump away and let the door slam closed. There was a strong possibility the door was going to end up smacking her on the head one of these days, if she didn't move fast enough, but so far she'd been lucky.

She hauled the two bags across the lot and braced herself, gripping the first bag tightly.

Fling door open.

Toss bag in.

Jump back.

Success! One more bag and she'd be able to go back to her warm, almost-finished apartment and get off her aching feet. She took a deep breath and wrapped her fingers tightly around the top of the bag while trying to ignore the sting of cold air in her lungs.

Fling door open.

Toss bag in.

Land on her back on the hard, cold pavement.

That had definitely *not* been part of the plan. She didn't realize she'd been standing on black ice until her feet shot out from under her when she twisted to throw the bag through the opening the second time. The impact knocked the air from her lungs, leaving her gasping like a fish out of water. She closed her eyes and took a silent inventory, starting by wiggling her toes, then moving up her body until she was tentatively turning her head back and forth. Everything seemed to be in working order, other than a dull ache in her lower back. More specifically, her butt. She could almost feel the bruises forming there.

"Open your eyes and look at me."

She was so surprised to hear the deep voice right above her face that her eyes snapped open and she started to sit up, a soft moan of pain escaping her lips.

"Easy, easy. Don't move until we know if you're injured."

Asher Peyton's hands gently held her shoulders down, his eyes staring straight into hers. He was on one knee at her side, and he looked worried. About her.

"It's cold. Let me up." His presence here was

confusing, and she was too tired and sore to deal with confusion well.

"Yes, it is cold. That's why people in the North wear *coats* outside when it's only fifteen degrees." He glanced down at the old sneakers she was wearing. "And boots that give you traction on ice. Tell me where it hurts."

His fingers were still holding her shoulders, and she did her best to ignore the sizzle she felt. There could be no sizzle between her and the man who hated her daughter. She pushed his hands away.

"I'm fine. Let me up."

"Nora…" The way he said her name, with an intensity she didn't think he even realized, made her stay still. She didn't want to feel the flutter in her chest when he spoke, but there it was. Why did it have to be *this* man, of all men, who made her react this way?

"I'm fine. Really." She needed to get away from him.

He sat back and watched as she carefully got to a sitting position and stretched. When she didn't feel any surprises, she moved to stand. Asher stood with her, supporting her with one arm until she was on her feet, then he stepped away. But only after draping his coat over her shoulders. She couldn't resist pulling it tight around her to soak up its warmth.

She noticed the trash bag hadn't made it into the metal box. She reached for it, but Asher stopped her, muttering something under his breath. With one smooth move, he tossed the bag inside, then slowly closed the heavy door. Nora burned with irritation.

"I could have done that." She was pretty sure she saw the corner of his mouth lift in a half smile.

"Of course you could have." Something in his tone screamed sarcasm, and she bristled.

"I've been tossing out the trash from the shop all week."

"Yeah, I know."

What did *that* mean?

"Why are you even here?"

He hesitated before answering. "I saw you fall. I wasn't going to leave you lying there."

Nora glanced up at the small window overlooking the lot from above Asher's studio. She had a similar small window in her place, and it was located in her utility room. Assuming they had similar floor plans, he'd been watching her from his laundry room.

She turned to glare at him, knowing her annoyance was partially fueled by exhaustion and hunger, but she got no satisfaction from it. He was busy staring at the green bin with a great deal of concentration.

"You need a platform with a step or two to be able to reach the door." He kicked at the frozen ground, and his voice dropped as if speaking to himself. "It would need to be level."

"Yeah, well, until the garbage company decides to supply us with a trash bin with stairs, or even better, a door that someone under six feet tall can manage, I'll just have to make do."

"I could make something."

"You... Why would you do that?"

He looked at her in surprise. "Because I can build something that will make it safer for you..."

"I thought you hated me."

His hands rose in a frustrated gesture. "I've never once said that. Look, it wouldn't matter if it was you or if it was Carl at the liquor store. It's not a safe setup."

"So you don't hate me?"

His head dropped until his chin almost hit his chest. "I have definitely forgotten the joys of trying to talk logic with a woman."

"I beg your pardon?"

"Never mind. I'm just trying to be a good neighbor. Don't turn it into some evil plot."

Nora crossed her arms. "Says the man who thinks my pregnant daughter and I are plotting to trap his son into marriage."

Asher rubbed the back of his neck, his lips thinning in anger. "Let's leave our dumbass kids out of this, okay? Christ, I'm sorry I even came out here." He reached his hand toward her. "Why don't you get off that…"

Nora finished the sentence in her head. He was going to tell her to get off her high horse, just like Paul always used to say. *Get off that high horse you're always on.* Just because she was organized and liked things under control, didn't mean she was some kind of uptight snob. What had Asher called her back in November? A *fixer*? Well, she'd fix him. She slapped his hand away.

Which was a bad idea, because she was still standing on black ice. The quick movement sent her feet skittering, and she threw out her arms to catch her balance. Asher muttered something and grabbed her. Instead of being thankful for the save, she struggled to pull away.

"Get your hands off me!" She pushed him away, resisting the urge to stomp her feet like a child. The man made her completely irrational. "And don't tell me to get off my high horse, because I wasn't…"

"What?"

"Don't play dumb with me, Asher Peyton. Here, take your damn coat and good night." She whipped his warm jacket off her shoulders and moved to throw it at him, but because this apparently was her life now, she stepped on the edge of the ice again and started to lose her balance.

"Careful!" The jacket hit him in the face and he tossed it off, grabbing her arm for yet another rescue. Could this night get any more embarrassing?

Flashing blue lights lit up the parking lot.

Yes, apparently it could get a *lot* more embarrassing.

"Oh, my God! It's the police!"

ASHER LOOKED DOWN at the petite brunette spitting fire at him and almost laughed. Her chin-length hair was wild from all the flailing she'd been doing. It was usually tucked neatly behind her ears, but this softer look was good on her. There was nothing soft about those eyes, though. They were flashing gold in his direction, partly in anger and partly, he guessed, in panic at the sight of Dan's police cruiser.

Dan killed the flashing lights almost as soon as he'd turned them on. As he got out of the car, Asher wondered how long his friend had been watching. Nora yanked her arm away from him again, finally standing well away from the ice.

"Is there a problem here, folks?" Dan was trying to wear his sheriff face, but Asher could tell he was biting back laughter. Asher would never hear the end of this one.

Nora started talking a mile a minute. Surprise, surprise—Little Miss Goody Two-shoes was afraid of the police.

"No, no, Officer. There's nothing to worry about. Just a little accident and a misunderstanding, and I'm just heading inside now, so there's really nothing to see here…"

"Did you really just say 'there's nothing to see here' to a cop?" Asher bent over to pick his jacket up off the ground, thankful he could hide his uncharacteristic smile from her. No one else could make him smile so damned much. "Could you sound any *more* guilty?"

In the soft glow of the single parking lot light, he saw her eyes go wide. Was she really afraid of being arrested by Dan?

"I didn't mean it that way!" She shot a glare at him before turning to Dan, her hands fluttering in front of her. She forced out a laugh. "I'm sorry if that sounded… Really, though…there's nothing to see…here." She closed her eyes and groaned. "I'm just going to shut up now."

Dan laughed. "Yes, ma'am. I would advise you to stay silent during any future run-ins with law enforcement." Nora swallowed hard, and Dan shook his head. "Relax! I only hit the lights to let you know I was here." He gave Asher a curious look. "No one's going to jail tonight, unless one of you wants to press charges?"

He couldn't help himself. "Yeah, I'm pressing charges for verbal and physical abuse."

Nora's head whipped around and her mouth

dropped open. "This is nothing to joke about, for God's sake. The man is a *sheriff*! Besides, you're the one who physically abused me."

Dan's eyebrows rose, but he still wore an amused smile. "Is that true, Mr. Peyton?"

"Only if you call saving a woman from cracking her stubborn head open on the ice abuse. And for thanks, I got my coat thrown in my face and was falsely accused of insulting her." Nora rested her hands on her hips. The motion pulled her knit top tight across her breasts, and, well, it was cold out here. Asher's eyes lingered on her chest until Dan cleared his throat loudly, snapping him back to the conversation. "Um, yeah. I tried to tell her to get off the ice, and she assumed I was saying something else entirely."

He watched the emotions flit across her face and wondered who it was that had accused her of being on a high horse to begin with. It must have happened a lot for her to automatically assume that was where he was going.

The thought made his stomach twist for some reason. They hadn't exactly gotten off on the best foot at Thanksgiving, what with both their children being idiots and all, but she was now his neighbor. He wouldn't accomplish anything by antagonizing her. And he *had* been missing his morning cups of coffee from the café. He'd avoided the place since Nora bought it.

She bit her lower lip, and some of the fire faded from her eyes. The sight of her, small and shivering, chewing her lip and looking up at him with those golden eyes, made something funny happen in his chest. Not funny ha ha, but funny like his heart was racing uncontrollably in a really weird way. Maybe he'd be better off making his own damned coffee.

Dan cleared his throat again, and Asher and Nora quickly broke their intense stare. They'd been gazing at each other the whole time he'd been lost in thought. Interesting. And dangerous. Dan stepped forward and extended his hand to Nora.

"I'm Deputy Sheriff Dan Adams, ma'am. And this lunkhead here is a friend of mine." Asher rolled his eyes. "Sorry if I startled you with the lights. I was pulling in to see him when I saw two people struggling by the trash bin and a coat went flying, so I figured I'd announce my presence." He gave Asher another intense look, as if he'd like to be interrogating him. "And then I saw who it was. You're Nora Bradford, right? The new owner of Caffeine Cathy's?"

Regaining some of her composure, she shook Dan's hand. "Yes, I'm Nora. And the coffee shop is called the Gallant Brew now. I fell on the ice, and Mr. Peyton came to assist me. There was a minor misunderstanding after that." She looked at Asher with narrowed eyes.

"About Michael and your daughter?" Nora stiffened, and Dan laughed softly. "It's a small town, Nora. I haven't met your daughter yet, but I hear she's a nice girl."

She glanced at Asher, and he realized Dan was still holding Nora's small hand in his. He wasn't sure what was more annoying—his feelings about Dan holding her hand, or the direction the conversation was taking.

"I assume you didn't hear that from your friend?"

The last thing Asher wanted to talk about was what was or was not happening with Michael and Nora's daughter. What was her name? Barbara? Betty? Becky. That was it, Becky. He spoke up before Dan could respond.

"I hate to break up this little social hour, but it's not exactly warm enough to hang around outdoors and chitchat. Nora, why don't you get back inside? Dan, you're welcome to join me for a nightcap." Nora's eyes widened. "Relax. He's off duty in five minutes."

Dan smiled at Nora and she returned it. The shared smiles made Asher's stomach churn for some reason. Dan was divorced. Nora was widowed. Why should Asher care if they became friends, or more than friends, for that matter?

"It was nice to meet you, Nora. I'll definitely stop by for coffee sometime." Dan gave Asher a quick grin as he finally let go of Nora's hand. Had his friend just been playing with him?

"It was nice to meet you, too, Dan. And please do stop by. I'm having pastries delivered every day from the bakery in Windham, and they're delicious." She started to turn toward the building, tossing her parting comment over her shoulder. "Good night, Asher. Thanks for trying to be a gentleman."

Before he could ask if she was insulting him or not—*trying?*—she was hurrying through her back door. The lock clicked behind her.

"So," Dan said, "you want to tell me what *that* was all about?"

"What?" Asher was staring up at the light that had just come on in the third-floor window. He'd been inside the apartment when Cathy owned it and knew the layout. Nora was in the loft. Was she using it as her bedroom?

"You're almost as bad as her with the whole 'there's nothing to see here' act. Why were you hanging on to her, and why was she throwing things at you?"

Asher walked toward the back door to his shop, digging his keys out of his pocket. "It was no big deal. She fell on the ice trying to get her trash into the Dumpster. I tried to help her, but she's Little

Miss Independent. Every time she tried to show me how tough she was, she slipped on more ice. I really *was* trying to keep her from cracking her stubborn skull open."

"And she thanked you by throwing your coat at you?"

"She was returning it. And yes." Asher stepped inside, but Dan didn't follow right away.

"There definitely seems to be some weird vibe between the two of you."

Asher narrowed his eyes. "You mean like a my-son-and-her-daughter-got-pregnant-together-and-neither-of-us-are-happy-about-it vibe? Yes, definitely."

Dan glanced at his watch and stepped inside, officially off duty. "No, I sensed a completely different kind of vibe."

Asher told himself he didn't know what the hell Dan was referring to.

But he'd felt it, too. A vibe. A Nora Bradford vibe.

CHAPTER EIGHT

NORA SCRUBBED THE last of the guest-room paint from around her fingernails and wiped down the utility sink in the laundry room. Now that she'd spent a few weeks actually living in the apartment, it was finally starting to come together as a home. She'd painted the few nonbrick walls a soft yellow. The kitchen cupboards wore several coats of glossy black paint, and she'd replaced the ancient Formica countertops with white quartz. The old island had been expanded to accommodate room for four barstools. New stainless-steel appliances had arrived yesterday, and bright cherry-red accessories added a jaunty tone to the space.

She'd thought Amanda was crazy when she suggested the diner-esque color scheme for the kitchen, but it looked just right in the brick loft, and it made her smile whenever she walked in. The rest of the apartment had been transformed, too, with long striped drapes at the windows and her old furniture artfully arranged to create a living room and small office area.

"Nora!" Amanda's voice no longer echoed in the loft now that they'd arranged oriental rugs on the plank floors and hung pictures on the walls. Her designer cousin had worked miracles with this former greenhouse. Nora looked up into the bedroom loft, where Amanda was sitting, her feet hanging over the edge twelve feet above the living-room floor. Her arms rested on the lower horizontal iron railing, now also wearing a glossy coat of black paint.

"Come on up and see your new oasis!"

The pounding of hammers and the heavy footsteps of Blake and his contractor, Bobby, had stopped over an hour ago. Nora, under strict orders from her cousin, had been using the downstairs bathroom, and she hadn't peeked once into the tiny loft bath while Amanda transformed it.

She hurried up the steps, groaning only slightly at the strain in her legs. After three weeks of running the coffee shop, she was starting to get into shape. Those first days had been horrible, and the pain in her legs when she'd finally sat down at night often left her in tears. But it was getting better.

They'd decided on soft blues for the bedroom, and it looked lovely now that the bedding had arrived and her furniture was in place. When she woke up in the mornings, she sat up and looked through the big arched window right out to Gallant Lake across the street.

"Are you ready to see your new en suite?" Amanda's ponytail was bouncing as she rocked back and forth on her heels. She was more excited about this than Nora was. "Now remember, we didn't have a lot of space to work with, and you did lose a couple feet of closet space, but I think it's totally going to be worth it." Without waiting for any response from Nora, she opened the door.

The small bathroom, which had been painted bright orange originally, was now covered in gleaming white marble, from the floor tiles to the walls to the expanded shower, now enclosed in glass instead of a ragged old shower curtain. The only thing that wasn't white was the vanity. It was an antique cabinet Amanda had found and converted for this room. A clear vessel sink sat on top under a silver gilded mirror on the wall.

"Amanda… I'm speechless." Nora stepped in and looked around. It was still compact, but the elegance factor was off the charts. "This looks like a miniature version of some old-time movie star's bathroom. It's beautiful!"

Amanda grinned. "I know, right? As soon as I saw this little cabinet, I knew it would be perfect. There was no way to squeeze a tub in here, of course, but you have a tub downstairs. And at least you can turn around in the shower now!"

Amanda jumped into the shower to prove her point. "This rainwater shower head will be nearly as relaxing as a bath."

Nora looked up and agreed. The square shower head almost covered the entire top of the small shower. "I love it. The place finally feels like home."

Amanda tipped her head to the side. "Does it? Are you settling in? Has your neighbor called the cops on you again since that first time?"

Nora swatted at her cousin with a hand towel as they walked out of the bathroom. "Shut up! He didn't call the cops. The sheriff is a friend of his." Nora had noticed Dan Adams's cruiser in the lot several times since her little run-in with Asher two weeks ago.

Amanda glanced back at her as they went down to the living room. "Blake said the steps Asher built by the trash bin are sturdy enough to withstand an earthquake."

It was only two nights after her fall that she'd lugged the trash outside and found the sturdy platform with a railing and two steps leading up to it. It put her at the perfect height to be able to open the heavy door and drop her trash bag inside without twisting herself into a knot. Amanda was still talking, but Nora had no clue what she'd just said.

"I'm sorry, what?"

"The steps Asher made? You know, that guy next door who makes you all blushy and absentminded?"

Right on cue, Nora's cheeks warmed.

"I don't know what you're talking about. He did a nice neighborly thing and I thanked him for it." Not in person, of course. She'd left a bag of fresh pastries hanging on his shop door the next morning, with a short note of thanks. "Let's not forget he once suggested my daughter get rid of the child she's carrying. *His* grandchild."

"Okay, I get that. But I also see the way you react whenever his name comes up. In some little corner of your brain, he's still Hot Produce Guy."

Nora picked up her clipboard from the kitchen counter. She wasn't about to acknowledge the accuracy of Amanda's statement. "With the bathroom done, the only project left is cleaning out that mess of a laundry room." She checked off a line on her lengthy moving-in to-do list. "But that can wait. Five in the morning comes awfully early, and I'm exhausted."

"I don't know how you do it. Don't you think it's time you got some help with the shop?"

"Yes, actually. I'm going to look for some parttime staff, and Becky's offered to help on the weekends."

Amanda stopped in the middle of pulling on

her down jacket. "Really? So she's accepted your presence in Gallant Lake?"

"It sort of depends on what day of the week it is. She still thinks I came here to spy on her and Michael, so I can secretly run their lives." Amanda's eyebrows climbed toward her hairline, but Nora waved her laughter away. "Yeah, yeah, I know. It's partly true. She doesn't know the main reason I left Atlanta was to protect her from any stories about her dad. And, besides, *she's* the one who told me to start living my own life. So here I am, doing that."

"You *are* doing that. And she's got to be proud of you, even if she won't say it out loud yet. The coffee shop looks great and everyone is talking about it. The ski season is almost over, but when the summer tourist traffic hits, you're going to do fantastic. And you have very stubbornly done most of it on your own." Amanda gestured around the apartment. "I mean, look at this place! You turned a pot farm into a home straight out of a design magazine."

"Oh, God, stop reminding me about the pot plants. I swear I can still smell them sometimes."

"Cathy didn't happen to leave any samples, did she?"

Nora shooed Amanda to the door with a startled laugh. "No! The only thing she left behind was dirt and creepy crawlies."

"Creepy crawlies? In the middle of winter?"

"She kept this place the temperature of a hot-house, and a bunch of spiders and flies decided to snowbird right here above the coffee shop." Nora suppressed a shudder. When the contractors were cleaning, they told her they'd cleared quite a few spiderwebs, and some of them were pretty big. Since then, she'd been killing flies and, much to her horror, a variety of smallish spiders, but the number seemed to be diminishing.

She said good-night to Amanda and turned, leaning against the closed door and looking around the apartment suspiciously. Big scary spiders were something she hadn't minded leaving behind in the South. Surely they didn't grow that big up here.

Did they?

ASHER WAS SURPRISED to see his son's red Jeep driving up the steep mountain road. He didn't get a lot of visitors when he was on Gallant Mountain, and Michael hadn't been up here in months. Not since right after Christmas.

He set down the sander and brushed the sawdust off the front of his T-shirt and out of his hair. The thick slab of cherry he'd chosen for the mantel on the fieldstone fireplace was ready for a clear coat of stain now that it was sanded smooth.

"Dad? Where are you?" Michael's voice echoed in the large, empty space.

Asher met him in the kitchen. "Hey, son. What brings you up here?"

Michael looked around and gave a low whistle. "You've been busy this winter. It's looking good, Dad."

Asher followed Michael's gaze. The kitchen opened to the great room, which had a soaring vaulted ceiling and one wall lined with windows overlooking Gallant Lake and the snowy mountains beyond. The recovered antique plank floors were scarred and weathered. There were three bedrooms beyond the living room, and a wide circular staircase led up to the master suite.

Nothing was finished. The rooms were basically raw wood and unprimed drywall. The only exception was the kitchen, which was at least partially completed. He'd hung the hickory cabinets last week and topped them with finely grained marble in dark gray. Appliances would arrive next week.

"It's coming along." Even in the kitchen, the floors were still plywood. He looked through the large windows to the outside, purposely avoiding the incompleteness indoors. He once thought he'd raise his family here, but his ex-wife had been less than enthusiastic. Amy said it was too long a commute to White Plains, so they'd agreed it would be a vacation home. But that had never happened, either. Now it was just a place to stay busy when he had spare time.

"I like the kitchen," Michael said.

"It's not done."

"It's a lot more done than it was in December."

"I suppose."

This conversation was going nowhere fast.

"Why are you here, Michael?" Maybe there was trouble in paradise, and his son was ready to accept Asher's California offer. The rush of adrenaline he felt at that thought was quickly followed by something resembling regret. Before he could examine that any further, Michael turned and leaned back against the large island, crossing his arms and looking Asher straight in the eye.

"We need to talk, Dad." Asher didn't know how to read Michael's body language anymore. Was this going to be a good kind of talk or another lecture on how to behave?

"Talk about what?"

Both men had been careful to keep their voices devoid of emotion, but now Michael's arms swung wide as he exploded in anger. "Seriously, Dad? How about all the things we haven't talked about in months? Things like my fiancée and the baby we're going to have. My wedding. School. The money pit I rented and need your help with."

Michael's brown eyes shone with what ap-

peared to be unshed tears, and that hit Asher
right in the center of his chest. He had to grind
his teeth to keep from reaching out to his only
remaining child. He wanted to ask Michael what
had happened. Why was he here now, after so
much time? Was everything okay? What could
Asher do to help? But those weren't the words
that ground through his clenched teeth. Instead,
he said the same words he'd said to Michael before. And to Dan. And to Nora.

"There isn't going to be a wedding."

Michael dropped his head until his heavy beard
brushed his chest, and he stared at the floor for
a long moment before speaking. His voice was
low but firm.

"You can't stop this with words, Dad. I get
that you're unhappy. But you can't just wish it
away." Michael glanced at the bottle of bourbon
on the kitchen counter and the empty glass next
to it. "You can't drink it away, either. You can't
drink *me* away. I'm standing right here in front
of you asking you for some support. *Please.*" Michael looked up and ran his fingers through his
dark hair. "I miss you. I'm asking you to be my
dad again."

Asher struggled to come up with a response.
He was still determined to protect his son from
this terrible mistake he was making with his life.
He had to stop this marriage and get Michael as

far away from this girl as possible. It was for his own good.

"I've never stopped being your dad, Michael."

"Then be *happy* for me, damn it!" Usually the most composed person in the room, Michael started pacing the kitchen in agitation. "I know our timing is a little off, but I'm in love with a terrific girl, and we're having a baby together. We're starting a life right here in Gallant Lake. I gave her a ring—Grandma Walker's ring—and we're planning a wedding. I want you to be a part of all that, Dad."

"You know I can't be."

"Why the hell not?" Michael walked up and planted his feet right in front of Asher, as if daring him to deny his presence. Asher held his ground, but his heart stuttered and he blinked away from his son's face, trying to refocus. He was doing the right thing here. He had to be.

"You're twenty years old. You don't understand what you're doing, starting a family before either of you have your degrees. Before either of you have a job."

"We're both going to transfer."

"What?"

"Albany has a law program for me, and it's only an hour away in good weather. And Becky's looking at a state university program where a lot of the work can be done online. When the baby's a little older, we'll find him a good day care program so Becky can catch up on her studies."

"And how are you planning on paying for all this? Because I'm not…" Michael's words finally registered. "Wait, did you say *him*?"

Michael smiled slowly. "You're going to have a grandson, Dad. As far as money goes, we'll be up to our eyeballs in student-loan debt, just like every other college graduate out there. Hopefully we'll grab some scholarships, and Mom's helping with the rent on the house. I've got my job with Judge Wilkes and Becky's working part-time."

You're going to have a grandson…

Of all Michael's words, those were the only ones he'd heard. A baby boy. A blue-wrapped bundle handed over in a hospital nursery, carrying hopes and dreams for a future that might never happen. Been there. Done that. He stepped back and shook his head sharply.

"No."

"No?"

"I mean…no, I won't pay for college if you stay here. My offer still stands for Stanford, Michael. But not here in New York."

Michael let out a harsh breath, then turned away. "When I said I wanted your support, I wasn't talking about your damned money. I want you to know your future daughter-in-law. I want you to know your grandson. I want us to be a *family*."

Family.

There was no way for his son to understand how much pain that one word caused him. The panic it induced. The sorrow that welled up and threatened to drown him.

He scrubbed both hands down his face, trying to compose himself and swallow the tide of emotion barreling his way. He knew his words would hurt Michael. But he couldn't stand by and watch his son suffer the pain that a child could bring.

"I'm sorry, Michael. I really am. But I can't do it. I won't. This is a mistake."

Michael stared at him long and hard before heading to the door with swift, angry strides. His parting words hung in the air long after his Jeep had roared down the driveway.

"You're right, Dad. This *is* a mistake. And you're the one making it."

CHAPTER NINE

NORA PULLED ANOTHER stack of boxes from the back of her laundry room. From the clanking sound, she'd guess it contained more coffee mugs. Cathy must have gotten one heck of a discount on the brightly colored porcelain mugs she'd bought for the café, because there were cases full of them *everywhere*. Not only were there cases of extra mugs in the storage room downstairs, there was also a wall full of boxes up here in the apartment.

It was after ten o'clock, and Nora was exhausted. But she'd have the rare luxury of being able to sleep in tomorrow, so she was determined to get this last room cleaned and painted. The oak floor had already been sanded down to bare wood, and she was going to stain it after she finished painting the walls. She carried the boxes out into the hallway.

She *hated* clutter and disorganization. The café downstairs was finally gleaming and completely organized in every nook and cranny. The apartment was turning into a lovely home. And once she took care of this room, she'd be able to relax.

She'd hired the most unlikely part-time employee to open the shop three days a week: Cathy Meadows. Caffeine Cathy had shown up yesterday with the ad in hand, claiming she was bored and restless without having the shop to come to. And Cathy *loved* mornings. Nora did not. So Nora hired her, but only after having a lengthy discussion about hygiene and abiding by the rules. Just to be sure, Nora had hung numerous little signs where customers couldn't see them, reminding Cathy to wash her hands and use plastic gloves when handling food.

With Becky helping on the weekends, Nora's time was going to be a lot more manageable. Once she finally caught up on her sleep, which right now felt like it might take weeks, she could actually have this new life of hers right where she wanted it—under control.

After she finished up in this room, everything on her most recent list would be checked off. Which meant, of course, she'd have to start a new list.

The little house the kids had rented on the edge of town was in worse shape than this apartment. On the plus side, it did have a charming front porch and a picket-fenced backyard, although the fence was leaning in several spots and needed painting. Their landlord had given them permission to make improvements, so Nora would work on that to-do list, too.

She wiped down the built-in shelves, then started sanding the surfaces smooth enough for painting. The shelves were deep and ran around the corner in the back of the room, creating areas that were hard for her arms to reach. She pulled a wooden crate over and stood on it so she could clean the top shelves. Creating mental lists always relaxed her, and she started humming to herself as she thought of things to do. Becky and Michael would need nursery furniture, clothes, toys, diapers, outlet covers. She'd look for a bassinet for her apartment, too, so the baby would have a place to sleep when they visited.

Nora smiled. She was going to have a grandson. Becky had given her *that* news yesterday. A little boy was on his way. The timing wasn't ideal, but there was nothing they could do about that now. Ready or not, a new family was being created. And Nora would make sure they were ready. She reached under the shelf in the corner with the sanding block.

And a spider dropped down onto her hand.

Nora froze. She was afraid of all spiders, but this was the scariest one she'd ever seen. It had a small black head and a bulbous body that reminded her of the evil spider from *The Lord of the Rings*. Furry, almost two inches long and with sharply jointed legs expanding its overall size, this was an eight-legged horror show.

And right now it was sitting on the back of her hand.

She let out a piercing scream as she jumped off the crate, shaking the spider off. Scrambling backward, she bumped into the stack of boxes filled with mugs, sending the top two crashing to the floor. The spider landed in the center of the laundry room, apparently unharmed and unfazed. Nora shook her hands wildly—she could still feel that thing crawling on her skin.

"Oh, my God! Oh, my God! Oh, my *God*!" she wailed. The spider took a few slow steps in her direction, and Nora let out another scream. Her heart was beating so wildly she could hear her pulse pounding in her ears.

She couldn't turn her back on the spider. If it disappeared in here, she'd have no choice but to move out of the apartment. And burn it to the ground. There was no way she'd ever be able to sleep knowing this thing was crawling around. And if she tried to kill it and failed, it would surely seek revenge on her. Everyone knew that was how spiders worked.

But how was she going to get rid of it? There was a loud noise behind her, probably another box of mugs landing on the floor. She flinched but never took her eyes off the spider, which seemed to be sharing her dilemma. It was just standing there in the middle of the floor, as if it didn't know what to do next.

"Nora! What the hell?"

Asher's deep, urgent voice was right behind her, but she didn't respond. She was too busy trying to breathe. She hugged herself tightly, hoping to regain some semblance of control. She didn't know where he'd come from or how he'd gotten into her apartment, but he assessed the situation quickly. His voice softened as he stepped closer.

"Okay. Alright. It's just a spider—it's not going to hurt you." He put his hands gently on her shoulders. "Breathe. It's okay."

Just a spider? *Just?*

Nora took a ragged breath, "It was on me! It was *on* me! That son of a bitch was *on* me!" She ignored the smile that quickly flashed across his face at her furious outburst. Her hands were reflexively shaking at her sides, trying to dispose of invisible monsters.

He patted her shoulder and moved past her. He raised his foot, preparing to crush the spider under the sole of his well-worn leather shoe.

"No!" Nora yelled, unable to stop herself. "That's bare wood—it'll stain!" She didn't even want to think of the fluids that would come out of that grotesque body.

His mouth dropped open and he looked at her in consternation.

"Oh, for chrissakes…" He opened the small window above the washing machine, letting in a blast of cold, damp air. He grabbed a wooden paint stirrer lying next to the paint can on the dryer, put one end under the fat spider, lifted it and quickly flipped the creature right out the window. From the looks of the trajectory, the spider had flown over the fire escape and down to the icy parking lot. Thankfully her car was parked across the lot and not next to the building.

Nora watched him pull the window closed, then buried her face in her hands and, much to her horror, burst into tears. She didn't know if it was from fear, relief or embarrassment. Even more shocking, she felt Asher's arms move around her and draw her against his very solid chest.

He made soothing sounds as his mouth brushed against her hair, and she was able to start breathing at last. He smelled like wood and whiskey, and she liked it. A lot. She let herself just soak in his essence for a minute before reality hit. A spider. A scream. And *Asher*, of all people, breaking in to her home to save her.

She started to giggle. Then she laughed out loud. He pulled his head back and looked down at her as if he feared she was having some kind of breakdown.

"Oh, my God," she gasped, unable to stop laughing. "I can't believe that just happened!" She sniffled at her remaining tears, wiping her face unglamorously with the back of her arm. She looked up and smiled at him. Her hands rested lightly on his chest. "I don't like spiders."

His voice was dry as he responded. "Really? You had me completely fooled…"

That made her laugh even harder, and now he started to chuckle, too. This close to each other, she could see that his eyes were an incredible blue with the tiniest flecks of silver. And he had a very nice smile.

She was admiring that smile, that mouth, those lips…when something happened. It was hard to define, really, but something shifted in her chest. Her gaze moved back up to his eyes. He knew she'd been staring at his mouth. He knew she'd been thinking about kissing him. Their smiles faded and the atmosphere went from light laughter to…something. She couldn't look away from him, and Asher was apparently caught in the same net. His arms tightened, pulling her closer, and she didn't resist.

It felt like she was having an out-of-body experience, like she was watching the scene play out from somewhere up above. She saw their bodies pressing against each other, both making unconscious adjustments to find full contact, from legs to hips to chest. She saw his head lower toward hers, and she knew he was going to kiss her. And she wanted him to. Her eyes closed and her breathing slowed. This was going to be good.

And then he was gone, stepping away abruptly. Her eyes snapped open and she felt a sting of loss. It had been a long time since she'd been held by a man. And she'd never felt like *that* in any man's arms—as if the entire world had fallen away at their feet. Asher was shaking his head, likely trying to regain his bearings. She knew just how he felt.

His eyes had been dark with heat just seconds earlier, but she watched them cool as he took another step away. Fear was in those eyes now, and she wasn't sure where it had come from. She only knew she wanted to take that fear away.

Jumping back into his arms and kissing him senseless, no matter how tempting, wasn't a good plan, though. She'd need something more logical, but her planning skills were temporarily short-circuited. Beyond his broad shoulders, she saw her back door standing wide-open. She'd locked it earlier, and she didn't see any signs of damage to the door frame.

"Wait—why are you here?"

He seemed relieved at the change of subject. Not that they'd spoken a word while he'd held her, but a whole lot of communication had gone on nevertheless. The corner of his mouth tipped up into a crooked smile.

"A gentleman is duty bound to respond to a woman's bloodcurdling screams. It's in the manual."

She pressed her hands to her heated cheeks in humiliation. "I'm sorry. When that thing landed on my hand…" She shuddered and looked up at him. "I'm grateful, but how did you get inside?"

He shuffled his feet uncomfortably, then held up a key. "Cathy and I exchanged keys a while ago, in case we lost ours or needed something. I was hoping you hadn't changed the locks."

Nora's mouth fell open. "You have a key to my apartment?"

"I'm guessing you have a key to mine, too." He pushed the back door closed and looked at the row of keys hanging on the wall behind it. "Yup—here it is." He picked up a wooden key chain shaped like a fish, with the words Gallant Lake printed in blue. "If it makes you feel better, you also have a key to Carl's place right here, and I'm sure he has keys to ours. It's nothing sinister, just being good small-town neighbors."

Nora looked at this tall, handsome man standing in the narrow hallway inside her home. She thought about the night he'd come out in the cold to help when she fell on the ice. The stairs he'd built so she could use the giant trash receptacle safely. The way he'd rushed over when he heard her screaming. A good small-town neighbor. A neighbor she should definitely *not* want to be kissing.

"Right. Neighbors. I can't imagine what you must have thought when you heard me."

His face sobered. "I didn't know what to think. I just grabbed the key and ran. But now that your hairy visitor is gone, I'll head back…"

"Would you like a cup of coffee? Or something stronger? I think I have some Kentucky bourbon in the cabinet. You drink bourbon, right?"

She didn't know why she'd said any of that, but the words were out there now. He stared at her long enough to make her uncomfortable, but instead of retracting the invitation, she defended it. Out loud, in an avalanche of words. "I mean, it's the least I can do after you came running to my rescue. I don't even think I've said the words *thank you* yet. Seriously, thank you so much. I have no idea what I would have done left here alone with that thing, short of burning the place down."

She looked around the utility room, wondering if that spider had any relatives left in here. The thought made her shudder.

"Plug in the vacuum cleaner."

"What?"

Asher pointed to the vacuum behind her.

"You're worried about finding more of them. Plug it in, and I'll vacuum all the seams and corners and make sure the room is clear." His mouth quirked into a half smile. "And then I'll toss the bag outside and stomp on it. While I'm doing that, you can pour me a shot of bourbon. Neat."

She wanted to tell him it wasn't necessary for him to vacuum, but she couldn't. The truth was, she'd sleep better knowing the room was free of the spider's avenging relatives. So she nodded and plugged in the cleaner, handing it to him. Then she left this complicated neighbor of hers vacuuming her laundry room while she went to pour him a drink.

THE WHINE OF the vacuum in the small room did nothing to calm Asher's racing mind. What the hell was he doing here, in Nora Bradford's apartment, running a vacuum cleaner, so late at night? Was he in some alternate reality? Was he dreaming? Something bumped up the hose of the cleaner, reminding him of why he was here. He swallowed hard and focused on what he was doing. Cathy had always called the spiders that gathered in the overheated apartment her fly traps. Asher would rather have the flies.

Something else bumped its way up the vacuum cleaner hose, not as loudly as the last one. Could have been a piece of dirt. He glanced up and saw a spiderweb arching under the top shelf. Maybe not a piece of dirt. He pulled the wooden crate closer and stood on it, being careful to cover every inch over and under and around the shelves. Then he dropped to his knees and made sure the lower spaces were free of surprises, too. When he was finished, he stuffed the vacuum bag into a plastic grocery bag and tied it shut.

Nora's screams had easily taken ten years off his life tonight. He'd just poured himself a third glass of whiskey when he heard her. At first he'd just stopped, instantly sober. Then he'd heard the loud crash and another scream, and his blood had run ice-cold, then raging hot. Convinced someone was hurting her, he hadn't hesitated in grabbing the key and running out the back door. Once he was inside, he'd seen two cases of Cathy's mugs smashed on the hall floor. And Nora, pale and trembling, having a stare down with one of the biggest, ugliest spiders he'd ever seen.

He *hated* spiders.

If that thing had moved while he held it on the paint stick, he probably would have dropped it and run. But it didn't, so he'd ended up looking like a hero. He frowned. Or like a crazy stalker neighbor she didn't know had a key to her home.

But she hadn't seemed to mind being in his arms. She'd moved right in, and damned if he didn't like the way her petite body had felt pressed against his, her hair wild around her face. It wasn't until his head was dropping down to kiss her that he'd come to his senses.

There'd been a few women since Amy gave up on him, but nothing serious. In the beginning, he'd sought a diversion from the shit storm his life had turned into. But sex wasn't a long-term painkiller. It also wasn't worth the emotional entanglements when a woman wanted more of him than he was capable of giving.

Nora, though, even for the brief moment she was in his arms, had felt very different from those casual hookups. Which meant she was dangerous. Getting into some emotional knot with the mother of his son's…whatever…was a colossally bad idea.

He stepped into the hallway and looked at the cases of mugs stacked there. The boxes had been on those back shelves, which was also where the spiders were. Probably not a good idea to leave them inside. He put the plastic bag on top of the stack, opened the back door and slid them all out onto the walkway. He'd figure out how to deal with them tomorrow. Probably with a big can of bug killer.

He should just close the door behind him and go home. That would be the smart thing to do. Nora's invitation to share a drink had surprised him so much that he'd agreed without a thought.

She might be offended if he left, but so what? It wasn't like he needed her to be his friend, or anything else, for that matter.

"Asher?"

She was standing in the hallway. Her dark hair was tucked behind her ears, neat and tidy again. With her brightly colored leggings—were those unicorns?—and a lime-green top, she looked more like a student than a woman about to become a grandmother. That reminder of their tenuous relationship was enough to stop his perusal of her. He should not be ogling this woman. But, instead of leaving, he stepped back inside and closed the door behind him. Because he was that much of an idiot.

"I thought you left without having your drink. Come on, I warmed up some leftover scones from the shop. I bet they go great with bourbon." She gave him a bright smile, and he realized just how foolish it was for him to be here with her. She was his adversary when it came to protecting his son. And her smile had the power to turn his resolve into dust.

He should have left, but instead, he followed her down the hall like a lost puppy.

CHAPTER TEN

NORA HANDED ASHER his glass of bourbon and quietly admired him as he took a sip and looked around her home with interest. His faded T-shirt still had a wet spot on the front from her tears. Seeing that made something deep inside her hum. His jeans hung low on his hips and clung deliciously to his very fine backside.

Whoa. What was she doing thinking about anyone's backside, especially Asher Peyton's? She gave herself a firm mental shake to snap herself out of it and took a sip of her red wine.

"The place looks good."

"Thanks. A little different from Cathy's style?"

He snorted. "You could say that." He looked up at the loft, and her face warmed. Her bed might not be visible from this angle, but he was still basically looking right into her bedroom. "I always thought this could be a great living space, but Cathy had other ideas."

"You knew about her clandestine growing operation up here?"

He smirked as he took another sip of bourbon.

"I'm surprised *you* do. She always makes it sound more serious than it really was, though. She had maybe two or three plants that weren't exactly legal. The rest were tomatoes and herbs."

That was news. Maybe it really *was* basil she'd been smelling. "Why wouldn't Cathy want to live right here over the shop?"

"She grew up here, and I don't think it holds good memories for her. She has a nice double-wide just outside town."

Nora took another sip of wine. It felt oddly comfortable to be sitting at her kitchen counter sharing drinks and scones with Asher. Who would have thought it possible? He stared up at the arched window, where they could see stars sparkling in the night sky.

"We don't have to be enemies, you know." She didn't realize she'd spoken her thought out loud until he turned to look at her, one brow arched.

"I don't think we're enemies." He paused, staring into his glass for a moment before continuing. "We're just on opposite sides of a situation." When he raised his head to meet her gaze head-on, she found herself unable to think clearly. He noticed her reaction, and his blue eyes darkened to cobalt. "What? No greeting-card quote for me tonight, Nora?"

There. That. The way he said her name, all soft and low and lingering. He'd done that out in the parking lot a few weeks ago. And now, sitting inside her home with the warmth of red wine in her veins, he hit her with it again. They stayed perfectly still, gazing at each other in silence. That strange *something* was back, shifting the atmosphere and shifting her heart. She found herself leaning forward. He did the same.

Then his phone buzzed and pinged in his pocket, snapping the moment so abruptly that they both sat back as if they'd been stung. Nora's face flamed, and Asher grumbled as he pulled the phone from his pocket and swiped it. It was on speaker, and the man's voice was loud and clear.

"Dude, are you okay?"

Asher gave Nora a chagrined smile. "I'm fine, Officer Dan. Did someone request a wellness check on me?"

"Yeah, *I* requested it," Dan answered. "I'm at your place. Your car's here. Your lights are on. Your back door is open. And you're nowhere to be found. If you've been kidnapped, give me a code word."

"The code word is *spider*." Nora giggled, and Asher took the phone off speaker and put it to his ear.

"That was my neighbor...Yes, *that* neighbor... Stop grilling me like I'm a suspect in something. I got rid of a spider for the lady and she offered me a drink." Asher rolled his eyes and rose to his feet. "I'll be right home, *Mom*." Then he ended the call.

Nora took another sip of wine as Asher drained his shot glass. The atmosphere had gone from flat-out sizzling to awkward.

"Does Dan stop by for drinks with you every night?"

Asher set his empty glass on the counter and gave her that crooked grin. His weatherworn face and long, dark hair gave him a devilish look that sent her heart racing again.

"We're not involved, if that's what you're suggesting."

She couldn't hold back another laugh. "That's not what I meant, although that would be fine with me." Other than the fact that she'd be ridiculously jealous of Dan. "He just seems to show up here a lot."

Asher shrugged. "It started with him feeling like he had to check on me. Then it just became a habit. And I keep my fridge stocked with his favorite beer."

He turned for the back hall, but Nora reached out and stopped him with her hand on his arm. She'd done the same thing a few months ago in his studio, when all hell broke loose between Asher and his son and her daughter. He stared at her hand in consternation, just as he had that first time. As if he wasn't used to being touched.

"Why did Dan feel like he needed to check on you?"

Asher looked toward the back door, probably wishing he was on the other side of it, but he didn't pull away.

"I did a stupid thing a few years ago. I couldn't sleep, so I went for a drive in the middle of the night." He turned to face her. "I'd had a few drinks and had no business being behind the wheel. Dan found me asleep in the car, engine still running, parked at the overlook outside town."

"He gave you a DUI?"

Asher shook his head. "No. We talked for a while, and he gave me a ride home. He said he couldn't prove I'd driven under the influence, since I was parked when he found me. Which was bullshit, of course. After that, he'd swing by to make sure I was doing my drinking at home." Asher reached for the door. "Then he started dropping in when he was off duty to have a beer with me. Or coffee. Depending on what kind of shift he's had."

"Sounds like a good friend."

He hesitated, then nodded, reaching for the door.

"The only one I have."

Those five words hit Nora hard. For some strange reason, she wanted to make things better for him.

"You and I just had drinks and a conversation. Friendships have started on less."

He stared deep into her eyes, as if he was searching for something there.

"You're going all Hallmark on me again. Don't try to fix me, Nora. You'd be wasting your time. I gotta go…"

"Asher."

"No, Nora. I have to go."

But he didn't open the door. Instead, he turned toward her. She didn't wait for an invitation, stepping in and leaning against his strong, hard chest. He hesitated for a split second, then folded his arms around her, and it felt so…right. She tipped her head back. His gaze fell to her lips and she silently begged him to finish the job this time and kiss her. Her whole body vibrated with the need of it. But he just rested his forehead on hers, shaking it back and forth.

"No, no, no." Was he talking to her or himself? "I am *not* going to kiss the mother of my son's girlfriend, no matter how much I want to. It's way too complicated." He gently pushed her away. "Whatever's happening here tonight, it's just adrenaline from the spider, or the booze, or… I don't know. But I am *not* going to kiss you, Nora. Good night." And he was gone.

She stood staring at the closed door for a long time. Asher could be rude and annoying, but he'd come running to her rescue tonight. He'd built those steps by the trash bin. And she'd seen him spreading salt on the lot when it was icy. He did all of that for her. He acted like he hated the world, but tonight she'd seen a spark of something there in his eyes. Loneliness. Fear. And temptation.

He'd said he wasn't going to kiss her.

But he'd also said he wanted to.

DAN WAS SITTING at the counter in Asher's kitchen with a half-empty bottle of beer in front of him. He gave Asher a huge grin when he walked in. He probably should have taken his truck and left for the mountain instead of coming back here to face Dan's abuse. But, even though he'd felt sober from the moment he heard Nora scream, he didn't trust his blood-alcohol level enough to try it.

His young friend slid a shot of whiskey in Asher's direction, chuckling to himself like he was in on the world's biggest joke.

Asher finally ran out of patience. "Go ahead. Have your fun."

Dan laughed out loud. "Oh, trust me, I'm already having fun. A *spider* emergency, huh? This I gotta hear." He waved his hand, gesturing for Asher to start talking. So he filled Dan in on the highlights of spider hunting but left out any mention of Nora burying her face against his chest.

He didn't tell Dan she'd smelled of coffee beans and a citrusy perfume. He didn't tell him she'd felt just about perfect in his arms.

He also didn't tell Dan about that moment when the air left the room and there was nothing but the two of them staring into each other's eyes. There was something magnetic about the way their bodies had pressed together, as if the pull was completely out of their control.

"So, let me get this straight. She screamed so loud over a *spider* that you felt you just had to go running over there and let yourself in?" Dan's brows bunched together. "You never gave your key back to Cathy?"

"I forgot about the damned thing until I heard her screaming. And it was a big freakin' spider, okay?" Asher sat back, rubbing his neck. "When I heard her...I thought she was being assaulted, damn it. What was I supposed to do?"

Dan tipped his head to the side. "Oh, I don't know...maybe call the *police*? What if there *was* someone in her place? Were you armed with anything?"

Asher shook his head. "She was right next door. And screaming. Do you really think I should have made a phone call instead of helping?"

"How about making the phone call *before* helping? At least I could have been on my way as reinforcement."

"It was a *spider.*"

Dan tried to bite back a grin but failed.

"A big one, huh? Did you tell her you don't do spiders?"

"And give up my man card? No. I just sent that sucker flying out the window. With any luck you ran over him when you pulled in. Did you feel a bump?"

Dan laughed and shook his head. "Is that why all those boxes are outside on the landing?"

"Yeah. I didn't want to take any chances his relatives might have taken up residence. I don't think my heart could take hearing Nora scream again."

Dan leaned back on his barstool, tipping it precariously on its back legs. One of these days the guy was going to go right over backward and smack his head.

"And she thanked you with bourbon and scones. That's quite a neighbor you have there. Did you forget she's on the opposing team? Or are you finally coming to your senses about Michael and Becky?"

Asher scowled. Every conversation seemed to come back to Michael and that girl. Nora's daughter. He had a harder time demonizing the girl when he thought of her that way. But his son was still making a big mistake.

"I haven't changed my mind about anything. I don't want Michael starting a family."

"Sooner or later he was probably going to want kids, Ash. And your grandson or granddaughter is now coming sooner, whether you want it to or not."

"Grandson." Saying that word out loud held a surprising amount of weight for Asher.

"What?"

"Michael told me it's a boy."

Dan held out his hand. "Congratulations! A grandson! That's awesome news."

Asher didn't take his friend's hand. He couldn't accept congratulations for this.

Dan looked down, then lowered his hand. "You're not happy about a Peyton baby boy? Come on, man, your son is having a son. It's the miracle of life and all that."

Asher envisioned a toddler in blue, with Michael's dark hair and Nora's golden eyes. Then he saw that boy in a hospital bed, hooked up to tubes and monitors. He emptied his glass in one swallow, keeping his eyes tightly closed and trying to force the thought out of his head. The effort was too much on top of everything else.

"Don't you get it? Michael's going to fall in love with that baby, and when it dies…"

Dan sat up and the front legs of the stool hit the floor with a smack. "What makes you think this baby's going to die? That's crazy!" Dan put his hand on Asher's shoulder, but he shrugged it away. He didn't want sympathy. Or logic. And he could tell Dan was about to give him both. "I know you lost a son, but that doesn't mean Michael will. You know that, right?"

He just shook his head. He wouldn't listen to this.

"This conversation is over."

"Asher, you know that, right? You have a kid who lived."

"I also have one who *didn't* live! And I lost more than a son when Dylan died. I lost everything. My family. My career. My faith. My heart. Everything. It's my job to protect Michael from that."

The two men stood, staring at each other. Dan's mouth opened and closed a few times before he blew out a long breath and turned toward the back door.

"There are so many things wrong with your logic that I don't know where to start. You really should talk to someone, man. A professional someone. Your son needs you, and you can't stop him from falling in love and having this baby. You can't stop him from living."

There was a corner of Asher's brain that was

nodding vigorously in agreement with Dan's words. But he ignored it.

"I can try."

CHAPTER ELEVEN

"So, ASH USED his key the other night?" Cathy Meadows stacked a rack of freshly washed mugs next to the espresso maker. "He's a good boy, that one."

Nora was wiping down the counter. The early-morning rush of commuters heading off to work had passed, and now there were just a couple of customers sitting at tables while reading their papers and sipping coffee. Lunchtime would bring another flurry of activity. The older woman was getting used to Nora's cleanliness requirements, even if she did make fun of all the handwritten signs around the shop that said things like *Did You Wash Your Hands? Are You Wearing Gloves? Put Things in Their Proper Place!*

The shop looked good. Other than the mugs, the bright colors were gone, replaced with warm tones of natural wood and brick. The tables and chairs were painted black. Local art was back on the walls, including the painting Nora saw on her first day here, with the sailing ship heading for a monster-filled abyss. But she hadn't brought back Cathy's silly poster about life being about the journey. That was lying on top of some boxes in the storage room. Nora was a firm believer in having goals. Speaking of which, she reached for her planner.

Ignoring Cathy's opinion of Asher's behavior three nights earlier, she flipped to her to-do list. "Okay, this week's goal is finding someplace to display that old brass espresso maker. I was thinking of putting it in the window, but I don't want people getting fingerprints all over it."

Cathy shook her head. "Nora, you really have to stop worrying so much. You're going to be old before your time. If you want the coffee maker by the window, put it by the window. Who cares if someone touches the darn thing?"

"*I* care. And please, Cathy, there's nothing wrong with having goals and a plan to achieve them." Nora knew she sounded self-righteous and defensive, but darn it all, planning was something she was good at, and she didn't see it as a weakness.

Cathy gave her a one-shouldered shrug. "Maybe not. But how do you plan for the detours? I mean, life always throws you detours, right? Like your daughter and Mikey falling in love. That detour bounced you right out of Georgia and all the way to Gallant Lake. I bet you didn't plan on *that*, did you?"

"I definitely did not. Did you just call him Mikey?"

"Yes, but I wouldn't recommend it. Drives the boy nuts."

"Then why do it?" Nora hated making people uncomfortable.

Cathy was preparing a cappuccino, and she waited for the whir of the frothing machine to stop before answering. "I like keeping people a little off balance. That's when they show their true colors, you know? Take you." Cathy gestured toward Nora. "You swear by your planners and your lists and your goals. But I don't trust that version of Nora. I want to see Nora when she hits a pothole and has to react to something she *didn't* plan on."

"Yeah, well, don't hold your breath." Nora held up her planner. "I pride myself on being prepared for anything." She heard footsteps behind her and turned. She found herself staring into the silver-blue eyes of Asher Peyton.

He stood on the other side of the counter and stared right back, not saying a word. Nora's body started heating from her toes right to the top of her head, and if there hadn't been an audience, she would have fanned her face like a blushing debutante. Behind her, Cathy was whispering.

"Well, hel-lo, detour…"

Asher's eyes softened, and his mouth curved into the suggestion of a smile.

"Are you going to take my order, or should I step back there and make it myself, like I used to?"

Cathy laughed. "Asher, you wouldn't know what to do with this fancy machine Nora put back here, but it does make a fine cup of espresso. Let me get it for you, since Nora seems to have taken a mental *detour*." Cathy elbowed Nora hard enough to snap her out of her stupor.

"I…I'm sorry. I was just surprised to see you. This is the first time you've been in."

"Nope. Second." Asher seemed amused by her confusion. "I came over two mornings ago when Cathy was here." He'd come to the shop the morning after he'd been in her apartment. What did that mean? He glanced around, then at the back of Cathy's head, before lowering his voice. "Place looks…different."

Cathy gave a sharp laugh as she added two scoops of raw sugar to the black coffee in the insulated paper cup, then dumped in a shot of espresso. "Go ahead and say it, Ash. You won't hurt my feelings. When it was mine, it reflected me. But it's Nora's now, so it should reflect her. It's very organized." Cathy winked at Nora. "Just like its owner."

He took the cup from Cathy without looking away from Nora.

"You're right, Cathy, the shop does reflect her. It's pretty in here, and…comfortable."

His unexpected compliment made Nora's skin feel tight, and her pulse jumped. Cathy murmured an audible "Wow." Asher looked away, rubbing the back of his neck, as if he'd been caught off guard by his own words. He fumbled in his pocket and placed a few crumpled bills on the counter. He'd started to turn away when Cathy stopped him.

"Hey, Ash, you might be able to help your pretty neighbor. She wants to put that brass espresso machine in the front window as a conversation piece or marketing or whatever." Cathy's hand gestures made it clear she didn't share Nora's vision. "But she doesn't want people to touch it. Any ideas on how she could showcase it?"

As Asher's dark brows furrowed, Nora jumped in to speak, giving Cathy a quick glare to shut her up. "Oh, no, don't worry about it! I haven't even designed what I need yet."

Cathy's hand rested on Nora's shoulder. "Honey, you do know he's an architect, right? Like, the kind of architect who can design skyscrapers?"

Nora looked up at Asher in surprise. "But you build furniture."

"I do now. But, yes, I *used* to be an architect." He gave Cathy a pointed look. "And I still dabble in a few projects. In fact, I'm working with your cousin and Blake right now on a remodel of the resort's lobby."

Funny how Amanda never mentioned that little detail about the remodeling project she'd been talking so much about. "Regardless," Nora said with a nervous wave of her hand, "I haven't even made my mind up about where to put the espresso machine yet, but it's on my list."

"Your list?"

Cathy answered before Nora could. "Oh, honey, this girl has a list for *everything*. And a schedule for everything on her list. Then it's all worked out in her planner, with stickers and special colors, and God forbid if you touch that planner. She'll cut your hand off!"

Asher grinned and Nora felt her face flame. He now knew another part of her, while she knew so little about him.

"Well, let me know if you want my help." He raised his cup and nodded to Cathy. "Thanks for the brew, ladies."

"So, you really think we can do Amanda's staircase concept?"

Asher looked around the lobby of the Gallant

Lake Resort. "You can do anything you want, as long as you're willing to spend the money." He ignored Blake's grunt. "Amanda said she wants it to look like a tree growing right through the center of the lobby. My plans have the center being a large wooden column carved to resemble a tree trunk. It'll run three stories up, right to the ceiling. Then we'll wrap the open staircase around it, with raw-edged wooden steps. I know a guy who can create an iron railing with a copper leaf design. He'll also create a sculpture that will hang from the ceiling, looking like branches and leaves. It isn't that difficult to make Amanda's vision work."

Asher bit back an unexpected burp. His stomach had been off since lunch. He'd met with a potential client down in White Plains before coming to the resort, and the sushi wasn't agreeing with him. He'd never been a big fan of raw fish, anyway, but the guy insisted that the little restaurant was a hidden gem. Hidden petri dish was more like it.

Blake Randall frowned at the drawings spread out on the table in front of them. "I know my wife is good at what she does, but her woodsy plans for the lobby make me nervous."

Randall had purchased the aging resort several years earlier, with the intention of demolishing it and the adjoining mansion so he could build a massive casino. The residents had gone to court to have the property declared a historic landmark. That was when Amanda, an interior designer, showed up and convinced him not only to leave the resort and mansion standing, but to make it their home. Amanda Randall was petite, like Nora, but blonde and blue eyed instead of a brunette. Where Nora was careful and conservative, her younger cousin was bubbly and free-spirited.

"Don't worry, Blake. It will be very upscale once it's finished, and your guests will love it. The rustic wood of the stairs will just highlight all of…" Asher turned, intending to point to Amanda's sketches, and the room tilted for a minute. *What the hell?* He hesitated, and his equilibrium returned as quickly as it had left.

"You okay, man?" Blake looked concerned. They weren't exactly close friends, but during the warmer months they'd played golf together a few times at the resort's new course, and the lobby was the second project Asher had been hired for. The first had been designing the new clubhouse for the golf course, which would be completed by the time the course officially opened in the spring.

"Yeah, I'm fine. It's just been a long day."

"Well, we're about wrapped up here. As soon

as you finish your architectural specs, I'll get my contractor working on it." Blake stopped, leaning in closer. "Are you sure you're okay? You look a little gray."

Asher tried to ignore his roiling stomach. Something was definitely staging a rebellion down there. "I think my lunch disagreed with me. Freakin' sushi."

Blake groaned. "Oh, I learned that lesson a long time ago. No sushi lunches. There's something about daytime sushi that's just not right. You better get on home."

Asher felt a rush of heat, and he broke into a sweat under the collar of his shirt.

"Yeah, sorry. I'll call you when the specs are ready."

The short drive home was torture. He was hot, cold, then hot again. His skin was clammy, and by the time he parked his truck, he wasn't sure he'd be able to make it inside. But the cold air braced him momentarily. He was just unlocking the back door when he saw movement on his right.

"Asher? Are you okay?" Nora's soft Southern accent was a balm to the war going on in his stomach. But he knew he was only minutes away from the internal war turning into a very external one, and he didn't want to be spewing his guts out here on the deck. And he *really* didn't want it to happen in front of Nora. His key turned and the door swung open. He was ten steps from the downstairs bathroom. He could do ten steps. He just had to get rid of any potential witnesses.

"I'm fine. Ate something bad. G'night."

He closed the door and dashed to the bathroom, barely hitting his knees before it was too late. He lost all track of time as wave after wave of nausea washed over him. After spending who knew how long on the bathroom floor, he lifted his shaking head. He was light-headed and feverish, and he knew he was badly dehydrated. The kitchen was just down the hall. He could make it that far. There was ginger ale in the fridge. He got to his feet and headed down the hallway. If he could just get some cold ginger ale in his system, he'd feel better.

He didn't remember the hallway being this long. Or this…curvy. Was it tilting? Should he turn around and try to make it back to the bathroom, or should he press on to the kitchen, which now seemed an impossible distance away? The hallway swirled again, but he caught sight of the barstools. If he could just sit down and rest for a second, he'd be fine. If only the hallway would stop dipping and twisting.

He reached his hand out to grab a stool, but his hand closed on nothing but air. That was weird.

He reached again, putting more effort into it this time, and there was a crashing sound just before everything went dark and silent.

CHAPTER TWELVE

WHEN ASHER OPENED his eyes again, he wasn't in the hallway anymore. Or the kitchen. Or the bathroom. He turned his head to get his bearings in the dark and moaned as a stab of pain shot through his skull. He was in his own bed. Upstairs. It was nighttime. He shifted and his stomach protested. Moving was definitely not a good thing right now.

He had no memory of coming upstairs. There was a bottle of Pedialyte on his nightstand. He hadn't seen that stuff since the boys were young. Dylan used to drink it by the case after chemotherapy. A hard shiver swept from his feet to his head. He whispered his son's name. Was he dreaming? If this was a dream, Dylan might be in it. He hadn't dreamed of him in so long. Someone was sitting in the chair by the window, and they stood, walking toward him in the dark. A cool, gentle hand touched his forehead.

"Dylan?" Asher didn't whisper it this time; his voice cracked as he blurted the word out. His lips were dry and stiff. He wanted to see his son's face again. He tried to focus, but a soft voice with a distinct Southern accent shushed him as a hand ran through his hair and rested on his cheek.

"Go to sleep, Asher. Go back to sleep."

He shook his head, but the pain and nausea crippled him to the point where he just closed his eyes and gave in. Maybe if he slept, he'd see Dylan again. Gentle fingers caressed his face as he drifted back into a restless slumber.

The pink glow of dawn was visible behind the pulled curtains the next time he woke. He moved his head slowly, testing the pain level. The headache was more manageable than before. His stomach was sore, a little queasy and very empty, but it no longer threatened to explode.

"Welcome back to the living."

He couldn't believe the voice that spoke those words.

"Nora?" Sure enough, there she was, sitting on the edge of his bed. She was dressed in leggings—were those dancing frogs?—and a long, loose T-shirt. *His* T-shirt. He must still be dreaming, because he couldn't imagine any real-life scenario that would bring Nora Bradford into his bedroom wearing one of his shirts. Well, he could imagine one, but it was highly unlikely, and he hated to think he'd ever forget having her in his bed. She gave him a small, somewhat nervous smile.

"You're recognizing people again. That's a positive sign." She reached out and put the back of her hand on his forehead, as if such an intimate act was completely normal between them. Yeah, he was definitely dreaming. Except…he could feel the coolness of her touch on his skin.

"Are you really here?" The words came out of his mouth before he could stop them.

Nora laughed, and he remembered how much he'd liked her laugh the other night after the spider episode at her place. Her laughter was soft, but there was a huskiness to it that hinted at strength. This woman was tougher than she looked, for sure.

"Yes, I'm really here, Asher. You had quite a night. What's the last thing you remember?"

He frowned. "I was sick. *Really* sick. I went to the kitchen for ginger ale… I don't remember much after that." There were fragments of memory coming back to him now. Nora's voice calling his name, sounding panicked. Someone else helping him up the stairs. Who *was* that? And then he remembered getting sick again, in his own bathroom and even…in the bed? He looked down at the sheets. They weren't the ones that had been on the bed yesterday. He looked back to his T-shirt on Nora. Oh, *hell* no.

"Please, God, tell me I didn't throw up on you."

Her hand moved from his forehead to pat him playfully on the cheek.

"Well, not exactly." How could she sound so amused by all this? "It's not as bad as you're thinking. But I did need to change my shirt and I wasn't about to leave you alone again, so I borrowed one of yours."

He wasn't sure how any of this could *not* be as bad as he was thinking, but he focused on one word she said.

"Again?"

She nodded, pulling her hand away, which caused a surprising sense of loss. She pulled her legs up under herself, looking like a little wood sprite perched on the edge of his bed. Her dark hair was pinned back at the sides, and he was tempted to reach up and pull those barrettes out to let it fall around her face.

"I left you here in bed while I cleaned things up downstairs, and you decided to go into your bathroom alone and nearly split your head open on the edge of the sink. You're going to have a bump there, I'm sure. I thought I was going to have to call Dan again to get you back in bed. You were a bit of a mess, and that's when my shirt got…um…dirty."

"*Dan* saw me like this?" Oh, great, could this get any worse?

Nora smiled, temporarily rendering him incapable of caring how bad the night had been. There was something about her being here, in his room, in his shirt, that did something to his chest. Or to the organ that resided inside his chest. An organ that hadn't reacted to anyone for a very long time.

"Let me fill in the blanks for you." Her hands fluttered, and he realized she talked with her hands a lot.

"I knew something was wrong when I saw you come home. You were so green you were almost glowing, Asher. But you told me you were fine and slammed the door before I could do anything. You were far from fine, but a stomach bug isn't usually fatal, so I figured I'd check on you in the morning."

Her face grew serious. "And then I heard that god-awful crash. That's when I remembered the key you showed me with the fish on it. I used it to let myself in and found you passed out on the floor next to the two barstools you'd knocked over. I almost dialed 911, but Dan came in right about then."

"Dan got me upstairs?"

She nodded. "I hadn't bothered to close the back door when I ran in and saw you. Once he realized I hadn't assaulted you…" She winked playfully, and Asher's heart did that weird thing again. "We managed to get you into bed. Then I sent him out to buy you some electrolytes. Between the fever and the dehydration, you were really out of it."

She shifted on the bed, moving closer to his legs, and for the first time he wondered what he was wearing under these sheets. He was definitely shirtless. Had she undressed him? Had she seen him undressed? Had he seen her undressed when she changed into his T-shirt? And why couldn't he remember any of this?

"Here, drink some more Pedialyte. You need to keep taking in fluids." She leaned forward and reached for the bottle, causing the T-shirt to cling to her curves. He was pretty sure she wasn't wearing a bra. Was it crazy to be jealous of his T-shirt? He took the bottle from her and emptied it, needing the distraction as much as he needed the liquid. When he was done, she took it from him and patted his hand as if he were a child. That was enough to annoy him and remove the weird attraction.

"Look, I appreciate what you did, but I'm fine…" He sat up and moved to leave the bed, but two things stopped him—the fact that he was clearly only wearing his boxer briefs and the fact that the bedroom was revolving around him.

"Oh, no, you don't!" Nora laughed and put her hands on his shoulders. She didn't have to work very hard to push him back against the pillows. "You are staying in bed today. You're still a little green around the edges, and I've done all the cleanup I can handle, thank you very much."

He closed his eyes and groaned in embarrassment.

"I'm sorry, Asher. I shouldn't tease you about it. I'm sure Dan will do enough of that when you're better." Her smile faded. "You had me worried for a while. The fever had you totally out of it. You kept talking and talking, but a lot of it didn't make sense."

Something shook in his stomach, and it had nothing to do with the food poisoning. He tried, and failed, to keep his voice steady.

"Yeah? What did I talk about?"

She looked at him with solemn golden eyes.

"You talked about Dylan."

NORA WATCHED AS Asher struggled to control the panic and anger that raced across his face. His eyes narrowed and he forced his words through a tightly clenched jaw.

"I don't ever talk about Dyl… I don't talk about my son."

She looked down at her hands, folded tightly in her lap. Asher's pain was a living, breathing thing in this room, and her heart broke from the weight of it. How did he get through his days, carrying this burden?

"You talked about Dylan last night."

Asher shook his head vigorously in denial. "No. I couldn't have."

"How else would I know about the son you lost?" What little color Asher had recovered drained from his face when she said the word *lost*, and she immediately regretted it. She rested her hand on his arm, but he pulled away and sat up, leaning against the headboard and closing his eyes as if that simple move had exhausted him.

"What did I say?"

"When I found you on the floor, you kept calling me Dylan, and saying you were sorry. When Dan came, I asked him who Dylan was."

Asher's eyes snapped open. "*Dan* talked to you about my son?"

He couldn't even say the boy's name. This couldn't be healthy.

"About *Dylan*? Yes, but only to say he was your youngest son, and that he died several years ago. He said it was your story to tell." She shifted on the bed, pulling her feet in tight under her body. "But I was able to fill in a lot of the gaps as the night went on. You rambled on about how sick Dylan was, and how you hated that he suffered." Her heart had broken when she found him sobbing on the bathroom floor, saying he wished he'd been the one who'd died. "You said the word *chemo* a few times. Dylan had cancer?"

His mouth thinned in anger, and his only response was a single nod. His entire body was tight with tension.

"You called him your little warrior. How old was he when…?"

"I told you, I don't talk about him. Ever."

"Asher, have you talked to *anyone*? A therapist? A pastor? A friend? You can't hold this all in…"

"The last thing I need right now is another greeting-card moment from you, Nora. Just go home and leave me the hell alone, okay?"

He was hurting so much. She just wanted to hold him tight and make the pain stop.

He ran a slightly trembling hand through his tousled hair, refusing to meet her eyes. His skin was still the color of flour paste. He didn't need her stressing him any further. She noticed his obvious relief when she unfolded her legs and stood. He thought she was leaving as he'd asked her to. He didn't know her very well.

"Let's compromise," she said, holding up her hand to stop his protest. "You need more sleep and liquids and, eventually, food. Once you've accomplished all three of those things, I'll leave. In the meantime, I'll be downstairs finishing the cleanup."

"I'm a grown-ass man, and I can do my own cleaning. Please just go."

She pursed her lips as if considering it, then

shrugged. "I think the jury is out on the grown-ass man thing, and you're not well enough to be left alone yet. Unless you'd prefer I call Dan to come sit with you?" He hesitated, then shook his head again. "Okay, then. Get some sleep, and call out if you need anything."

She couldn't help asking one more question before leaving him.

"Do you and Michael talk about Dylan?"

He glared at her in response.

"That's not good for either of you. You know that, right?"

The glare intensified until she could almost see blue flames in his eyes.

"Okay, okay. No more advice. I'm leaving." She laughed when his expression brightened. "I'm leaving the *room*. I'm not leaving this apartment until you sleep, drink and eat. In that order."

It was four hours before she heard movement upstairs. His place had the same basic layout as hers downstairs, but instead of an open loft, his was a traditional two-story, with a full second floor. She heard the shower in his bathroom come on. That was a good sign. Not only was he strong enough to get into the shower, he was also healthy enough to *want* to shower and dress.

She stirred the large pot of soup she'd made. It had required a couple of mad dashes to her place for ingredients, since his kitchen was definitely that of a bachelor, with lots of cereal boxes and frozen meals.

She'd looked in on him every time she came back, to be sure he was still safely sleeping. She even allowed herself one last touch, resting her hand on his face to check for fever. He'd probably try to evict her as soon as he came downstairs, but at least he'd have some healthy homemade chicken soup to eat later.

She wiped her suddenly sweating palms on the front of her jeans. She'd changed clothes on the first trip back to her place. She'd intended to bring his T-shirt back, but it was still hanging on the end of her bed. Would he notice if she kept it? She shook her head. Why on earth would she keep his shirt? Just because it smelled like him and felt soft and oh, so comfortable? That would be silly. She'd bring it back later. If she remembered.

The sight of him stepping off the staircase, shirtless, with the top button of his jeans unbuttoned so they hung low on his hips, made heat curl down her spine. His hair was still damp, his eyes dark and guarded. He pulled up short when he saw her, a shirt dangling from his hand.

"I thought you'd left."

"I told you I wouldn't. Not as long as you need me." Emotion burned in his eyes, then dimmed. "I made you some soup for later, but right now, why don't you have some water? How are you feeling?"

His skin still had an ashen undertone. Shower or not, he wasn't out of the woods yet.

"I'm fine." He rolled his shoulders, then stepped forward to take the water. "Thanks for…everything. But I can handle it from here."

"Nice try, neighbor, but I gave you the conditions that have to be met before I leave. Sleep, which you've done. Hydration, which you're doing now." She nodded as he drained the glass. "And I need to see you keep food down."

The corner of his mouth lifted. "As opposed to not keeping it down?"

Her laughter bubbled up. "Yes, definitely. We've had enough of that."

He watched her refill his glass with more water. "I don't embarrass easily, but knowing what you must have dealt with last night…"

"We've both raised children, Asher. We've both seen our share of unpleasant body fluids."

His face reddened, but he nodded. "True."

She couldn't resist one last try at getting him to open up. "You went through a lot more of that than I did, I suppose. With Dylan."

His jaw went so tight she could see the cords of muscle in his neck.

"I don't talk about that."

That. He was talking about his *son*, not a thing. Nora had a lecture on the tip of her tongue, but she held it in. He wouldn't listen, anyway, and she wasn't going to argue with him while he was still feeling ill. She needed a better plan. What he was doing wasn't healthy emotionally. No wonder the man was angry all the time.

"Okay. Is your stomach good enough to try some soup?"

He tugged his shirt on and sat at the counter across from her. She decided that was a yes and put a single ladle of soup in a small bowl, sprinkling a handful of oyster crackers on top. Asher stared at it, obviously hesitant.

"Don't eat if you don't think you're ready. But remember—the sooner you eat, the sooner you get rid of me and my nosy questions." She saw a hint of a smile before he took a spoonful of soup. He blew on it gently, then sipped just the broth through his lips. Nora was inappropriately fascinated with watching his mouth shaped like that. Like a kiss. She watched as he took a second sip and tentatively swallowed a few pieces of chicken and some noodles. He sat back and frowned.

"That was a mistake."

"Not ready?"

He shook his head and blew out a long breath. "I'm okay. But I definitely don't want any more food right now."

"Try to get a few sips of the broth, at least."

"Nora, I don't need a nurse. Or a mother." His temper was back. "You don't need to fix me. You must have something to do at home or in the café. Anywhere but here." Despite all his protests, he slurped more of the broth. "I just need a little more sleep and I'll be fine." He gave her a firm look. "I need to be alone."

"Okay." She nodded. "Why don't you go lie down on the sofa, and I'll clean up in here real quick."

He started to argue, but she turned away before he had a chance. She turned off the stove and found a container for the soup. Eventually she heard him settle onto the leather sofa in the very masculine living room. This whole apartment was a giant beige man cave, with lots of leather and wood, but very little color and no artwork on the walls. And one fiercely independent man who was now settling in to sleep in the middle of it all while she tidied up his kitchen.

This was what Cathy might call a most unexpected detour.

CHAPTER THIRTEEN

WHEN ASHER WOKE on his sofa, his first thought was that he was starving. That had to be a good sign. His second thought was that Nora Bradford looked damned fine sleeping over there in his chair, curled up under a blue-and-white football blanket Michael had given him. Her hair covered half her face, soft and loose the way he liked it. Her lips were barely parted as she breathed in and out.

She'd been cleaning the kitchen when he came in here to lie down. Then she was going back to her place. Asher frowned. Did she actually say she was leaving, or was that just his wishful thinking? The sofa leather creaked beneath him as he sat up. It was enough to disturb Nora's sleep, and he froze. Her face scrunched up, and she adjusted her position before settling back to sleep with a sigh.

She made him smile. Even in her sleep, she had the surprising ability to make him smile. His feisty little Southern belle. Well, not *his*. Not really. Okay, not at all. Last night's fever was muddling his thinking. Of course she wasn't his. She was a nice neighbor who liked to fix everybody and everything. He opened his eyes and looked at her once more. She wanted to fix *him*—he'd seen it on her face this morning. But that was impossible. What was broken in him was broken for good. She'd only get hurt if she tried to change that.

Very carefully, he got up from the sofa without making any more noise. Nora didn't move as he tiptoed past her and headed toward the kitchen. His stomach was grumbling, and this time it wasn't in protest of anything other than plain old hunger. He glanced at the time. Three o'clock in the afternoon. He'd slept the entire day away, never opening the shop. That was a first.

He pulled Nora's soup out of the fridge and dropped a couple of slices of bread into the toaster. He was hungry, but cautious, so he nibbled on the dry toast as the soup warmed. Just about the time he was ready to pour it into a bowl, he heard a sound behind him. Nora was sitting on one of the counter stools, still looking sleepy.

"You're feeling better." It was a statement, not a question.

He just nodded, oddly tongue-tied. She stood.

"Well, that was the goal, so I can check off the last item on my list. I'll give you your wish and leave you alone."

"You could join me…" She looked up at him in surprise. "For dinner. It's your soup, after all."

She hesitated, and he wondered at the shadows he saw in her eyes. Had he spoken again in his sleep? Did he say something to upset her? Was she coming down with his stomach bug? But he was sure he'd had food poisoning. Why the hell did he care so much about what was bothering her?

"No, thanks. A deal's a deal. You wanted me to go, so I'll go." She gave him a smile. She really had to stop doing that smiling thing, because it was breaking down walls he thought would never crumble. "Take it easy tonight, and I bet you'll be back to a hundred percent in the morning."

"Nora…"

But she shook her head, stopping him.

"I need to go, Asher. Call if you need me."

I need you.

He didn't say the words out loud, because they couldn't possibly be true. Instead, he gave her what she seemed to want: a quick exit.

"Okay. Goodbye, Nora. And thank you. Really."

She looked at him silently, as if trying to read his mind or see into his soul. Her brain was definitely busy with something. Then she nodded, and there was something just a bit sly about the smile she gave him before turning away.

"Bye, Asher."

Two days later, Nora was still lost in thoughts
of what to do with the guy next door. The man
clearly needed to deal with his youngest son's
death. She'd heard it said that the first steps of
the grieving process were anger and denial, and
she suspected Asher had never gotten any further,
frozen there for years now. She frowned as she
swept the café floor. It was impossible to imagine the pain of losing a child. So how could she
know how to help him?

"Mom? You okay?"

Becky was behind the counter, wiping it down
after a big lunchtime crowd. The café was beginning to build a reputation for good coffee and
good pastries. She'd love to find a local bakery,
but Gallant Lake's only bakery had closed over
a year ago. Maybe she could ask Asher for a rec-
ommendation. But why would Asher know anything about bakeries? And why did he manage to
work his way into her every thought?

"Mom?"

"Sorry, honey." She chased him out of her head
again. "I'm fine. Just a little tired."

"Why don't you go upstairs? I can finish here."
Becky smiled, and Nora's heart cracked a little
at the hesitancy she saw there. Things had been
so terribly, tensely polite between her and her
daughter in the month since she'd moved here.
Becky was still skeptical of her motives, and it

felt as if she was judging Nora's every word and action. No matter how careful she was, Nora still managed to say the wrong thing often enough to annoy her daughter. Some days it seemed like *everything* was the wrong thing. And Michael had carefully avoided her, wisely not wanting to be in the middle of whatever was going on between mother and daughter. Becky rubbed the soft swell of her belly, as if cuddling the child inside.

"I think you should be the one resting, Rebecca."

And there went Becky's eyes, rolling skyward in exasperation.

"Seriously, Mom? I'm *fine*." With that, she turned away and went into the kitchen.

Nora watched her leave, wondering how they were ever going to break out of this strained relationship. Becky seemed to feel that everyone was against her and Michael, and she'd grown so prickly about it.

"You need to talk to her, you know."

Cathy put her hand on Nora's shoulder.

"I don't know *how* to talk to her anymore. If I worry, she thinks I'm being negative. If I make a suggestion, I'm too controlling. If I look at her wrong, she thinks I'm disappointed in her. She thinks I'm crazy for coming here and trying to run a coffee shop. And maybe I am. I just can't figure out how to fix things." Nora looked at Cathy and was surprised to see tears glistening in her eyes. "Cathy, what's wrong?"

"You're what's wrong, Nora." Cathy pulled her to the sofa by the window to sit. "Becky's *here*. She *offered* to work for you. She just asked you if you were okay. She *cares*. You two need to stop tiptoeing around each other and *talk*. Before it's too late." Cathy looked out the window at the gray sky, threatening more raw March weather.

"Too late? What do you mean?"

Cathy sighed. She was wearing a long denim skirt with a bright sweater, giving in to Nora's demands that her clothing be clean and neat. Her long silver hair was pulled back into a braid, and silver hoops hung from her ears. A lone tear escaped from the corner of her eye.

"You talk about losing your daughter, Nora, but you have no idea what that really means. I do."

Cathy hadn't said anything about her family since the surprising revelation that she'd sold the shop to help a granddaughter she'd only recently learned she had. And Nora hadn't wanted to push. Nora never wanted to push, never wanted to be inappropriate or rude. She didn't press Asher further than he wanted to go when it came to talking about his son. She didn't press Becky for fear of losing her. She hadn't pressed Cathy because she figured the woman's past wasn't her concern.

Maybe it was time to stop being so damned careful all the time.

"Tell me about your daughter, Cathy."

Cathy wiped away the tear and smiled. "Paisley was a beautiful kid."

"Paisley? That was her name?"

"Yes. She hated it, but it was the only piece of her daddy I could give her." Cathy smiled at Nora's confusion. "I was a bit of a wild child, and I had the same lousy taste in men that my mama had. But her men were worse." Cathy's eyes dulled. "Some of Mama's men were much worse."

Becky was whistling as she worked in the kitchen. She'd picked that habit up from Michael, who was constantly whistling to himself.

Cathy continued. "I met Paisley's daddy at a hotel bar in Chicago. He was a businessman, and he always wore a suit and tie—always a paisley tie. I thought I'd finally found The One, but when he heard I was pregnant, he dropped me like a hot rock. Turns out he already had a wife and kid, and I was just his walk on the wild side. He gave me money to get rid of the pregnancy, but I used it to pay for a bus ticket to San Francisco. That's where Paisley was born."

Nora's eyes were suddenly moist, and she blinked rapidly. "I think it's a lovely name. Where is she now?"

"She died over ten years ago. I didn't even know until last summer."

"Oh, Cathy, I'm so sorry."

Cathy shrugged. "She hated being dragged around the country while I chased after bad men and crazy dreams. So she buried herself in her schoolwork to escape the chaos I thrived in, and she got herself a scholarship. The morning after she turned eighteen, she was gone. Got a job, rented a room, went to school and made a life for herself that didn't include me. And I let her go, because I figured she was better off without me."

"When did you see her last?"

"I showed up for her college graduation. It took every penny I had to get there. She was standing with her smart friends and their fancy parents. She saw me in my wrinkled clothes from the bus ride and my crazy hair—I think it was pink then. I'd had a little liquid courage before I got there, and she knew it. She turned her back to me like I was a stranger, and I was so humiliated that I just left." Cathy looked around the café, so different now than when she'd owned it. "A few years later I came back here to take care of my mom when she got sick. I figured if Paisley eventually wanted to see me, she'd be able to find me here, and she'd be proud because I finally stayed in one place, I was a business owner and I didn't have a stupid man in my life. But she never came."

"And you didn't reach out to her?"

Cathy shook her head sadly.

"I sent a few letters and postcards at first, but after a while they started getting returned. I found out last year she was gone." Cathy took a deep breath, straightened her shoulders and glanced toward the back of the shop before meeting Nora's gaze.

"Her in-laws called me. Turns out Paisley married their son twenty-some years ago, and they'd died together in a car accident. But they had a little girl that the grandparents had raised. They didn't know Paisley had any family until they found a postcard from me tucked into a poetry book she had. She'd never mentioned me." Cathy shrugged. "They didn't want me to upset the girl by suddenly showing up in her life, and I agreed. She wants to be a veterinarian. I know that's expensive, so I decided to help without her knowin' about it."

"That's why you sold the shop—to pay for her college?"

"I had to do something, you know? Even if her mama didn't want her to know me."

"But Paisley held on to that postcard from you. That means something, right?"

"Maybe. But I'll never know, will I? It's too late for me, but it's not too late for the two of you." Nora followed Cathy's gaze to see Becky standing by the counter. She didn't know how long she'd been listening, but, judging from the dampness on her cheeks, she'd heard enough. A mother and daughter torn apart forever because of fear and pride.

Here she'd been worrying about how much *Asher* needed family, when her own daughter was standing right there in front of her, needing family, too. She smiled at Becky, doing her best to hide her fear.

"Why don't you and Michael come over for dinner tonight?"

The shock on Becky's face gave Nora a stab of guilt. She should have done this sooner.

"With you? And Michael, too?"

"Yes. Tonight. With Michael. After all, the two of you are expecting my grandson, and it's time we all got better acquainted, don't you think?"

Becky grinned. "Mom, are you pulling a smile and a plan on me?"

"Maybe." Nora walked to Becky and took her hands. "Look, I know things have been hard between us. I'm sorry we argued at Bree's wedding. I'm sorry you felt I was too negative or controlling. I'm just sorry, period." She gestured down to Becky's round stomach. "This…this has been a bit of a shock for your old mom, and I haven't handled it as well as I should have. But I want you to be happy, sweetheart. That's all I've ever wanted."

When she looked up, Becky was crying harder, and Cathy was sniffling behind her. Nora opened her arms and Becky stepped into the hug.

"Oh, Mom, I'm sorry, too! I don't know how to have a baby or be a wife, and I don't want to screw this up..."

Much of the relentless weight that had been pressing down on Nora since Thanksgiving vanished as she held her daughter tight and consoled her. They were going to be okay.

A few hours later she was just checking off the last thing on her dinner list when Michael and Becky arrived at the apartment. Becky's favorite shrimp toast appetizers? Check. Becky's favorite Caesar salad with homemade dressing, including anchovies? Check. Becky's favorite baked ziti casserole? Check. And, last, Becky's favorite dessert, the pineapple upside-down cake, was fresh out of the oven. Check.

Nora usually ate at the kitchen counter, so this was the first time the dining table had been set since she moved in, and it glowed in the light of a dozen different pillar candles arranged on a silver tray in the center. Too much? Maybe. But this was step one in Nora's plan to create a complete and functioning family, and everything had to be perfect.

Becky started laughing as soon as she walked in. She'd been up to the apartment a few times since Nora moved in, but never for more than a few minutes.

"OMG, is that your baked ziti?" Becky rushed to the kitchen. "And my favorite cake, too? Oh, Michael, be prepared to have your mind blown."

The young man in question stood uncomfortably in the doorway. His eyes warmed when Becky spoke his name, but when he looked at Nora, she could see the shutters coming down. His own father had turned him away, and Nora and Becky had been arguing so much. The guy had every reason to be distrustful.

"Come inside, Michael! Take off your jacket and try one of those shrimp things on the counter while I finish putting the salad together."

Her voice was too loud and overly cheerful, and Becky and Michael were exchanging uneasy glances in the kitchen. She took a deep breath and tried to shake off her nerves. "Okay, let's get this part over with. Do I wish my daughter hadn't gotten pregnant at eighteen? Of course! But it's happened. And I couldn't possibly want anything to happen to that precious baby you're carrying. I love him already. With a little help, you and Michael are going to be great parents. This child will know nothing but love from *all* of us." Nora saw the sadness that shadowed Michael's eyes. He looked like a wounded animal. She remembered having the same impression of Asher after he and Michael argued back in November—that Asher looked like a cornered, frightened animal. Both men had known too much pain. It was time to start fixing that.

"Michael, you and I don't know each other that well yet, but you'll learn when I put my mind to making something happen, it generally happens." Becky coughed out a laugh behind her. "So I'm telling you right now that when I say your son will be loved by all of us, I mean by your father, too."

Michael's eyes went wide in surprise, then he shook his head sadly. "I don't think so, Nora."

"Your dad is a good man, Michael. I know he's still grieving Dylan's loss, but together we can help Asher deal with becoming a grandpa."

Michael's face paled.

"There's no way my father told you about Dylan." Michael's voice was hard. Her heart broke for the wounded young man in front of her.

"Mom, why are you calling him *Asher* like that? Like you're friends or something."

"Let's eat while dinner's hot."

They sat obediently, but their suspicious expressions made Nora laugh, which didn't seem to help their moods any.

"Guys, Asher and I are neighbors. He helped me with a spider problem. I helped him when he was sick." She loaded their plates and brought them to the table. "He didn't intend to tell me about Dylan, and he certainly didn't tell me much." She sat at the table and turned to Michael. "His loss must have hurt so much. How old were you?"

There was only a brief pause before he answered. "Sixteen."

"And Dylan?"

"Twelve."

Nora winced. His death had left its mark on the entire family.

"Tell me about your little brother, Michael."

He didn't answer right away, as if skeptical of her interest. Then Becky set her hand on his and gave it a squeeze. He looked at her and the two had a silent conversation loaded so heavily with love and compassion that Nora could feel it across the table. Michael looked up and gave her a crooked smile so much like Asher's she had to force herself to focus on what the young man was saying.

"Dylan was the coolest kid. He could make anyone laugh, and he did. All the time. I helped him set up a motion sensor in his hospital room one Halloween, and he scared a nurse half to death when this recording of spooky music started playing and lights started flickering. She let out a scream and everyone came running." Michael started to laugh. "And that was nothing.

When he was only seven, he got his hands on a paintball gun…"

The rest of the meal was filled with stories of a young boy with a big heart and a sharp wit. The more Michael talked about his brother, the more his shoulders relaxed and the more animated he became. Finally, after devouring two pieces of upside-down cake, he leaned back in his chair and rolled his neck.

"Damn, I haven't talked that much about him in a long, long time."

"Your mom doesn't talk about him, either?"

Michael shrugged. "She doesn't avoid it, like Dad does, but she's not here, you know? It's not something that comes up on phone calls. She's trying to focus on her new life in California."

"How long have your parents been divorced?" She knew the pressures of having a sick child could break the best of marriages.

"Officially? Two years. But they separated six months after Dylan…" Michael gave Becky a small smile of gratitude when she reached over to hold his hand.

"They didn't get divorced until *after* he died? After they'd been through so much together? How sad…" Nora stopped herself. This was none of her business. Becky gave her a curious look, apparently thinking the same thing.

"Mom and Dad were a solid team the whole

time Dylan was alive. We called ourselves the Warrior Clan and Dylan was…"

"He was your Little Warrior." Nora finished the sentence, remembering Asher's fevered words in the middle of the night.

Michael raised his brows. "That's right. But once Dylan was gone, Mom and Dad were pretty much gone, too. Dad worked at my grandfather's architectural firm. It's where he and Mom met. But he quit when Dylan died. He started drinking and just withdrew from everything. Mom did the total opposite. She hadn't worked in the office for years, but she started doing eighty-hour weeks all of a sudden. She needed to be constantly busy, and Dad didn't want to move a muscle. As the old cliché goes, they grew apart."

Nora stared at Michael, thinking about what he'd just described. A family blown to pieces by the death of a child. The father hiding in a bottle. The mother hiding in her work. And a sixteen-year-old boy alone in the middle.

She didn't trust herself to say anything without shedding tears, so she stood and started to clear the table. Becky jumped up to help in the kitchen, while Michael walked to the windows and stared out over Main Street. The two women worked without speaking for a while before Nora put her hand over Becky's.

"He's quite an impressive young man."

Becky grinned. "I know, right? We had something in common from the start, with him losing Dylan and me losing Daddy, and everything just grew from there."

Nora nodded. "I'm glad you had each other to talk to."

"We could tell each other anything without being judged." Nora tensed, and Becky was quick to explain. "Mom, whenever I talk about Daddy, you get all tweaky about it. Michael just *listens*. And he can't talk about Dylan with his parents, but I was there. Listening."

Michael was walking back toward them when Nora answered. "When times get tough, be sure to remember what brought you two together. Trust and listening."

The kids were getting ready to leave shortly after that, loaded down with leftovers to reheat. A family reunited. As Michael opened the back door, Nora thought of Asher. He was the one piece of the family puzzle still missing.

Michael stepped outside and stopped so quickly that Becky bumped into him. He was staring to the right, his shoulders tense.

"Dad?"

CHAPTER FOURTEEN

ASHER RECOGNIZED HIS son's Jeep when he pulled into the lot behind his building. Michael had a key to the apartment, but he hadn't used it in ages. What was he doing here so late? Was something wrong? Was he here to accept Asher's offer for Stanford?

He whipped his truck into a parking space and took the metal stairs two at a time. But his apartment was locked up tight. He glanced back to the lot. That was definitely Michael's Jeep—it still had the dent on the driver's side from when Michael hit a deer last summer.

Muffled voices and laughter came from Nora's apartment as her door opened. Michael stepped out. Nora's daughter was right behind him.

"Dad?"

He hadn't seen Michael since their argument at the mountain house ten days ago. And now here he was, apparently attending an intimate little dinner right freaking next door to him.

"What the hell are you doing here?"

He saw the pained reaction on Michael's face

and cursed under his breath. This was not the way he wanted things to be. But he'd dug himself into this hole and didn't seem capable of getting out.

Michael's voice was cool. "Nora had us over for a family meal." He held up a bag full of leftovers. "You remember family meals, don't you, Dad?"

Nora's voice came from the hallway. "Michael, stop it."

Asher's internal reaction was quick and hot. What right did this woman have to correct his son? What right did she have to be inviting him into her home like he was part of her family? Why were the three of them laughing together like they were all lifelong friends? His lips curled into a snarl, but before he could speak, Michael gave him a dismissive up and down look.

"It's okay, Nora." Michael glanced over his shoulder into the apartment and smiled. After the look Asher had just gotten, Michael *smiled* at her. "My fiancée and I are leaving. Thanks for a great meal and a really cathartic conversation." Michael gave Asher a look filled with resentment. "It was great to talk about Dylan."

That name froze Asher in place, speechless.

Michael moved to allow Nora's daughter, Becky—there, he remembered her name—to precede him down the steps. As she moved past, her long coat swung open, revealing her rounded stomach. Her hand raised to rest on the swell. His grandson. The sight made him withdraw into his doorway, his chest constricting with emotions he couldn't begin to identify. He watched them drive away, his throat thick with sorrow.

"Asher, I'm so sorry. He shouldn't have said…" Nora's words faded when he glared at her. He was still struggling to contain all the feelings crashing around inside him, suddenly loose from their cages and looking to tear someone apart. He took a menacing step toward the only target in sight.

"You shut the hell up." He waved his finger right in front of her face, forcing her to lean away, but she didn't move her feet. "You stay the hell away from my family, do you understand?" He was shouting now, and still she didn't retreat. He grudgingly admired her fearlessness.

"Or what?"

The words were spoken as softly as a lullaby, but there was steel behind them. He wanted to rend his own shirt from his body in fury and scream to the heavens to get this pressure out of his empty chest cavity. But no sound came out when he opened his mouth.

"Yeah, that's what I figured." She nodded, and her shoulders relaxed. Had she been afraid of him? The thought soured his stomach. Damn it, would he ever stop hurting people? She pushed past him into his place uninvited, and he was too busy beating himself up to object. "Come on, show me where you keep your bourbon."

"You and Michael talked over dinner. About my family." His voice sounded heavy and leaden in his own head. He was suddenly bone tired.

"Yes." Nora was in the kitchen, opening and closing cupboards until she found the liquor. It looked as if she'd dressed up for dinner with his son, wearing a swirly skirt that brushed her calves and a clingy peach-colored sweater. Two sparkling clips held her hair back, one on either side of her face. She took down two glasses and poured amber liquid into both. He accepted a glass, but he wasn't done arguing. The problem? He seemed to be alone in this fight. His uninvited guest was unfazed, sipping daintily from her glass before screwing her face into a grimace at the strong drink.

"I mean it, Nora. Don't interfere with my family. And stay away from my son. You have no right to be discussing…"

"Dylan?" The boy's name came so smoothly from her lips that it almost dulled the impact it had on Asher.

"You know what? I don't need this shit. Go home. And stay the fu…"

"Don't." An edge crept into her voice. "Don't tell me again to stay away from 'your' family." She made air quotes with her fingers. "Like it or not, Michael is now part of *my* family, too. He's going to be the father of my grandson and also my son-in-law."

"That is *not* going to happen."

Nora's hands flew up in frustration. "Oh, my *God*, Asher! You keep saying that and saying it and saying it, but you don't get to just make a wish. There is no magic lamp to rub. You can't twitch your nose and make the baby disappear. There's no time machine to go back and stop Michael and Becky from falling in love. I saw you look at her belly. You know damned well that's *your* grandson in there. How can you not feel anything for that baby?"

Oh, he felt plenty. He just didn't want to. He did his best to keep his voice steady.

"Go home, Nora."

She stood there staring at him, eyes shining bright with unshed tears. Those tears, if they fell, might be the death of his self-control, and he looked away rather than take the chance.

"Fine." She blew out a long breath. "I'll go. I'll leave you here to stew in your own misery, Asher. You keep trying to convince the whole world, including yourself, that you've got this all under control. And people call *me* a control freak!" She gestured wildly before walking past him. He caught a whiff of fruit and sugar as she went by. She wasn't done with her lecture.

"You think if you just deny things, then they aren't happening. Your son *needs* you, Asher. But you refuse to see it. You're like an ostrich, sticking your head in the sand and hoping the world will leave you alone."

She spun, working up a good temper now, and this time it was *her* finger in *his* face. "Michael needs to talk about Dylan. And Lord knows, *you* need to talk about Dylan. But you pretend you never lost a son, just like you're trying to pretend you're not going to be a grandfather." Her gold eyes were on fire, anger making her cheeks bright pink. The more she raged, the thicker her Southern accent became. "You live in a constant state of denial. You've closed off all your feelings."

"That's not exactly true."

"Bull*shit* it's not true."

That was pretty harsh language for the Southern beauty to be spitting out. She was almost to the door before the words escaped.

"I can prove it."

"What?" Her eyes grew wide when he started walking toward her.

"I can prove I haven't closed off *all* my feelings. That I can't deny *every* truth."

Her back was to the door, and he didn't stop walking until his chest brushed against hers. She pressed back, her arms at her sides, hands flat against the door. Her lips parted, and she took a shaky breath as he lowered his head. Her pulse was jumping in the little vein at the base of her neck. He liked Nora best when she was knocked off-kilter, not so prim and smart and nosy.

"Wh-what are you doing?"

"I can't control the feeling that I want to kiss you, Nora Bradford. Can you deny that you want me to?"

Was kissing this woman the stupidest thing he could possibly do? Yes. But when her hands came up and cupped the back of his head, when she stood on her toes to press her lips to his, he no longer gave a damn.

ASHER'S LIPS WERE hard and tender at the same time as Nora lifted up onto her toes and kissed him. She *kissed* him! Because he was right. She wanted this as much as he did.

At first they were gentle, tentative. Butterfly kisses, teasing and tempting. Making contact, then pulling back. But when his hands moved to her waist, up and around, slipping under her sweater, the feel of his calloused hands moving across her skin unlocked something inside her she'd never known existed, and suddenly she was on fire. Her fingers twisted in his hair and her lips parted. She felt the vibration in his chest as he growled before moving his tongue across her teeth and into her mouth.

Their heads turned and bumped as their tongues twisted together and pushed against each other. Was that him moaning in pleasure or was it her? She didn't care. She just wanted more. Their mouths came apart only long enough to gasp for air before crashing together again. Her arms tightened around his neck and she pulled herself higher, fairly climbing the poor guy, and he didn't object. In fact, his hands dropped to cup her buttocks and he lifted her, pinning her against the door. His mouth moved down her neck, devouring her inch by inch, and she lifted her chin to give him full access. He sucked at the base of her throat, and a loud groan echoed in the hallway. Oh, God, that was her!

"Asher…"

She didn't have any words other than that. She just needed to say his name out loud. How had she come to be here in his arms, moaning his name like some wild woman? It didn't matter. The only thing that mattered was the feel of his lips on her skin, of his fingers gripping her, of her own name being whispered over and over as if he was breathing her in and out.

He lifted his head and stared hard into her eyes. She wasn't going to stop him, and he knew it. His mouth met hers again, but it was different this time. Less desperate, yet deeper somehow. He lowered her legs until she was standing, but his lips never left hers. His hands roamed up over her body until he was cupping her face, kissing her into oblivion. This. This moment meant something. Her hands dropped to rest on the waistband of his jeans. Mindlessly, wordlessly, her fingers started searching for a buckle. For an opening. He groaned her name again and her heart tightened. Her fingers found the buckle and feverishly went to work.

The ringing of a phone brought them both to a sudden stop. It was Nora's phone. It was Amanda's ringtone. It was almost eleven o'clock at night.

She removed her hand from Asher's belt and he blew out a sigh. The moment was broken, and they both knew it.

"It's my cousin. I have to…"

His head was next to hers, and he nodded against her. She pulled the phone from her pocket and stepped away. He leaned against one wall and she leaned against the opposite one, both left shaking from that kiss.

"Hey, what's up?" Nora thought she'd covered her scrambled emotions, but apparently not.

"Nora? Why are you out of breath?"

"I'm fine." The corner of Asher's mouth tipped up and he nodded in agreement. She waved him off, trying not to laugh. "Why are you calling so late? What do you need?"

"Are you okay? You sound weird." Amanda

waited, but Nora didn't answer. She wasn't sure if she'd ever be okay again. "Anyway, Becky and Michael just stopped by to pick up those curtains I ordered for their place." Amanda had some great contacts in the design world who owed her a few favors, and she'd been calling in those favors to help decorate the kids' bungalow.

Asher slowly slid down the wall until he was sitting on the hallway floor, and Nora followed suit with a knowing smile. She was just as legless as he was. Amanda kept talking.

"Becky told me about your dinner tonight, and I just wanted to say yay, you. I'm so glad you guys are working things out. She also told me what happened with Michael and his dad on the way out. I can't believe what a jerk Asher was."

His brows knit together, and she knew he'd heard Amanda's words in the empty hallway. "No, he really wasn't. They just have some things to work through, like Becky and I did."

"Look, I know he helped you with a spider and all, but he's still the same guy who doesn't want Becky to have that baby." Amanda had no idea how close she and Asher had come to kissing in the laundry room that night. And judging from his reaction when he saw Becky's rounded stomach this evening, Asher no longer had any desire to end the pregnancy. He'd been more frightened than angry. She looked up and met his dark gaze. He wasn't frightened now. He rose to his knees and crawled toward her, brushing a strand of hair from her face and leaning in as if to kiss her again.

Yes, please.

"Amanda, things have changed. We'll talk tomorrow, okay?"

"What is going on with you? Oh, my God, is he there in your apartment right now?"

Nora looked into his blue eyes, so close to hers, and smiled.

"He's not in my apartment." Her voice sounded ridiculously breathy.

"Holy hell, are you in *his* apartment? Are you two a *thing*?" Amanda's voice rose, and Nora could hear Blake's voice in the background questioning her, and the muffled response. "Nora and *Asher Peyton*, Blake. Together. Now." Amanda refocused on Nora. "Are you drunk? You're the one who called him a…"

Asher's lips brushed against hers, and she never heard the end of the sentence.

"Was that a *kiss* I just heard? Are you seriously talking to me and *kissing* him? You do remember he's the grandfather of your grandchild, right? Isn't that, like…incest or something?"

Asher took the phone from Nora's hand.

"Not incest, Mrs. Randall. But definitely something."

Amanda started to shout. "Don't you Mrs. Randall me! I'm on my way over there, and you'd better have my cousin back in her apartment by the time…" He swiped his finger across the screen and set the phone on the floor.

They shared one more toe-curling kiss before Nora started shaking her head.

"She's not kidding, you know. She's on her way, and she only lives five minutes from here. She might be petite, but…"

They stared at each other in silence, then Asher grinned and rose to his feet, pulling her up with him.

"If she's anything like you, her size has no relation to her power." He leaned in to kiss her again but stopped himself, stepping back with a grimace. He glanced around. "Look at us, making out in the hallway like a couple of kids. You should go."

With those words, she felt him retreating from her. Closing her out again. This man's mood swings could give a woman whiplash.

"Asher, don't."

"Don't what? Don't act like a grown man instead of some horny kid?" He stepped back, physically telling her what she already knew. But his next words suggested he wasn't completely shutting her out. "We'll be continuing this...*discussion* later. I just don't feel like being verbally assaulted by *two* women tonight."

It wasn't until she heard a distant car door closing that Nora nodded and left his apartment. None of this was in her plan to help Asher. Not the argument. And definitely not the kiss that had turned into something so much...*more*. She hadn't planned on *more* with anyone ever again. The last time she did, she ended up a betrayed, broke single mom. But for the first time in years, she wondered if a change of plans might be a good thing.

Or a complete disaster no one would recover from.

CHAPTER FIFTEEN

NORA STOOD IN front of the shiny red espresso machine the next morning, tapping her foot impatiently. Would this thing *ever* heat up enough for her to get a much-needed shot of caffeine?

Maybe two or three shots.

All in one cup.

After being interrogated for an hour by Amanda last night, she'd fallen into bed but not to sleep. Her cousin wasn't so much put out that Nora and Asher had kissed as she was by the fact that she hadn't had any inkling there was a possibility of that happening. Nora had calmly explained that *she* didn't have an inkling it would happen, either, but Amanda immediately called BS on that.

"Kisses don't just come out of nowhere. There has to be chemistry first—some kind of mutual attraction energy going on—or it's not a kiss, it's assault. So fess up, Nora. What's been going on between you and Asher that you haven't been sharing?"

Nora had started at the very beginning, with

her out-of-character attraction to a grumpy guy in a grocery store back in November. The icy parking lot. The spider incident. Caring for him when he was ill. And, yes, the amazing kiss last night when she climbed his body in the hallway.

Amanda knew about some of these things in general, but Nora hadn't conveyed what she *felt* while they were happening. The undercurrent of…*something*…that wove through every encounter she had with Asher. The way her heart skipped at the sound of his voice. The way her skin warmed when he looked at her with those intense eyes of his. The way her knees went weak when he held her in his arms. The way his pain became her pain when she tried to get him to deal with Dylan and Michael and Becky and the baby.

By the time she'd finished, Amanda was sitting at the kitchen counter staring at her with wide blue eyes and an open mouth.

"So, all this time I've been planning on setting up my prim and proper Southern cousin with a nice quiet high school history teacher, you've been having the hots for your bad-boy neighbor? I never thought I'd see the day you'd fall head over heels for a guy like that."

Nora had tried to deny it, explaining she couldn't possibly be head over heels for a man so complicated and unpredictable. But Amanda wouldn't listen and was still laughing when she finally headed for the door, apparently satisfied Nora wasn't drunk or being victimized.

"I can see it in your eyes, honey. You're gone for this guy." That was when Amanda grew serious. "Be careful, okay? I like Asher, but he's got some deep stuff going on. His shadows have shadows. I know you like to fix things, but I don't want to see you get hurt." Her smile returned. "But, then again, a guy who can't stop kissing you, even while you're on the phone, might be worth the risk."

The light blinked on the espresso machine, snapping Nora back to the present. She made a mug of her favorite beverage: a mocha latte with a dash of toasted marshmallow syrup. And an extra shot of espresso, of course. She sat at the counter in the silent café, still an hour from opening.

Her phone pinged a few minutes later. It was Bree, texting from North Carolina. Apparently Amanda hadn't wasted any time spreading the word among the cousins.

Kissing the Hot Produce Guy from next door? You go, girl!

Nora couldn't help but laugh as she typed a response.

Don't make too much of it, okay?

Hard not to when our cautious little Mother Hen finally spreads her wings. I told you to be careful around sexy grumpy neighbors! ;-)

Nora rolled her neck and sighed. Her lack of sleep last night combined with her nosy cousins were going to make for a long day. She glanced at the clock behind the counter and started typing.

Why are you up so early? I have to open the shop, but you should be sleeping!

She watched the wavering lines as Bree typed a response.

Cole's up and out early this time of year, doing his farmer thing. Lately I've been feeling queasy in the mornings and I can't get back to sleep. Been going on for a week or two.

Nora smiled. Bree and Cole had met last summer when Bree hid from a stalker in his tiny Carolina farm town. Although they'd argued nonstop in the beginning, Bree eventually left her glamorous life in Hollywood and moved to Cole's farm. She'd never seen her cousin happier, and the news that Bree was now feeling sick in the mornings just made her smile all the more.

Bree may not have put the pieces together yet, but Nora had. She started typing.

Keep some saltines on your nightstand, and try nibbling one as soon as you wake up. That should help.

The answer came quickly.

Thanks *Mom*. Tell me about kissing Hot Produce Guy.

Nora set her mug down and raised her fingers to her lips. They were still soft and swollen from his passionate kisses last night, but the caffeine was bringing her to her senses. It was a mistake to go any further with Asher. She was trying to bring the family *together*, not set off a nuclear bomb in the middle of it. What would Michael and Becky think of her and Asher having a relationship? What would happen if things worked out? What would happen if they didn't? She couldn't take that chance, even if her desire to kiss him again made her body burn. Her fingers started typing.

No more kisses with Hot Produce Guy. Things are messy enough.

It took so long for Bree to reply that Nora wondered if she'd fallen asleep. But finally the words appeared.

Hmmm. Messy can be fun. Don't be afraid of messy.

That was ridiculous. Messy couldn't be controlled. She needed to get Michael and Asher back together and bring Asher into the family unit being created by this grandson of theirs. That was her plan, and she was done taking messy detours. Before she could type her reply, another text came in.

Ugh. Gotta go. Feel sick. Call you later.

Nora pictured Bree running for the bathroom. Should she tell her to pick up a pregnancy test the next time she went to the store? Nah—Bree and Cole would figure it out sooner or later.

Four hours into a busy Saturday morning, Nora, Cathy and Becky finally had a chance to catch a breath. It was a raw, windy day, with the sun ducking in and out of dark clouds, playing tag with the showers that swept through every half hour or so.

Business had been brisk, and three tables were still occupied with customers chatting quietly, or in the case of the two older gentlemen in the corner, playing checkers. Becky was cleaning up the kitchen. Cathy took a smoke break. Nora hoped her employee wasn't smoking a sample of her clandestine harvest. Was she growing pot at home now, or had she given up the hobby, as she'd said she would?

The sound of boxes being dragged across the floor of the storage room made her smile. Becky had said something to Michael about how challenging the oddly shaped room was to work in. He'd come in this morning to take a look, and he'd been restacking boxes and sliding shelf units around for a couple of hours now, whistling the entire time.

The bell tinkled over the front door, and Nora turned. Asher stood in the doorway, looking at her with brooding, hooded eyes. His flannel shirt was open to reveal a dark rugby shirt underneath. He looked as exhausted as she felt and just as troubled. She knew why *she* thought last night was a mistake: too messy and too far off plan. But why did *he* seem so full of regret?

A customer walked in behind him, propelling Asher toward the counter. He nodded at Nora.

"I'll have a…"

"Large black coffee in a to-go cup with a shot of espresso and two raw sugars?" she said, finishing his order for him. His right brow arched, and a smile teased the corner of his mouth.

"You know me too well."

She shrugged. "Or maybe not well enough."

"You know more than most."

"But not more than all?"

He gave her a crooked grin, finally letting down his guard. They were *flirting* with each other. Not only were they flirting, but there was an extra level of heat behind their words after last night. Someone cleared their throat firmly, and Nora flushed when she realized she'd been so busy staring at Asher that she'd ignored the people who came in behind him. She prepared his coffee, then assisted the other customers. He stood off to the side, waiting for her to be free. Was he looking to flirt some more? Was it crazy for her to hope he was?

The customers took their coffees to the sofa by the window. This time it was Asher clearing his throat. His voice was low, meant just for her ears.

"Look, if I was out of line kissing you last night, I'm sorry."

She studied him, knowing the smart thing would be to say they'd both been out of line and it should never happen again. But she was having too much fun with the flirting thing.

"If I remember correctly, I'm the one who kissed you, so…"

"You *kissed* my dad?"

It wasn't the first time Nora had cursed the acoustics in the shop that made conversations so easy to overhear. Michael was scowling at them both, and there was more than just anger in his eyes. He was hurt and confused.

"*Who* kissed your dad?" Becky stepped up behind Michael, laughing. Her laughter died a violent death when she saw Nora and Asher standing there.

This was worse than bad. Unimaginably worse.

"Mom?"

The word was said with all the horrified censure a teenager could muster. Nora's cheeks burned as if she'd been caught kissing Asher right there at the counter.

"What, are you two *living* here now?" Asher's angry words distracted Nora, and that was a relief. She'd rather deal with his grumpiness than the mortification on her daughter's face. Michael bristled, forgetting the kissing comment for the moment. Hopefully Becky would do the same.

"And what if we *are* living here, Dad? Maybe I'm getting more attention and parenting from Nora than from you."

Okay, maybe they'd be better off talking about the kissing.

"And now you're making a move on her? Are

you just looking for ways to turn *everything* in my life to shit? What kind of father does that?"

Michael's challenge hung in the air as a hush fell over the café.

"Mom, did you really kiss him? For months you've been on your high-and-mighty judge's seat about me and Michael, and now you're hooking up with Michael's *father*?" Her face screwed up in disgust. "That is so…*gross*! How could you?"

The two men continued their own conversation over the women's heads.

"Here's a news flash for you, son. It takes more than warm and fuzzy greeting-card sentiments to be a parent. Making you feel good is not my job."

Nora winced. Was that a dig at her?

"Calm down," she hissed at Becky. "There are customers listening to every word."

"Oh, sure, Mom. *Now* you care what people think, but what about when you were kissing him?" Becky gestured toward Asher, and the movement pulled her apron tight across the baby bump. Asher's eyes dropped, and he paled. This wasn't the first time Nora had seen him react with fear when he saw evidence of the baby. He'd jumped back from Becky last night as if he'd been stung.

"For heaven's sake, Rebecca, I didn't kiss him out here in public!"

"Oh, great. Where *did* you kiss him?"

She opened her mouth to answer, stuttering over whether to tell the truth or not, but Michael talked right over her to his father.

"Yeah? Well, don't worry, Dad. There's no chance of you leaving your own self-pity party long enough to *ever* try to make me feel good again."

She saw in his eyes the moment his son's words made a direct hit. Becky was still complaining loudly about double standards, but Nora couldn't take her eyes off Asher.

His shadows have shadows.

She turned to face Michael. "That's enough! What's done is done. Hurting him is not going to make things any better."

Becky snorted behind her. "But kissing him will, right, Mom?"

At that point, Cathy walked in and stopped short.

"Whoa! What did I miss?"

Michael and Becky both started talking at once, while Asher just stared at Becky's rounded stomach. A muscle twitched in his cheek. Their children were getting louder and louder with Cathy.

Even the most proper of Southern ladies has their breaking point, and Nora reached hers.

"That's *it*!" Her don't-mess-with-me voice rang out and her hand slammed down so hard on the counter the glass display panel rattled. Becky jumped back when Nora pointed a finger at her.

"You keep telling me you want to be treated like an adult who's living her own life. Well, guess what? *I'm* also an adult who wants to live *my* own life. Frankly, who I do and do not choose to kiss is none of your business."

Becky's mouth dropped open, but Nora spun to Michael before she could speak. He didn't jump back, but he definitely leaned away, looking down at her with a mix of surprise and resentment.

"And you! You say you're ready to become a husband and a father, and then you resort to playing stupid, childish games with your own father, who's doing the best he can with all of this. And let me tell you from experience, *this…*" She gestured wildly at the two of them. "This is not easy for a parent to handle, okay? So why don't you both grow up and cut Asher and me a damned break?"

She turned to confront the last of the troublemakers, but Asher was gone. All she saw were the faces of her customers, staring at her, wideeyed and uncomfortable. Cathy came to the rescue, clapping her hands together loudly.

"Okay, folks. That concludes today's melodrama." One of the old guys playing checkers started to laugh. "Refills are on the house, and I'll be serving free samples of our new white chocolate chip cookies."

She leaned over to speak in Nora's ear.

"I'll handle things here, including these idiot kids of yours. You might still catch him if you run."

And that was what Nora did.

She ran.

CHAPTER SIXTEEN

SATURDAY WAS USUALLY his best day for walk-in business, but Asher didn't give a damn. He flipped the window sign over to the Closed side and turned the deadbolt so hard it sounded like a gunshot going off.

He thought of how Becky's hand had rested so protectively over the baby during the argument, as if shielding him from all the anger in the room. It wasn't Michael's words that had made him leave. They'd stung, yeah, but not enough to chase him off. It wasn't Nora's temper tantrum that had propelled him out the door. That was kind of cute, actually.

No. It was the realization that Becky was shielding the baby from *him* that made him run. She'd done the same thing last night when she walked past him to the stairs. Her hand had been raised like a barrier between him and his grandson.

His grandson...

All the twisted emotions that had been assailing him since last night burned like acid in his chest. And they scared the hell out of him. He had to get away from here before…before something happened. He didn't know what. He just knew he might not survive it. He was opening the truck door when he heard Nora calling his name, but he didn't turn around. Right now, his feelings were so close to the surface that just seeing her might destroy the dam holding everything tightly in place. He yanked the door open and got in, pushing the key into the ignition.

"Asher! Wait!" Her feet were splashing across the wet parking lot. "Don't you dare drive away from me, Asher Peyton! I wasn't done with you!"

A surprising warmth hit him. He liked Nora's angry voice. A lot. But he couldn't stay. He started to pull away but hit the brakes when he saw her in the rearview mirror, running around the back of the truck and falling so fast it was as if she'd vanished into thin air.

"Shit." He jumped out of the truck. She was just getting up, brushing dirt off her hands onto her bright green apron. Little circles of mud dotted her jeans at the knees. Her hair had been knocked free of its barrettes, and she pushed it behind her ears impatiently. He put his hands on her shoulders, and she looked up in surprise, out of breath.

"Damn it, Nora, are you alright?"

She nodded quickly. "Fine. I'm fine. Stupid

black ice. When does spring arrive in this god-forsaken place?"

Panic was still clawing at him, but he had to smile. "Officially? In about ten days. In reality? Don't be surprised to see snow flurries for the next month, so pay attention when you're out here. Especially wearing those shoes." She was wearing silly little ballet flats. It was too cold for her to be out here in nothing but jeans and a little knit top.

"Go back inside, Nora."

"Not without you."

He shook his head. "What did I tell you about trying to fix me? Just let me go. I'll be fine." That lie always fell so easily from his lips. He'd been telling it to himself for years now.

"Where are you going?"

"Away."

"Away sounds great. Take me with you."

"No. Seriously, stay here."

"With my horrified daughter and your furious son? No, thanks. Either you come back in so we can face them together, or you take me with you. No way are you sticking me with those two alone."

To Asher's surprise, a laugh bubbled up in his chest. He laughed out loud, staring first up at the mountains, where a patch of sunlight was glancing along the trees, then back to her. He was a goner with this woman.

"Get in." Nora wasted no time getting inside the vehicle.

They were halfway up the mountain before she said a word.

"You're not secretly some crazed mountain man kidnapping me and taking me to your remote cabin in the woods, are you?"

"Not exactly."

She gave a short laugh. "Oh, that's reassuring." Her head dropped back against the seat and she closed her eyes with a sigh. "Six months ago I was a respectable single mother who'd managed to get her daughter through high school and into college. I scraped and saved and planned, and everything was working so perfectly. And then…poof! All my plans went up in a cloud of baby powder. My little girl is pregnant." Nora's eyes opened, but she wasn't looking at him. Her fingers tapped nervously on her thigh, and her words came faster and faster. She was having this conversation with herself, so he stayed out of it.

"And I can't even hate the guy who got her pregnant, because he's so damned nice! And the two of them together are so sweet it makes my teeth hurt. And now I'm living here in the frozen North, and Becky thinks I came here because of the baby, but I didn't and I can't tell her the real reason. I didn't plan on any of this. Not one bit of it. And I don't like the unexpected. I like to have plans. It makes me happy when things go according to those plans. No surprises. And then there's you."

He could see her glaring at his profile, but he needed to keep his eyes on the twisting mountain road. "The father of the guy who got my daughter pregnant. A surly, hot bundle of manliness who lives right next door. And I should hate you, too, but I can't."

Hot bundle of manliness? He tried to keep a straight face but failed.

"Because I'm so damned sweet?"

"What?"

"The reason you can't hate me. Is it because I'm so damned sweet, like Michael?"

"Don't flatter yourself. You make my teeth hurt, but it's from grinding them together in frustration, not from sweetness. But speaking of Michael..."

She was suddenly distracted, from what he knew would be a lecture on his parenting skills, when he abruptly turned onto a dirt road even steeper than the pavement had been.

"Where are you taking me?"

"To my secret secluded cabin in the woods."

She gripped the door as the truck rocked back and forth. As soon as the weather broke, he would have to haul more stone up here to level this out. A branch swished along her side of the truck and she flinched.

"Uh…just so you know, Becky didn't get her love of hiking and skiing from me, okay? I don't do wilderness well."

So, the girl Michael had fallen for loved hiking and skiing just as much as he did. Asher had been looking at the two of them as if the pregnancy was the only thing holding them together, probably because it was the only thing he could see.

"You're the one who insisted on coming along. So sit back and enjoy the ride."

Bringing Nora here was a mistake. And it was probably a big one. He should have just taken her for a drive. But it was too late now. She was still busy complaining about the wilderness when he drove around the final corner and brought his truck to a stop.

The sudden silence was almost funny as he turned off the truck and turned to watch her. She was staring out the windshield at the log house, all three thousand square feet of it, nestled into the forest on the side of the mountain. He'd enlarged the small clearing into about an acre of level, grassy land in front of the house. Beyond that, Gallant Lake sprawled beneath them, with blue-gray mountains receding into the distance.

The rain had stopped for the moment, and the sun was trying to break through.

She got out of the truck without saying a word and walked across the lawn to the fieldstone wall along the drop-off. Then she turned to look back at the house, with its faded and weathered logs. A wooden deck stretched the length of the house on the first floor, with a balcony above it that could only be accessed through the master suite. It was all topped by a dark green metal roof that matched the pines behind it.

Hands in his pockets, he followed her, trying to see the place through her eyes and feeling oddly anxious about what she thought of it all. Amy never wanted to live up here, but Michael and…

He took a quiet breath to steady himself. Both of his boys loved this piece of land, and he couldn't part with it.

"This is yours?" She sounded in awe.

He nodded, his eyes never leaving her face, trying to read her thoughts.

"You built it yourself?" He nodded again. "Designed it yourself?" Another nod. "So you own all this—" she gestured from the view to the house itself "—and you live in that apartment above your shop? *Why?*"

He paused for a moment before answering. "It's not ready."

She tilted her head to the side and arched her

brow. "*It's* not ready, or *you're* not ready? How long ago did you start?"

"I laid the foundation seven years ago."

"Seven years?"

This was starting to feel an awful lot like an interrogation, and he was about to tell her just that when a gust of wind came up the side of the mountain, bringing another sweep of rain with it. Nora shivered and stepped toward him for shelter, her apron fluttering around her hips. He took his flannel shirt off and wrapped it around her shoulders.

"Come on. Let's get inside."

Once in the house, he gave her a quick tour of the main floor, and by the time they reached the upstairs master suite, her silence was wearing on him. She'd taken everything in: the almost-finished kitchen, the half-finished great room and the unfinished bedrooms downstairs. At least the master suite had primed drywall and a vaulted ceiling lined with cedar. The attached bath was nearly complete, with all the fixtures and a heated slate floor installed. But no paint yet.

Very few people had been up the mountain in recent years. The occasional contractor he'd hired for things like wiring and plumbing. Michael, of course. Dan. Blake Randall once. But never a woman. Never *this* woman. It mattered far more to him than it should that Nora like this house.

She shivered, and he kicked himself. He kept the furnace set just high enough to keep the pipes from freezing, which wasn't warm enough for a cold, wet woman. He moved to the fireplace, where logs were stacked and ready.

He lit the fire without saying a word, then went to the bookshelves he'd built to one side of the fireplace and pulled down a bottle of cognac. He had no glasses in the bedroom, so he took a drink straight from the bottle and handed it to her. She took it, drinking down several swallows before returning it. She looked around the room and gave a heavy sigh. He couldn't take her silence any longer.

"What are you thinking, Nora? What's wrong?"

"There's nothing *wrong*. I mean, the house is gorgeous. It could easily be in *Architectural Digest* someday. And the setting is incredible." She looked out over the lake, now shining blue under sunshine that had chased away the rain temporarily. "But all these years, Asher. And it's still unfinished. Were you planning on living here with your family? Is that why you let it sit?"

He pretended to study the view outside.

"I planned on a lot of things that never happened."

She looked around. "It's such an empty shell. There's no life here. There's no feeling of family or love or…"

His defenses rose. "Stop. It's a building. Wood and nails and stone. It doesn't have a personality."

"Maybe not. But a home reflects its owner. And this place is frozen in time, just like you are."

"Don't psychoanalyze me, Nora."

She huffed in response. "It doesn't take a psychoanalyst to see what you're doing."

He wasn't sure what annoyed him most. The fact that she'd said the words or the fact that they were undeniably true. She stared into the fire, which was now crackling nicely and warming up the room.

He looked around, trying to see the place through her eyes. Dusty, unfinished and colorless. Except for the woman who stood right in front of him. Her hair was drying in dark twisting waves. His blue flannel shirt hung off her shoulders, exposing her bright knit top and the green apron she still wore over her jeans. The fire, and perhaps her temper, had turned her cheeks cherry red.

Nora was a burst of color and life, and the contrast between her and the surroundings was almost too much to bear. He didn't realize he'd moved closer until she turned her head and looked up at him, her lips parting just enough to capture his full attention.

"Still got that bottle handy?" Her question surprised him, but it was better than her telling him to back off. She took the bottle and drank deeply, blowing out a breath as the liquid warmed her insides. Her eyes never left his, deepening from gold to dark bronze.

The woman poked and prodded at him until he was ready to lose his freaking mind. She got under his skin and into his head until he couldn't think clearly. She was dangerous. He set the bottle on the mantel and flinched in surprise when her hand touched his back. He turned, and her mouth trembled ever so slightly. The tip of her tongue moved across her bottom lip, moistening it and freezing him in place.

"You and I are quite the pair, aren't we?"

"How so?"

"We're complete opposites. I criticize you for being frozen in the past." He braced himself for a lecture he really didn't need. "But who am I to say anything, when I live only for the future? I spend all my time planning for tomorrow, next week, next month, next year. I set goals and figure out how to get there, and the end goal is all that matters. Get our finances in order. Get Becky through school. Plan her dream trip to England. Even now, I'm planning for the baby and setting goals for the business. My cousin Bree was right. When do I start living for myself? When do I start living for today?"

He pulled her into his arms, and she moved against him as if it was the most natural place for her to be, resting her cheek on his chest and sliding her hands around his waist. He waited, knowing she wasn't finished working this out in her head.

"Cathy had a poster in the café that I thought was so stupid. She was mad when I didn't hang it back up after I remodeled. It said that life is about the journey, not the destination."

He nodded, his chin resting on her head. He remembered the poster—it used to hang right behind the cash register.

Nora tipped her head back, looking up at him with wide eyes. "But maybe that poster is right. Maybe it *is* about the journey, about living in the moment, and I've been doing it *wrong* all this time! Maybe you and I both need to live in the moment, instead of looking backward *or* forward."

Her hands twisted in his shirt, and she moved her body tightly against his. There was no way she could miss his physical response, and she gave him a playful grin. "What do you think, Asher? Do we need to live in the moment, you and I?"

He pressed his lips against her forehead just long enough to dismiss the last of his doubts, answering right before he kissed her mouth, so soft and welcoming.

"I think this moment is as good as any."

NORA AGREED WITH a soft moan as Asher's tongue slid between her teeth. She didn't want to think anymore. She didn't want to worry and plan and fret and fix things for other people. She wanted to be right here, right now, in this moment, being kissed senseless by Asher Peyton. She trembled, and he drew her in closer, likely thinking she was cold. But she wasn't cold—she was burning up with need. And she was done denying herself. There'd be time for regrets later, but right now, she was going to live in this moment with him. *Their* moment.

He did that thing again, where he whispered her name over and over as if he never wanted to stop, running kisses along her chin and under her ear, then down her neck to the base of her throat. He was hard where she was pressed against him, and she couldn't resist moving. He responded by tightening his fingers against her hips, pulling her in even closer, grinding against her, zipper to zipper. His kisses turned to little bites on her skin, and her body responded in places he hadn't even touched yet.

He brushed his flannel shirt from her shoulders and it landed at her feet. His fingers hurriedly untied her apron—oh, God, she was still wearing her apron!—and then that was gone, too. He started to pull at the bottom of her shirt, but she wasn't going to let him win this race. She yanked the hem of his shirt up and he gave a rumbling laugh as he let her pull it over his head and toss it aside. She'd seen him shirtless, of course, but he'd been sick then. He definitely wasn't now, and she openly admired the breadth of his hard chest and the dark hair that curled down the center of it, leading to a sexy little happy trail that disappeared into his jeans.

"Your turn, princess." But she pushed his hands away, and his eyes darkened to cobalt as she pulled her own knit top up and off. She wished she was wearing sexy underwear instead of this simple cotton bra, but she'd had no idea this morning she'd end up stripping in front of Asher. Her momentary regret vanished when she saw the way he was staring at her. Like she was a goddess. She stood proud as she reached around to remove the bra. She didn't think twice about trusting this man who looked at her with such worship in his eyes.

When the bra fell to the floor, he whispered her name and stepped forward as if she was drawing him in with invisible cords. His hands cupped her breasts and she dropped her head back. He accepted her unspoken invitation, kissing her throat, her shoulders, then her breasts, back and forth, from one to the other. She dug her fingernails into his shoulders until he grunted, but his mouth never stopped. Finally, afraid he was going to make her come while still half-clothed, she gasped his name. He grinned at the desperation she knew was visible in her eyes, then he nibbled at her ear.

"What do you want, Nora?"

Her words came in breathy bursts. "You. I want you. Naked. Both of us. Naked. Right now."

His laughter tickled her neck. "For once, we are in total agreement." He lifted his head, glancing around the empty room, now warm from the fire. "Hang on." She couldn't stop the groan of loss as he stepped away. He pulled a mound of muslin drop cloths from the corner, piling them in front of the hearth until they looked like the most inviting nest she'd ever seen. By the time he looked up for her approval, she'd already pushed her jeans and panties to the floor. She didn't know who she was right now, but damn, it felt good to be bold. Still kneeling, Asher reached up and pulled her in.

"Holy hell, Nora, you're going to undo me before I even get inside of you. Come here." He kissed her stomach, then pulled her down until she was kneeling in front of him. The word *inside* triggered a more practical thought.

"Please tell me you have a condom…"

He'd been on the way to kiss her breast, but he stopped and grinned. "Yes, I'm a good Boy Scout."

He reached back and pulled out his wallet, extracting not one but two foil packets. "I'm prepared."

He tossed the wallet aside and unbuckled his belt. She'd never been an assertive lover, but she couldn't resist moving her hand down to stroke the firm bulge beneath his zipper. Asher sucked in a breath, then scrambled to get out of his clothes and lay her back on the makeshift bed. He stared down as if memorizing every inch of her, and her skin tingled everywhere his eyes caressed.

Some tiny spot in her brain registered that she, Nora Bradford, was lying naked on a pile of discarded drop cloths in an empty, unfinished shell of a house with a man she wasn't sure she knew at all. It was another out-of-body moment, where she could look down and see the two of them in front of the snapping fire, staring at each other without moving. She saw a glimmer of hesitation in Asher, as if he was having the same experience and questioning himself. She reached up and rested her hand along the side of his face.

"In the moment…" She whispered the mantra. He leaned into her hand and closed his eyes. When he opened them again, the hesitation was gone. He tore open the foil and lowered his body onto hers, kissing her deeply. He pushed himself against her, and she let him in with a soft sigh. They didn't move at first, just lay there, holding each other. She reveled in the feel of his body in hers. Her fingers curled against his back and he started to move. Cautiously at first, until she urged him on, not satisfied with slow. Not satisfied until he was moving hard and fast against her, swallowing her cries with his kisses until they both cried out at once and the room went so brightly, brilliantly white that she closed her eyes for fear she'd be blinded.

Asher continued moving gently against her as they both came down from the peak and started to breathe again. When he finally stopped, his face was buried in her neck. He released his hold on her bottom, and she knew she'd probably have marks from the firm grip he'd had while they were making love.

No. Not that. While they were having *sex*. She had to keep this real. It was just a moment. He moved his fingers up her sides, caressing and soothing as he went, until his hands were on both sides of her face. He looked down, and she saw a gentle warmth in his eyes she hadn't imagined possible.

"You will never again be able to say there's no life in this house, Nora. You just brought life to it."

CHAPTER SEVENTEEN

ASHER DIDN'T REALIZE he'd spoken his thoughts until he saw Nora's eyes go misty. A bashful smile tugged at her lips as if the compliment surprised and embarrassed her. Those high spots of pink he liked so much appeared on her cheeks, and he kissed them both. He couldn't quite wrap his head around the fact that he'd just had sex with Nora Bradford on the floor. And it had been amazing. He would remember every single moment of this for the rest of his life, in vivid images of her.

He'd remember looking up and seeing her standing there, naked, the curves of her body begging him to touch her. The look of her beneath him, brown hair splayed out around her head like a halo, looking at him with nothing but trust and desire. The sound of his name on her lips when she came. The way her body lifted against his, her legs wrapping around him as if she was afraid he'd get away. Even now, her legs were intertwined with his, and he, who'd never been much for cuddling, discovered he liked it a lot. With her.

One of the logs in the fireplace broke apart in a burst of sparks and flame. She blinked, and he saw the briefest glimmer of doubt in her eyes. He moved quickly to quell it.

"You're beautiful." She shook her head and opened her mouth, but he gave her a fast kiss to silence her. "You are beautiful. Do you trust me, Nora?" He did his best to ignore the hurt when she hesitated for a heartbeat before nodding. He dropped another kiss to her lips. "I don't want this moment to be over. So wait here, just like you are. I'm going to clean up and grab us some food from the kitchen, and maybe find some glasses…" He glanced at the cognac on the mantel. "I'll be right back, okay?"

She nodded again and gave him a shy grin. "We don't need glasses."

He pushed himself away, ignoring the protest from his body, which was already begging for more of her. "Straight from the bottle, eh? Okay. No glasses. You stay right here."

He pulled on his jeans and moved as fast as he could, but when he came back to the bedroom just ten minutes later, she was dozing. She must have gotten chilled, or perhaps felt a burst of modesty, because she'd pulled his flannel shirt over her like a blanket and was curled up tightly under it. He stood over her, unable to put words to the emotions running through him. He wanted to protect her. He wanted to make love to her... No, have sex... No, it was more than sex they'd just had.

Outside, the sun had finally lost its battle with the rain, which now beat steadily against the windows. Sunset was a few hours away, but shadows were already appearing in the corners of the room, currently lit only by the fireplace. For the first time ever, he wished he had more lights in this place instead of just a few cheap lamps with bare bulbs in them. He wished there were soft drapes at the windows, bringing color and warmth. He wished there was a big bed Nora could be nestled in, instead of sleeping there on his floor. He wished this was a home instead of a half-finished shell.

Before he could give that surprising revelation any more thought, Nora sighed and opened her eyes. She sat up, letting his shirt fall off one shoulder, and made room for him to sit with her. Damn, but she was beautiful.

He crossed his legs and sat, handing her the blanket he'd grabbed downstairs. Once in a while he'd sleep on a cot down there if he'd had too much to drink.

"I thought you might want something softer and cleaner than drop cloths." He handed her the plate of crackers and cheese. "I don't keep much food here, but there is a pizza in the freezer we can heat up later. It's not very fancy…"

Nora's fingers pressed against his mouth, silencing him. Laughter danced in her eyes.

"Are you feeling nervous or something, sitting here almost naked with me and offering crackers and cheese?"

Oh, he was definitely feeling something.

"I *like* sitting here almost naked with you." He ran his gaze up and down her body, taking a moment to appreciate her soft, pale skin and trembling smile. "But, yeah, it's a little…unexpected… to be here like this. With you. With anyone. Here. Now."

And he was devolving into single-word sentences again. He took a piece of cheese and ate it, just to shut himself up. As if she knew it, Nora giggled. He hadn't heard her nervous giggle since the spider incident.

"I think 'unexpected' is an understatement." She grinned and crunched on a cracker.

Without thinking, he bent over and kissed the crumbs from the corner of her mouth. She caught her breath sharply and he sat back, feeling a familiar panic rise up inside. They were getting way too cozy. Affectionate. Intimate. What the hell was he doing here with this woman?

"And there he goes."

"What?"

Her voice was soft and sad. "You're running again. Pulling away. Shutting me out."

His well-practiced defenses rose automatically. "This…what just happened…it isn't real life, Nora. It was amazing, and I sure as hell don't regret it. But trust me, I'm not relationship material. There's a long line of witnesses who can attest to that."

She pushed her arms into the sleeves of his shirt, drawing it around her and hiding the view he'd been enjoying.

"You used to be relationship material. You had a wife. Two sons."

He should have known she'd go down this road again. Dr. Phil had nothing on Nora Bradford. He pulled the cork from the bottle of cognac. He would need liquid courage for this conversation. "You just proved my point. None of those relationships still exist."

"The one with Michael does."

"No. It doesn't. You've seen how he reacts to me now. He hates me."

"Don't be ridiculous. Kids get hurt and lash out, but that doesn't mean they hate us. In fact, it's usually when they push us away that they need us the most." She blushed and smiled. "Okay, I know that was another greeting-card moment. But, seriously, when was the last time you two really talked?"

"It was here, at this house. A while ago."

"What happened?"

I offered him a bribe to dump your pregnant daughter.

"I don't know."

She stared at him long and hard, until he finally shifted restlessly. It was like she knew he was lying to her. She glanced around the room, then went straight for the kill shot.

"Dylan was still alive when you started building this. The boys must have been here together."

He resented the way his son's name fell so easily from her lips. All he could do was nod.

"Michael told me Dylan liked to play practical jokes."

He closed his eyes to keep from being ill. His fingers clenched the top of the bottle so hard he expected it to shatter in his hands. Then he felt the cool touch of her hand on his, and he was able to breathe again, barely. Eyes still closed, he listened to the wind and rain outside, the snapping and popping of the fire and the sound of his own blood rushing in his ears. He needed to walk away. No, he needed to run. He needed to get out of this room and run away from this woman.

NORA WATCHED THE color drain from Asher's face, then come rushing back again. His breathing was uneven and his pulse was leaping erratically in a little vein on the side of his neck. His hand beneath hers was trembling. She waited, expecting him to turn any moment and do one of the two things he did best: explode in anger or run. Whatever was going to happen, it was going to be his move. Not hers.

At first, she thought he was talking to himself. His eyes were still closed, and she had to lean in to hear.

"He had a big rubber spider with a string on it. He knew I hated spiders, and he was always putting the damn thing somewhere where I'd see it." The corner of his mouth lifted and his voice grew stronger. "He'd make it move with the string and laugh like hell when I jumped. And he constantly messed with our food. Black pepper in his mother's tea. Salt in the sugar bowl. Hot red pepper flakes in strawberry jam."

Asher opened his eyes slowly, looking into the fire as if he could see his youngest son in the flames.

"Michael said something about salting his toothbrush?" Nora asked.

Asher turned to her, the corner of his mouth twitching. "I forgot about that. Yeah, he'd wet the toothbrush and scrub salt into it, then put it back in the holder. Michael would go to brush his teeth and get a salty surprise. He'd chase Dylan all over the house…"

He stopped, and she knew why.

"How long has it been since you said Dylan's name?"

His brows knit together, and he took another swallow of cognac. "Other than when I had a raging fever? I don't know. A long time." His back straightened and he moved to stand. "We should go."

"No, Asher, don't stop. Tell me more." He was shutting her out again. It was so frustrating to get these glimpses of the man Asher could be, only to have him vanish like a mirage.

"I can't."

"Okay, don't tell me about Dylan. Tell me about Michael. What was he like as a boy?"

He hesitated, then started to talk again. "Michael started out as a little class clown and was a coconspirator in many of his baby brother's antics. He played baseball and football, but when he entered high school, he went from team sports to things he could do alone, like skiing and hiking." Nora felt her heart grow tight. Michael had changed when Dylan died. He became a loner. Just like his dad.

"How long have you been divorced?" She knew the answer already but thought it might keep him talking. He was done playing along, though.

"Enough. You've dragged more out of me in half an hour than anyone else has in years. Consider it a win, okay? Hell, are you this nosy about *everyone* you meet?"

His fingers raked through his hair, and she wanted to do the same, but she wasn't sure if she should touch him right now. He was tense, head down and shoulders hunched defensively. She took the bottle and had a drink to settle her frayed nerves. She was way out of her depth with this man and his secrets. But she couldn't leave him alone.

"Not with everyone, Asher." He stared at her, his body language easing somewhat.

"You know, Nora, you're really great at *asking* questions, but how about answering a few? You grill me every time we meet, and I know nothing about you."

She shrugged. "You've never asked."

"Why did you really move to Gallant Lake?"

She stuttered for a moment, then gave him her standard answer, ignoring the guilt digging at her. "Well…I moved here because of the baby."

"Bullshit."

"I beg your pardon?" Nora sounded so pompous she almost rolled her eyes at herself. She wasn't ashamed of her Southern accent, but it did get stronger at the most inconvenient times.

"You come at me for information like a damn piranha, snapping and ripping at me until I come clean." She was surprised to see disappointment in his eyes, and her cheeks burned. "And then you lie to me the first time I ask you a question."

"H-how do you know it's a lie?"

He shook his head. "When you were freaking out in the truck on the way up here, you said your daughter thought you moved here because of the baby, but you didn't. So why *did* you?"

He was right. She'd demanded his truth, so it was only fair that she trust him with hers.

"It's a really long story, but my late husband's past was about to rear its ugly head in Atlanta, and there are things Becky doesn't need to know about her father. The only way to make the story go away was for me to go away. There just happened to be a coffee shop for sale in the town where my daughter lives. And Amanda and Blake are here." She gave him her best attempt at a playful wink. "So, despite the neighbor I knew I was getting, here I am, living in the mountains of New York."

"You don't make impulsive decisions often, do you?"

"Hardly ever. I'm not big on surprises." She looked at him, sitting there. He was a surprise on every level, wasn't he? He hadn't bothered to fasten his jeans, so they hung low on his hips. She shivered, and he surprised her again by pulling her in close to his side and pulling the blanket up around her.

"What was in your husband's past that's so awful? I thought he was a politician... Oh."

"Yeah. Oh. He was a total cliché, and so was I."

Asher's fingers gripped her shoulder.

"Tell me what that means."

Now it was her turn to stiffen in resistance.

"I don't want to talk about this."

"That's ironic, coming from you."

The chirp of an incoming text broke the moment. Nora blinked and looked around. Where were her jeans? And when did it get so dark in here? What time was it, anyway? She leaned back and dragged her jeans over so she could dig the phone out. The text was from Cathy.

Locals are restless. Are you two okay?

Nora frowned. Which locals exactly?

Your girl. His boy. Your cousin. And Sheriff Dan.

She groaned and looked to Asher, but he was busy tapping away on his own phone. Reality was barging back into their lives.

We're fine.

You're at the cabin?

Leave it to Cathy to know where they were.

Yes.

I figured. But heads up. So did Michael and Dan.

Which meant they could be getting company any minute. Nora scrambled to her knees to grab her clothes, but a strong arm wrapped around her waist and pulled her back onto Asher's lap.

"They're coming…" It was one thing for her daughter to know she'd *kissed* Asher, but finding them naked was another.

"No. They're not. But you are."

His lips met hers and she forgot the rest of the world—until her phone pinged again.

"Leave it." Asher spoke the words against her mouth. But all Nora could think about was a caravan of vehicles headed up the mountain, bringing her daughter and her cousin and Asher's son and Sheriff Dan. She reluctantly pulled away, and his heavy sigh told her he wasn't happy about it.

This time the text was from Amanda.

You sure you know what you're doing?

Nora laughed out loud at that, and Asher leaned over to read the screen as she typed.

Of course not. But I'm going to keep doing it for a while.

Asher traced a kiss down her neck.

Can you keep everyone at bay?

She waited several minutes for a response.

Dan ordered us to stay away from there under threat of arrest. Becky's not happy, but I'll talk to her.

Nora was surprised she hadn't heard from Becky yet, but that mystery was solved with Amanda's next text.

Right now she's busy looking for her phone, which is safely in my pocket. I invited her and Michael to Halcyon for dinner, and that'll keep them occupied for a few hours. After that you're on your own!

"A few hours?" Asher kissed her shoulder. "I can work with that."

She tapped out a thanks to Amanda and turned in his arms, trying to ignore the thrilled *thump-thump-thump* of her heart when her eyes met his. One of them had to be the adult here.

"Our children are freaking out. We really should…"

Her sentence was ended by a kiss so deep and delicious she forgot what she'd intended to say. When he finally pulled away, it was only far enough to speak against her mouth.

"Our children managed to get themselves pregnant, so I think they have a pretty good idea of what's going on up here. What's the point in rushing back and pretending otherwise?"

She tried to come up with an argument, but she had none. He was right. Becky and Michael definitely knew what their parents were doing together. She looked at Asher, and something way down inside her warmed deliciously. She wrapped her arms around his neck. Who knew if this would ever happen again? A low growl escaped his throat as he spread the blanket behind her and laid her back.

His fingers traced along her cheekbone, then down her neck to her breasts, exposed by the open flannel shirt she still wore. His kisses followed the trail of his fingertips, and he breathed her name against her skin until she thought she'd be branded with it. Lower, and lower again, beyond her breasts and over her stomach. When he reached his goal, she whimpered with need, her body arching up to meet his mouth. One stroke of his tongue. One touch of his fingers. And she was gone, crying out so loudly her voice echoed in the empty room.

She barely registered the sound of tearing foil before he was over her, parting her legs and kissing her so wildly she thought she might just pass out from sensory overload. It was too much. And then he was inside her again, and all thoughts stopped. She was just feeling and moving and enjoying, as Asher's passion burned hot and fast. He shouted her name before they went over the edge together, grasping each other as if afraid of being torn apart in the fall.

His head lay on her shoulder and they stayed there, breathing heavily, as the fading fire crackled. Her fingers were still digging into his back. She should release him. But not yet. The first time had been exciting and naughty and sexy. But this time was different. The way he'd touched her. Kissed her. The way he'd taken control and managed her orgasms as efficiently as he constructed furniture. Something had shifted between them; something had flown free.

She was falling for Asher Peyton. Not just lusting after Hot Produce Guy, but falling for the *man* and falling hard. He was her daughter's future father-in-law. This was going to be a disaster. A tickle of panic worked its way up her spine, and he must have sensed it.

"Stop. Thinking." His head didn't move, and he

spoke the words into the blanket beneath them. "I don't have the strength to deal with any more Nora thoughts tonight, and I can feel them bubbling up inside of you. Don't think. Just stay here with me for a little while longer."

The last sentence came out as a plea, and she couldn't deny him. Asher had been chasing people away for years. That he wanted her to stay meant something. So she quietly traced her fingers back and forth across his solid back. The room grew dark and chilly as the fire died down to embers, but his body was keeping her warm. She shifted slightly and tried to pull the edge of the blanket up and over him, but her movement brought him out of his sex coma.

"Is there a problem?" He lifted his head and arched his brow at her.

"I was just trying to make sure you weren't chilled."

The corner of his mouth lifted. "Nora, I'm still buried inside you and we're wrapped around each other like vines. Cold is not a problem. Death from wild sex was a worry for a minute or two, but cold is not an issue." He frowned and started to move. "Unless *you're* cold?"

"No!" She gripped him more tightly, inspiring another grin. "You're perfect! I mean, you're keeping me perfectly warm...or something..." Her voice faded off. He really did feel perfect right now. He watched her closely, then started to move away as if he saw something he didn't want to see. He glanced around the room, and she knew he was pulling away emotionally as well as physically.

"Damn, what time is it? We should get going before the search parties arrive."

"Amanda's having the kids over to Halcyon for dinner, so they'll be distracted." She didn't want to leave this bubble just yet.

He shook his head and rose to his knees, allowing cool air to move across her exposed breasts. "Nothing's going to distract them for long now that they know their parents are doing the dirty."

"Doing the dirty?" Nora sat up with him and started to wiggle into her jeans.

"I'm sure that's how they'll see it."

She shrugged off his shirt and pulled her sweater over her head.

"And how do you see it?"

The silence grew heavy before he answered. "Nora, I don't know what to think." To soften the nonanswer, he laid the palm of his hand along the side of her face. "We did something impulsive here, and we're *both* going to have to deal with the fallout. So either I throw more logs on the fire and we stay here all night, while our friends and family lose their collective minds, or we go face the music."

She thought for a minute, then nodded. She wasn't the type of woman who'd actually *date* the father of her daughter's boyfriend. In her Atlanta circles, that behavior would be fodder for months of juicy gossip. But this was just a moment, not a long-term thing. Surely she was allowed to have a crazy afternoon with a hot, troubled neighbor. They were both adults, after all.

Perfectly capable of making grown-up decisions.

She hoped.

CHAPTER EIGHTEEN

THIS TIME ASHER *wasn't* surprised to find Michael's Jeep in the parking lot when he and Nora pulled in. He'd been hoping maybe this conversation could wait until morning, but no such luck. As he parked the truck, the passenger door of the Jeep opened. Apparently both kids had decided to wait for them. Nora's face was grim.

"We'd just started to patch things up, and now she's going to start hating me all over again."

Michael moved around the car and extended his arm so Becky could hold on to him as they crossed the muddy lot. Her baby bump jutted out through her open coat, and her free hand rubbed across it lightly. Twenty-some years ago, that could have been Asher and Amy together, expecting a child and having such high hopes for the baby, each other and the future. He'd been so oblivious back then to the kind of havoc the future would bring.

"Looks like we're being tag teamed." Nora appeared at his side, resting her hand on his arm. His blood pressure immediately settled and his breathing relaxed at her touch. She looked up at him. "Do we face them down together or divide and conquer?"

"You're the planner. You tell me."

She thought for a moment. "I know this will shock you, but I think we should let them take the lead here. It's understandable why they're upset. We're their parents and we're…well…you know. It's all a bit of a mess."

She frowned, looking away. She was having regrets about being with him. And that made her a smart woman. He pulled her in for a quick hug, dropping a kiss to the top of her head. He didn't let go until he heard Michael clearing his throat loudly in front of them. Nora stepped away from him, blushing in the dim glow of the single parking-lot light.

"Mom…" Becky's tone was disbelieving and angry.

Nora's shoulders sagged. He didn't want her to feel bad about what had happened between them. He pulled her back to his side, leaving his arm around her. Becky and Michael glanced at each other uncertainly, and Nora started to speak.

"I know today has complicated an already complicated situation…"

Michael barked out a humorless laugh. "You think?"

Asher stared hard at his son. "That's enough."

"Is it, Dad? Is it really enough, or are you just getting started? How much more damage can you do here? First you disown me…"

"For God's sake, Michael, I never disowned you…"

"Then you accuse Becky of plotting some marriage trap and you try to get me to…"

"Alright. I get it." Asher stopped Michael from finishing that sentence. He didn't know what Nora would think of his offer to get Michael to leave Gallant Lake. No, that wasn't true. He knew exactly what she'd think.

"You get it? Really? Because if you *got* it, you wouldn't be playing this game with Becky's mother."

"What the hell does that mean?"

"I don't know what your end game is here," Michael said, gesturing at Asher and Nora. "But I know you're up to something. And I'm not going to let you rip another family apart the way you did ours."

Asher's hand dropped from Nora's shoulder and he took a menacing step forward.

"What exactly are you accusing me of?"

Michael didn't move, other than to narrow his eyes. He just stood there, bristling with anger and distrust. Asher felt the sharp burn of regret. Had he created this? Did Michael really think he was manipulating the situation by being with Nora?

He blinked. Why *wouldn't* Michael believe that, since Asher had been trying to manipulate the situation between Michael and Becky since he learned of it?

Nora stepped between the two men, who both towered over her.

"Okay, now I'm the one saying that's enough." She put her hand on Asher's chest and gently pushed him back. "Why don't we all take a deep breath here before we say something unforgivable? I'm starting to think tonight isn't a good time for this discussion." She looked at Becky, whose eyes were shining with unshed tears. "I know you're confused, honey. Believe me, I'm a little confused, too. This wasn't in my plans." She turned to Michael. "I know you're mad at your father, but what's going on with Asher and me is not about you or Becky. He and I are two adults who are attracted to each other…"

"Eww." Becky's face scrunched up so much that Asher almost laughed out loud. But he was smart enough to know that would be a bad idea.

Nora fixed her daughter with a hard look. "That's pretty much the way I felt when I found out about you and Michael. I've done my best to respect your feelings. I'm asking the same in return."

Michael shook his head. "You don't know him, Nora. He'll hurt you."

Asher's teeth ground together in frustration. He wanted to deny it, but his son was right.

"Maybe. Or maybe I'll hurt him. That's how it works in relationships. I'm a grown woman, Michael, and I've been hurt before. I can take it." She nodded toward the Jeep. "But right now it's late and cold and you need to take care of my daughter. Give me and your dad a little time to figure out what we're doing, okay?"

"Mom, this is so messed up! He hates me..."

"I never said that, Becky." Everyone looked at him in surprise, and he realized he'd never before called her by name. This was a day full of firsts. "I don't hate you. I don't want you marrying my son, but it's not because I hate you." He paused, surprised that he couldn't remember *what* his reasoning was for a moment. Then he saw her hand resting on her stomach. Oh, yeah. Fear. That was why. "Your mom is right. This isn't the time or the place for this discussion."

Michael lowered his head and said something into Becky's ear. She took a deep breath and nodded. He looked up and draped his arm around Becky's shoulders. "Nora, let me know when you want to talk."

As they walked away, Asher swallowed hard, absorbing the sting of being dismissed by his only remaining child. A whisper of doubt rose in his mind. Was he doing the right thing for his son?

Was he wrong to want to protect him? And what the hell was he doing with Nora? How much more tangled could this situation get?

"Well, that was fun." Nora's sarcasm broke through his scrambled thoughts.

"Yeah. Lots of fun." He looked down at her. She was chewing on her lower lip, watching them drive away. He knew one surefire way to forget about their children. And it involved having Nora in his bed. He ran his lips along the curve of her ear and down her neck, smiling when she trembled. "I know where we *can* have some fun, though. Why don't you come up to my place?"

She pulled away, not meeting his gaze.

"Nora?" She held up her hands to keep him from tugging her back into his arms.

"Asher, our children are having a *baby* together. For us to start seeing each other is just adding fuel to an inferno, and I don't know how much more stress our families can handle. And how would it look to everyone else? You and I have businesses in this town. I need to think, and it's late, so… I'll catch up with you tomorrow, okay?"

He wanted to argue, but damn it, she was right. The two of them together would be a mess. And he didn't want to talk Nora into something that would only end up hurting her in the long run. So he nodded.

"Okay. If that's what you want." He followed her up the stairs to the outdoor landing and watched her slide her key into the lock and open her door. She turned to him and started to say something, but he was kissing her before she had the chance. The kiss was deep, but tender, too, and she melted into his arms. He took one last, long taste of her and stepped back, cupping her face with his hands.

"Going to bed alone is not what I want, Nora. But we probably both need some space. You pried open a lot of locked-up places inside my head today, and I need to sort it all out."

"No matter where you and I end up, holding all of that inside is bad for you." She gave him a soft smile. "Did I just sound like a greeting card again?"

He chuckled and kissed her forehead.

"Yes. Good night, Nora. Today was…a revelation, in a lot of ways. You were amazing. And, right or wrong, I don't think I'm done with you."

He left her standing there, bathed in the warm light from her apartment, and went to his place, which felt more empty than ever.

BECKY DIDN'T COME to work the next day. Nora wasn't exactly surprised, but it made for an extra busy Sunday morning. It didn't help that she'd had very little sleep the night before, as she lay awake and wondered what Asher was thinking about, knowing he was probably lying awake wondering the same about her.

I don't think I'm done with you.

Those words were on a repeating loop in her head. And then there was Cathy, who winked and giggled every time she looked at Nora.

"I *knew* it! I knew there was something between you two!"

Nora heard those words repeated at least a dozen times in the first three hours of business. She refused to acknowledge them with anything more than a roll of her eyes, and that just made Cathy laugh harder. Every time a customer gave Nora more than a passing glance, she'd burned with embarrassment, fearing the whole town somehow already knew she'd slept with the business owner next door. When the Sunday crowd slowed to a point where they could breathe and restock the counter, Nora finally responded to Cathy.

"How could you possibly know something *I* didn't even know?"

"Get real, Nora. When you two are in the same room, little lightning bolts flicker all around you. He ran to your rescue when there was a spider in your place, and that guy hates spiders more than any man I've ever met! You spent an entire night nursing him when he was sick. And then you *kissed* the man. And now you're telling me you had no idea you two had chemistry?"

Nora sighed. Cathy was right, of course. All the signs had been there.

"And judging from that dreamy look in your eyes, I'm guessing there was more than just chemistry happening on the mountain yesterday."

Nora's whole body lit up just thinking about herself and Asher on the floor in front of the hearth. Yeah, that was more than just chemistry.

"I'd like to know the answer to that, too."

Nora turned to find Amanda standing at the counter, wearing a grin that ran from ear to ear. She really had to do something about the acoustics in this place, since every conversation she had here was overheard by *someone*.

Amanda beckoned her with a crooked finger. "Pour two coffees and come sit with me, cuz."

There was no point in stalling, so she did as requested and followed her cousin across the shop. Amanda had pulled her hair up into the high ponytail she often wore, tied with a pink ribbon that matched her sweater. She and Amanda were both petite, but Amanda always looked like a little pixie with her baby blue eyes, wide smile and wild blond curls, while Nora just felt short. It was more than just the nine-year age difference. Amanda glowed with…life. The customers in the shop nodded and waved to her, asking about Zachary and Maddie.

For a woman who had been so traumatized by her youth that she'd once had a hard time being in public without experiencing a panic attack, Amanda had blossomed into a new woman after meeting Blake Randall. Nora felt dull in comparison and wondered what changes love might bring to her life—if she ever found it.

They sat at the corner table closest to the window and farthest from Cathy's curious ears.

"So you slept with the guy?"

Nora's cheeks burned. "Why don't you just put it on a billboard?"

Unperturbed, Amanda sipped her coffee. "Spill it, girl."

So Nora spilled. The argument with the kids. The drive to the mountain house. And even the sex, although she didn't share every little detail of that. She was pretty sure Amanda could read the details in her voice and face. When she got to the confrontation with Michael and Becky last night, her cousin's eyes were wide, her coffee forgotten and cold.

"Wow. I might need a cigarette after that story, and I don't even smoke. Holy shit, Nora. You're the sensible one among us. You can't walk across the street without having a written plan for how you'll do it."

Amanda's hands were moving through the air to punctuate each word. "I mean, I expected Bree to fall hard for someone like Cole, who's just as fierce as she is. And Melanie...well, who knows who Melanie might find, if she ever slows down long enough. But *you*? I thought for sure after that asshat you were married to, you'd be looking for some nice predictable man. But, no, you fall for Hot Produce Guy! Even after you find out he's Michael's dad, you..."

Amanda leaned forward and dropped her voice to a whisper. "You made love with him on the *floor*! I mean, I'm all for floor sex, but I never imagined *you*..."

"I'm forty, Amanda, not dead."

"Hey, don't get me wrong—I fully intend to be jumping Blake's bones on the floor every chance I get until I'm too old to get down there. I just..." Amanda sat back, shaking her head. "You know what? You're right. Why *wouldn't* you want floor sex with Hot Produce Guy?"

Nora couldn't help but smile. "It was amazing, but our kids are engaged to each other, for God's sake. What will people think? Just because it was great floor sex doesn't mean it should happen more than once." Amanda didn't answer, her focus on some spot over Nora's right shoulder. Was it Cathy behind her? Blake? Becky?

Warm breath slid across her ear, sending chills

down her spine that combusted into fire as Asher spoke so quietly she could barely hear him.

"Great floor sex should always happen more than once, Nora."

Face burning, she wondered who else had heard her comments, but a quick glance told her the tables around them were blessedly empty. She fixed her gaze back on Amanda.

"Thanks for the heads-up, cuz."

Amanda grinned. "What can I say? I'm a sucker for floor sex." She stood and her smile faded as she pointed a finger at Asher. "I know where you live, pal. I haven't decided yet if you deserve her, but I do know you'll regret it if you hurt her." She started walking past him, then stopped. Her voice softened. "And seriously, Asher, you have a great son. Quit being such a jerk to him."

"I'm not..."

But Amanda was gone before Asher could finish. Nora gestured for Asher to sit, but he shook his head.

"I don't want to feed the small-town gossip mill any more than we already have."

She glanced outside, where the sidewalks were getting busier as people left church and came downtown on what was turning into a rare sunny March day.

"Have you had lunch? I have sandwich fixings upstairs."

He hesitated. "The shop's open. I just came over for a quick coffee and to see if you were okay. I already missed a business day yesterday..." Their eyes met, and just like that, they were both laughing.

Two women came into the café and shot them a curious glance before going to order their coffee, heads together and whispering. Yeah, they needed to get out of here.

"Why don't I deliver lunch to you? Your shop has less traffic than mine."

Another hesitation made her wonder where his head had taken him last night. Then he nodded.

"The back door's open if you want to come in that way."

"And avoid the gossips?"

"I know that's important to you."

As brief as their conversation had been, they'd somehow managed to move so close to each other that Nora had to tip her head back to see his face. His gaze dropped to her mouth. They were standing in the middle of her café, in front of the windows, and she really, *really* wanted him to kiss her.

More customers came in, breaking the moment. Cathy signaled that Asher's coffee was on the corner of the counter, and he moved to get it, glancing over his shoulder at Nora.

"See you in a few?" She could only nod, still reeling.

Five minutes later, Cathy shooed her away after she asked if Cathy could handle the shop alone.

"Go. I've got this." She gave Nora an exaggerated wink. "Don't get any sawdust in shady places—that stuff can be nasty!"

So Nora went upstairs to get lunch for herself and Asher. Once the sandwiches were made, she packaged them up and headed down the back stairs to let herself into her neighbor's shop. He was kneeling in front of a small cherry dresser, tapping on something inside the opening where a drawer should be. The drawer was sitting on the floor by his side. He nodded to acknowledge her, but his focus was on the piece of furniture in front of him. She busied herself with the sandwiches, adding a handful of chips to each paper plate and setting out bottled water.

She hadn't been in his shop since November, so she took advantage of his distraction to look around. Bright sunshine flooded the room and Gallant Lake was blazing blue across the road, beyond a small park. The smaller pieces of furniture at the front of the shop were beautiful, each unique yet functional. Some were modern and sleek, while others were sturdier arts and crafts style. An oak Morris chair was near the entrance, upholstered in dark green leather, and Nora ran her hand along the top of the cushion. The leather was butter soft, and she stroked it again.

"I'm going to need you to stop doing that." Asher's voice sounded strained. He was standing nearby, and behind him she could see the dresser drawer was back in place. "If I have to watch you run your fingers across the leather with that dreamy look in your eyes too much longer, I can't be responsible for my actions."

"Really?" She moved her hand across the cushion again, exaggerating the motion. "Right here in front of the window?"

"Are you daring me? Because that would be a dangerous move."

"Dangerous for whom?"

He took a step closer, then caught himself and shook his head with a crooked smile.

"You're a tease, Nora Bradford. You are a gold-plated, certified tease." He turned away. "Let's eat lunch before we both get into trouble."

The conversation was everyday normal while they ate—weather, business, small-town news. It was all terribly civilized and friendly, but the longer she spent sharing the same space with him, the more her body hummed with desire.

His rough voice made her breath catch. His blue eyes caught hers and held them, and the conversation faded to silence. He reached out to brush her hair back behind her ear, and his fingers lingered there on her neck. They were leaning toward each other, and she hadn't even realized it.

"So did you figure out what to do with all those unlocked spaces in your head?" She did her best to sound unconcerned, but failed.

"There's a war going on inside there right now. I didn't sleep much, trying to figure it all out, but the only conclusion I came to was this." His hand cupped her face gently. "I should stay away from you, for a million valid reasons, but I can't. And what about you? Did you figure out whether we're worth the scandal?"

She pushed that horrified voice of doubt into a dark corner of her brain. There had to be a way to make this work. Because right now, being with him was worth everything.

"I…I think we should…um…take things slow. And I don't think we need to publicize our… um…relationship…"

"Slow works for me. And quiet, too." His thumb brushed across her cheek. "When you blush like that, your cheeks turn into little roses, all pink and sweet. It makes me lose my concentration, and all I want to do is this." He slid off the stool and stepped up to her. She parted her legs to let him come closer, and he pressed his body against hers. Then he kissed her—long and deep, slow and possessive—and she would have slid off her stool into a puddle on the floor if he hadn't been gripping her shoulders and holding her upright. Good God, this man could kiss!

The jingling of the bell over the shop door pulled them apart abruptly. She felt like a schoolgirl who'd been caught kissing the quarterback behind the bleachers.

Dan Adams stood in the doorway, in uniform, wearing a wide grin.

"Let me guess—Nora passed out and you decided she needed a little mouth-to-mouth?" Dan snapped his fingers. "No, I know what happened! She has a sore throat and you were checking her tonsils, right?"

CHAPTER NINETEEN

Damn Dan and his lousy timing. Asher stepped away from Nora. His body wasn't happy about it, but his brain functioned more clearly when he wasn't in her sexy little vortex. This place was his livelihood. He didn't need to be kissing the Coffee Shop Lady during business hours. Thinking of her as the Coffee Shop Lady reminded him of something her cousin said earlier.

"Hot Produce Guy?" He turned to Nora and watched her blush again. "Is that what you two called me when you were giggling about floor sex?"

Dan clapped his hands over his ears. "Please, for the love of God, do *not* answer that question while I'm in the building! I'm just here to do a wellness check. Your families were worried about you both yesterday."

Asher couldn't take his eyes off the pink in Nora's cheeks. "That's a pretty slow response time, Officer."

"Judging from all the talk about hotness and

floor…you know…I think you should be thanking me for not driving up the mountain yesterday."

Asher pulled himself away from watching Nora. "You're right. Thanks, man." He nodded to the minifridge in the back of the shop. "Soda?"

"Sure." Dan gave Nora a smile, and she smiled back. Asher fought back a bubble of jealous anger. His best friend was being nice to his… He frowned. What was Nora, exactly? His neighbor? More than that. His friend? After yesterday, definitely more than that. His girlfriend? Good Lord, he was in his forties. He couldn't have a girlfriend, could he? But if not that, what? *Sex buddy* didn't feel right. What was the term the kids used? Friends with benefits? No, those were more than just benefits they'd shared…

"And he's lost in his head again." Nora laughed. "I'll get your soda, Dan." She grabbed one of the root beers Asher kept stocked for his friend.

"Thanks, Nora. I'll leave you two to whatever fun thing you were doing when I came in." Dan winked at Asher, who still hadn't managed to speak. "I assume you don't want me letting myself into your place at the end of shift tonight, right?" Dan raised his root beer in salute. "Be careful, you two, and remember to use protection."

He was gone before Asher could react, but Nora's laughter settled his jangled nerves. She patted him on the arm affectionately.

"We definitely need a better plan for how to keep this quiet. I'm going back to my shop before we provide anyone else with a show. Dinner at my place tonight?"

He swallowed hard. "What are we doing, exactly?"

"Sometimes dinner is just dinner, Ash. What happens *after* dinner is up to you."

That evening, Asher was still trying to come up with a word or term for what he and Nora were doing. One thing he knew for certain was that Nora's lemon chicken was the best he'd ever tasted. Actually, the entire experience of dinner with Nora was the best. It had been years since he'd had a nice glass of wine with a meal instead of a shot of bourbon.

Conversation was easy, as it always seemed to be with her. They debated favorite movies—his was anything Star Wars related, hers was *The Notebook*. They talked about music. With Adele and Alicia Keyes playing in the background, it wasn't hard to figure out what Nora liked. But after dinner, as they moved to the sofa with their wine, Nora stopped by the iPod station and changed the playlist to Asher's genre—blues guitar. She sat on the sofa, but not too close.

"Come here." Her eyes went wide at his words, but she complied, sliding across the sofa until she was curled up with his arm around her. He kissed the top of her head. "You've been tiptoeing around me, playing hostess, and I want you to stop. I want you to be *with* me, not playing a role."

"I'm very good at playing roles, Asher. It's a tough habit to break."

"Because of your husband?" She stiffened, but he kept going. "All I know about you is you're from Atlanta, you're Becky's mom and your late husband was a politician."

She glanced up at him through thick lashes. "I think you know a little more about me than that."

He nodded, smiling at the memory of exploring every inch of her body in the glow of the fireplace. He definitely planned on doing more of that later, but first he wanted more of *her*.

"Tell me the real reason why you left Atlanta."

She chewed on her lower lip for a moment, then nodded and settled back against him. She stared toward the windows, where the last blush of the sunset was nearly gone.

"Everyone loved Paul. He was a handsome, outgoing guy who always had a smile on his face. Bigger than life, you know? We had a whirlwind love affair in college, and when I got pregnant at twenty, he didn't hesitate to propose, even though his mother hated me."

"Why would she hate you?" How could anyone hate Nora, who must have been downright adorable at twenty, all curvy and golden eyed?

"I didn't have any family connections she could use to reach her goal."

"Which was?"

Nora shrugged. "Meredith Bradford dreamed big for her boys. Senator. Governor. President. But she came to tolerate me after she found out I could organize a campaign better than anyone she'd have to pay."

That made sense, Asher thought. Nora was the most organized person he'd ever met.

"Meredith raised her precious boys to believe they could do anything they wanted, simply because they were Bradfords. The rules didn't apply to them."

"And which rules didn't apply to your husband?"

She was quiet.

"Nora?"

Her voice was thick with anger and regret as she told him about the man who'd racked up so much in gambling debts that he emptied his daughter's college fund and took out extra mortgages on their home. And he'd slept around, the bastard.

"How could you stay when he betrayed you like that?"

"I didn't know about the money until he was gone. I knew he played poker, but I didn't know how high the stakes were, and I had no idea how bad he was at it." Nora looked out through the dark windows. "The few times I allowed myself to wonder about other women, I convinced myself it was just a phase. Just the pressure of the campaign." She lifted a shoulder half-heartedly, defending him without putting much effort into it. "As his campaign organizer, I became the boss, telling him what to do all day long, and those women were there, all sweet and willing. I figured when the campaign was over, I'd find a way to save our family."

He could picture Nora doing that. She'd have a grand plan for fixing their relationship, because that was what Nora did. She fixed things.

"But then one night he told me he wanted a divorce as soon as the election was over, win or lose. I've never told *anyone* that. Not even my cousins."

She took a long, shuddering breath. "While I was busy pretending everything would work out fine, Paul graduated from random hookups to having a full-on affair. He fell in love. He expected me to be the smiling political wife out on the campaign trail, then quietly divorce him when it was over so he'd be free to marry this woman."

She looked up at Asher. "He died in a plane crash a few days after he told me. The news stories said he was headed to a fund-raiser, but like everything else, it was a lie. He was going to see her."

Asher didn't say a word, just ran his fingers through her silky hair and listened. She'd had to sell her home to cover the debts. There was a life insurance policy and a lawsuit settlement as a result of the crash, but she barely kept her head above water the first few years. That was when she became a superplanner, watching every penny so Becky wouldn't know the harsh reality of their situation.

She'd picked up freelance jobs writing grants and even managed a few local political campaigns. She created an elaborate mythology around her late husband's memory, making sure people—Becky, in particular—knew only about his charitable and environmental work. She covered up the ugly rumors and thought they were buried forever until some political hack tried to take the secrets public. That was why she'd left Georgia and ended up in Gallant Lake. What a mess.

"Wouldn't it be easier to just tell Becky the truth?" The girl had no idea what sacrifices her mother had made to keep the legend of Paul Bradford alive. Nora shook her head.

"Everyone asks me that, but I don't want to take her memories of her father away from her." She sat up and gave him a shaky smile. He was more than a little in awe of Nora Bradford.

"You got tough after he died." Adversity had tempered her and made her strong.

"I had to get tough. For Becky's sake." She hesitated, and her mouth twitched. "Speaking of *my* daughter who's pregnant with *your* son's baby…what are we going to do about them? And us?" She gestured between them. "You and I are probably a really bad idea. People will talk…"

Asher didn't want to think about their kids. He definitely didn't want to think about having a grandchild. And he didn't give a damn what other people talked about. There was only one way to stop this conversation.

He kissed her.

NORA WASN'T PREPARED for the kiss, but she went with it. She knew he was kissing her to shut her up. That was okay for now—she'd talked enough for one night. So she slid her arms around him and kissed him back. He grunted and pulled her onto his lap until she was straddling him. She kissed him as though she'd die if she didn't. Her tongue pushed into his mouth, making his fingers curl into her butt cheeks so tightly she knew there'd be bruises. And she didn't care.

She kissed him some more, barely registering that he was pulling her sweater up. When his fingers touched her bra, he pulled his head back and looked at the black lace that pushed her breasts higher.

"You wore that for me." He wasn't asking, but she nodded anyway. He dropped his mouth to her left breast and kissed it right through the lace. Then he took her nipple into his mouth and ran his tongue over the lacy covering, sending Nora's pulse jumping. She gasped his name, and he buried his head between her breasts, inhaling deeply.

"I swear to God you're killing me, Nora. You're so damned beautiful, and you're here in my arms, and I'm dying." He took a deep breath and glanced over her shoulder to the windows, growing briefly practical. "I think we'd have more privacy upstairs. And I definitely want privacy for what I'm going to do to you." He flashed another smile that turned her insides to molten lava. "I want you in a bed this time."

Sure, she could have told him she'd have to pull the blinds for privacy no matter where they ended up in the wide-open loft. But he wanted her in a bed, and she suddenly wanted to be in that bed with him more than anything in the world. On the way up the metal stairs, she hit the wall switch that drew the blinds closed with a soft whir of motors, silently thanking Amanda for suggesting the automated system.

They both started peeling off clothing as soon as they hit the top of the stairs, landing on the bed naked together, laughing. It was laughter that came from the almost childlike glee of "can you believe we're doing this?" She squealed and giggled when Asher tugged on her ankles to bring her lower in bed so he could trace his lips up the inside of her thigh.

Her laughter stopped when his mouth settled on her and her hips rose to meet him. She was gone almost immediately, shattering with a cry. Before she could catch her breath, he was over her, kissing her and entering her all at once. She hadn't even noticed him putting on protection, but he had and he was there inside her. He was everywhere, and she still couldn't breathe.

Her body was moving with his as if she'd been this powerful, sensuous woman all her life. She gasped his name against his mouth, but he didn't respond. He was gone, pushing harder and faster until she felt the fire building inside her again. She wasn't sure she could survive another orgasm, but she couldn't do a damn thing to stop it. Asher bit her skin lightly at the base of her neck and came with a loud, long groan of release. She dug her nails into his back as the sensation rolled through her and colors exploded behind her tightly closed eyes.

When she opened her eyes again, she was sure everything would look different. Perhaps the sky would be green now, and the grass purple. Her bedroom would turn into a fanciful sailing ship and her apartment into a palace. Because nothing could possibly be the same after that. *She'd* never be the same. She'd fallen in love with Asher Peyton.

He'd joked about a scandal earlier, but it was no joke. People were going to whisper and point, and it would affect her daughter and his son. Those relationships were already tenuous, and now she was in *love* with the man. What were they supposed to do—have a double wedding? This wasn't going to work. It was just sex. A little affair. No, she couldn't even sell that story to herself. This was way more than sex.

She turned her head and bumped into Asher's. His body lay heavily on hers, face down in the pillows. Was he asleep? Passed out? Affection welled up inside her, pushing the fear aside for now, and she kissed the top of his ear, eliciting a low groan.

"Leave me alone and let me die." His voice was muffled by the bedding. "I said you were killing me earlier, but I'm actually dying now, and it's okay, because that's definitely the way every man wants to go. Death by sex."

She put her hand against the front of his shoulder and pushed.

"If you don't move pretty soon, we'll *both* be dead. You from sex and me from asphyxiation."

He grunted an apology and rolled off, pulling her into him. She had no objection. His lips pressed against her temple, and he spoke into her skin so softly she strained to hear him.

"I don't know what that was, but we're definitely doing it again. First, I just need to lie here and hold you, okay?" She nodded. He did a quick shuffle to grab a tissue and dispose of his condom, somehow managing not to leave her side. She snuggled against his warmth and he wrapped both arms around her. "I just need to hold you, sweetheart." And he was asleep, his deep breaths blowing across the top of her head.

He'd called her sweetheart. It was a common enough endearment, but she suspected Asher rarely used endearments of any kind. Could he be falling in love, too? Would that be better or worse? It was too much to think they could really be together. It was not like they'd go double dating with their own children. He moaned softly and pulled her even closer. But they were together for now. She closed her eyes and soaked in his warmth.

Together for now would have to be enough.

CHAPTER TWENTY

THE WEATHER WAS a lot nicer the next time Nora was at the mountain house. After endless days of rain, the sun had returned.

She was dressed more appropriately this time, too, with sturdy walking shoes and several loose layers of clothing, including a lightweight jacket that was already off and tied around her waist. What would the Junior League ladies in Atlanta think if they saw her now? She tucked her hair behind her ear and turned to Asher, who was climbing the trail behind her.

"I look like a walking advertisement for L.L.Bean."

"You look perfect."

Her heart flipped and jumped, the way it did every time he came out with those random compliments. They were so unlike his usual serious conversation. They signaled an Asher she was seeing more frequently these days. One who smiled more easily, showed affection more openly and came up with crazy ideas like climbing Gallant Mountain. She liked to think this was *her*

Asher, and she treasured the moments when she caught a glimpse of him this way.

"You're only saying that because you're looking at my butt."

"Well, your butt *is* pretty perfect. But that's not why I said it. You look great in hiking clothes. We need to get you a whole wardrobe of them."

She'd started walking again and was glad he couldn't see her smile. She liked it when he said "we" like that. As if there was a future that included the two of them together. She was so distracted by that thought she didn't pay attention to where she was stepping, and her foot slid off a damp tree root that stretched across the path. She landed on one knee, and Asher's hands were helping her up before she could react.

"Nora, be careful!" He steadied her, worry clouding his eyes. "Are you getting tired? If this hike is too much for you, we can go back and do it another day."

"No, I'm fine." Her calves and thighs were screaming in protest, but she'd never let him know that. The hours she spent on her feet in the coffee shop hadn't been quite enough to prepare her for this steep climb. At least there was a clear trail to follow, and Asher insisted on staying behind her in case she fell, so she wouldn't roll all the way down the side of the mountain.

She smiled brightly at him and tried not to think about that possibility.

"As long as we don't have another five hours of this, I'll be okay."

He frowned, looking into the dense woods around them. "We're not going much farther, but you'd do a lot better with a walking stick. Stay here."

She leaned against the uphill side of a tree and watched as he strode through the woods, looking like he was born to be here. Born to be part of this mountain, strong and everlasting. He looked relaxed and at peace. His long legs covered the pine needle–covered forest bed quickly, his eyes scanning the ground. He stopped to pick up a long, straight stick. It was taller than he was, but he stepped on it and broke it off so it was just a little shorter than Nora. Looking very pleased with himself, he headed back toward her.

He stepped through a gap between two trees and recoiled abruptly. He grimaced and frantically wiped something from his face, brushing his clothing at the same time.

"Is it on me? Son of a bitch…" He was spinning in place now, his hands sweeping down his chest. "Damn it!"

Nora couldn't hold it any longer and started laughing. Asher glanced up, as if he'd forgotten he had an audience for his little dance. His face reddened. He *had* forgotten. That made her laugh even harder, wiping tears from her eyes when she spoke.

"Are you okay over there, mountain man?"

"Yeah, yeah. Laugh it up, missy. I walked into a damned spiderweb!" He said that as if it was a perfectly logical explanation for the dance routine he'd just finished. Her laughter grew as he continued brushing his clothing and searching himself. Cathy had told her Asher was afraid of spiders, and he'd mentioned it, too, but Nora had no idea it was *this* bad. Her laughter started to fade.

Once he'd decided there was no spider on him, he walked back to her, frowning at her expression.

"What?"

"You're *this* afraid of spiders and you still saved me from that creature in my utility room."

His forehead creased, but he nodded. "He was an ugly sucker, too. Maybe this was one of his relatives setting a trap for me."

Her laughter bubbled up again. There was something hysterically charming about Asher Peyton believing the same theory she did—that spiders *always* got revenge.

"You're kinda my hero right now—you know that, right?"

He handed her the walking stick he'd created. "Hero? For what? Humiliating myself in front of you?"

"No, although that *was* entertaining." His eyes narrowed, but his mouth slanted into a smile. "You're a hero because you saved me from a spider when you were probably just as afraid of it as I was. Isn't that one of the classic definitions of courage—acting brave when you're really afraid?"

"Would you please stop using the word *afraid* in reference to me? My manhood can't take it." He pointed up the trail. "I'm no hero, Nora. Start hiking."

She did as he asked, but smiled the entire time. He was braver than he knew. The trail brought them to a small clearing with a hulking boulder in the middle of it. There were rocks everywhere in these mountains, of course, but this was larger than most—the size of a motor home. It was only partially exposed, half buried in the mountainside, which continued to rise above them, more stone than soil at this point.

Nora bent and put her hands on her thighs, trying not to wheeze out loud. She hoped Asher wasn't going to ask her to climb any farther, since it looked like it might require actual rock-climbing skills.

His hand rested gently on her back, his fingers working into her aching muscles.

"We're here."

She straightened, looking up at the mountain.

"And where exactly is 'here'?"

"The Kissing Rock."

Her eyes went wide. "Why would anyone climb all the way up here just to kiss?"

"Turn around."

"Oh!" What little breath she had in her was taken away by the view. They were high on the mountain, looking almost straight down to Gallant Lake, which glittered in the sunlight. The town was to the left, and she could see the resort and the stone towers of Halcyon. She spotted the top of Asher's log house below, the dark green roof standing out as a sharp geometric shape in the midst of all the natural beauty.

"Oh, Asher! It's incredible!" She was whispering. It felt like being in church, as if the surroundings commanded that kind of reverence. His arm rested on her shoulders.

"Yes, it is." He wasn't looking at the vista in front of them. He was staring at her with a heat in his blue eyes she'd never seen before. It was more than desire. He pulled her in close and planted a kiss on her forehead.

"But why did you name this the Kissing Rock? Why not call it the Scenic Overlook Rock?"

"It's been called the Kissing Rock for generations. Kids sneak up here and sit on the rock to take in the view and spoon, or make out, or hook up, depending on the generation."

"So they have to climb through your land to get here?"

"No, there's an old logging road that comes up most of the way, and they walk over from there. And it's not my land. Your cousin and her husband own it. Blake bought most of the mountain a few years ago to protect the town from a casino developer." He took her hand and led her toward the boulder.

"I remember. He originally *wanted* the casino, but Amanda convinced him it would ruin the charm of Gallant Lake." Asher was helping her up the short, steep path to the top of the rock. The view was even more spectacular up there, but scarier, too. It felt as though they were standing on a cliff's edge, with the mountain falling away at their feet. Nora pointed to a mountain well to the north, with wide trails winding down through the trees. "What is that?"

"That's Hunter Mountain. Michael gives snowboarding lessons there in the winter." He frowned. "Apparently it's where he and Becky met."

She avoided that conversational land mine and pointed to a mountain closer to them, directly across the lake. It had similar trails winding through the trees, but they were more narrow and overgrown. "Is that another ski resort?"

"It used to be, but it's been closed for a while

now. I heard it's for sale, but it would take a fortune to bring it back."

They sat on the rock, which had been warmed by the sun. He was looking at the lake, seemingly lost in thought.

"Do you come up here often?"

He hesitated, then shook his head.

"I haven't been up here since Dylan died."

She waited for him to work through whatever was going through his head.

"The boys used to love coming up here. The three of us would climb the trail and sometimes go a little farther up the rock face." His eyes warmed. "Michael was always a natural at rock climbing, and he'd go so far up Dylan and I would lose sight of him. He'd have to whistle the entire time so we'd know he was okay." Nora smiled, thinking of the way Michael often whistled to himself.

"Thank you for bringing me here, Asher."

He nodded absently, his mind clearly still on memories of the boys. "We'll take our time going down. You'll probably be aching tomorrow."

They stood to leave, but she stopped him, resting her hand on his chest. "Wait—we haven't kissed. And this *is* the Kissing Rock, right?"

His melancholy faded and he started to smile

again. "Aren't we a little old for making out on the Kissing Rock?"

"If we weren't too old for floor sex, we're definitely not too old for this." She stood on her tiptoes and pressed a kiss to his lips. His arms wrapped around her and tightened. He deepened the kiss until their tongues were having a spirited dueling match. He lifted her off the ground, then nipped her bottom lip.

"You're not afraid someone will see us?" He liked to tease her about wanting to keep their relationship on the down low.

"I think we're safe up here today. Are you ready for some rock sex?"

"I vote for bed sex this time. Let's head back to my place. I'll sneak you in the back door." He was referring to his apartment in town, not the mountain house, which was still unfinished. It had been ten days since they spent an afternoon on the floor by the hearth, and they hadn't been back up to that bedroom since then. But they'd spent plenty of time in the bedrooms above their shops in town. He was going to have to deal with the unfinished business at the house and in his heart eventually. But when he started trailing kisses down the side of her neck, she decided that could wait for another day.

"Bed sex sounds like a great idea."

"So, THIS FIGURE includes the staircase and the metal railing, and the sculpture your friend is going to make?" Blake was studying Asher's estimate. "And you can have it done in time for the golf tournament in a few months?"

Asher nodded. "The quote covers everything, including installation. You've got a big charity tournament happening here, right?"

"Yes. Amanda's cousin Bree started a foundation to benefit veterans. She wants to do a fundraiser here as her first major event, and my lovely bride said yes before letting me in on the plans." Blake winked. "You'll find the Lowery girls are good at getting their way."

"Yeah, I'm beginning to sense that."

The fact that he was here in Blake's home office while Nora and Amanda giggled in the kitchen over dinner preparations was a prime example. He'd had no desire to turn this business meeting into a date night, but when Nora heard he had the quote ready, she'd promptly announced they *had* to have dinner with the Randalls.

As Michael had so bluntly pointed out, Asher didn't do family dinners. And yet here he was, making small talk with Nora's family. He'd been chafing at her insistence on keeping their relationship some big secret. But she'd been adamant, especially after old Mrs. Townsend said something to her in town about dating "the wood-worker" so soon after moving here.

If he pushed her, he was afraid she'd give in to her worries about the family entanglements and end things. He wasn't ready to lose her, even if it might be the logical and inevitable conclusion to what they were doing. So if she wanted to go public, at least in the confines of her cousin's home, he wasn't going to complain.

He wondered how much Blake knew about their relationship. After all, Blake was married to the woman who'd been discussing floor sex with Nora. His face heated. How many details had Amanda shared with her husband? Blake burst into loud laughter, jolting Asher out of his drifting thoughts.

"Holy shit, man, are you *blushing* right now? You'd best get over that if you're sticking with Nora. Trust me, there are no secrets between those girls. And I mean *no* secrets, if you catch my drift."

Asher didn't answer right away, caught on five words…*if you're sticking with Nora*. He wanted to stick, but he didn't know if he had it in him to start all over again. And then there was the whole mess with their children hating them right now, no matter how quiet they'd kept their activities.

Becky hadn't been back to work at the café, although Nora said she stopped by occasionally.

It was enough to give Nora hope, but Asher was skeptical. Michael was avoiding his father, as he had ever since Asher offered to pay his way to Stanford at Christmas. He frowned. That no longer seemed like such a great solution to the baby problem. The baby was due in two months, and he didn't like the thought of Michael leaving at this point. He should probably tell Michael that.

Blake shook his head. "You're in that I-don't-know-what-the-hell-just-hit-me phase, aren't you? She's got you spinning in circles and swatting at moonbeams, right? Falling when you absolutely don't want to fall?"

Asher barked out a laugh, thinking about the moment at the Kissing Rock just four days ago, when he'd looked at Nora, smiling up at him as if they didn't have a worry in the world, with Gallant Lake sparkling behind her. A long-forgotten emotion had flared up inside him then, and it was taking all of his strength to ignore it.

"That about covers it, yeah."

"I get it. The Cousins…" Blake raised his fingers into air quotes. "I always refer to the four of them in capital letters, like a secret society. The Cousins have the power to knock a man right to his knees. Amanda turned all my business and personal plans upside down with one toss of those pretty blond curls. She's a lot like Nora, small but mighty, you know?"

Yes, Asher knew.

"And Bree and Melanie are a lot alike—successful women chasing after the wrong things. Bree figured it out when she met Cole, but Mel's still a work in progress." He clapped Asher on the back. "Buckle up, buttercup, because if you're going after a Lowery woman, you're in for a wild ride."

"Daddy! Daddy!"

A two-foot-tall version of Amanda toddled into the paneled office, smiling with her arms upraised. A halo of white-blond curls surrounded her face. Asher took a step back as Blake scooped up his daughter and swung her through the air.

"Hey, Maddie! How's my favorite girl?"

"I thought *I* was your favorite girl." Amanda was laughing, standing in the doorway with Nora. She walked over to join her husband and daughter, but Nora stayed still, staring at Asher with a hungry fire in her eyes.

There was something else in her gaze. Something deeper. He'd noticed that look a few times. She was looking at him like he was her everything. With a shock, he realized how much he wanted to be exactly that.

"Oh, Blake, look how cute they are, gazing into each other's eyes like we're not standing right here." Amanda giggled. "Come on, you two lovebirds. Let's have a drink before dinner."

Asher took Nora's hand when he reached her, and they walked to the solarium off the main salon. He'd been to the Randalls' historic home before, and the place never failed to appeal to his builder's soul.

Built at the turn of the last century, it was an actual stone castle, complete with turrets and towers—one of many built by the rich throughout the Catskills and Adirondacks back then. Few still existed, and fewer still were actual family homes like Halcyon.

As an interior designer, Amanda had worked miracles with a place that had been long abandoned and faced demolition. Now it glowed with golden marble floors and polished mahogany ceilings, the rooms full of color and comfort.

"We have all our family meals out here." Amanda gestured to the glass-walled solarium. "It's more comfy than the big dining table. Honey, could you open the wine?"

It was all so normal, despite the elegant surroundings. A family meal, with the Randall children, Zach and Maddie, joining them. Laughter and conversation swirled around him while they ate.

Asher did his best to keep up. Did his best to smile and nod and participate. But Nora had been right the other day when she told him his social skills were so rusty they squeaked. Sure, he and Michael used to have meals together. They'd usually talk about sports or movies. He and Dan grabbed a pizza once in a while. And he and Nora shared dinner every night these days.

But two people was much different than six. He wasn't used to the ebb and flow of affectionate jokes and shared stories that filled the room. And there were children here. And one was a boy of twelve. The same age as Dylan when...

Nora's hand landed on his and squeezed. He turned to face her, blinking rapidly, trying to smile. The understanding in her eyes made his scalp prickle with shame. He was a basket case, and the fact that she knew it just made it worse. Zach was telling a story about something he and his friends did on the school bus, and Nora leaned in.

"I know this is a lot for you, but you handled the spider, and you can handle this." He stilled, remembering their conversation climbing Gallant Mountain. She'd called him her hero for facing his fear and dealing with a spider for her sake. Feeling not at all heroic, he nodded. This family meal was ripping at his heart, but bolting from the room wasn't an option—not when it meant running from Nora.

Later that night, back at her place, he held her as she slept. He thought long and hard about what she was doing to his life. Blake had said the Lowery women had the ability to make a man swat at moonbeams, and as silly as it sounded, Asher understood. His heart was turning inside out for this woman. He was feeling things he had never thought he'd feel again, like hope. And happiness. And every once in a while, like this moment in the dark listening to her breathe slowly through softly parted lips, he felt peace.

CHAPTER TWENTY-ONE

SPRING BEGAN IN earnest in Gallant Lake once April arrived. The morning sun sent reflections of light from the lake sliding across the walls of the café. Nora hummed to herself as she wiped down the counter. Business had been brisk earlier, but now she had time to think about last night in Asher's bed, and the memory made her body warm all over.

Cathy walked up behind her. "Oh, girl, you got it bad. You've been wiping the same spot on the counter for fifteen minutes now, just humming and smiling to yourself. You are completely besotted."

"Besotted? Cathy, have you been reading those historical romance novels again?" Nora moved to wipe down a table in the now-empty shop. "Did you order the pastries for this weekend? We need more napkins, too. And…"

Cathy started to laugh. "Yes, boss, I ordered the pastries and the napkins and more coffee beans and milk. Your ordering schedule is very clear, and everything on it has been checked and double-checked."

Cathy made fun of her checklists, but last week she'd admitted they made it a lot easier to keep track of things. Nora glanced at her employee, who was wearing jeans, sneakers and a green Gallant Brew T-shirt. Her salt-and-pepper hair was in its usual long braid. The tinkle of the bell over the door made Nora straighten from wiping the last table.

A young woman stood in the doorway, her expression uncertain. She was around Becky's age, possibly younger. She was tall, with bold facial features that looked familiar somehow. Her long, dark hair was loose, shining and perfectly straight. Her brown eyes were the same unusual shade as... Nora spun on her heel to look at Cathy, who was frozen in place at the cash register.

Cathy and the girl stared at each other in silence—grandmother and granddaughter seeing each other for the first time. Nora was thankful the shop was empty, allowing the two women to just stand and stare as long as they needed to. It was Cathy who spoke first, her voice thick with emotion.

"You look just like your mother."

The girl hesitated, then nodded. "Everyone says that. I think I look like you, too."

"True enough. I could never lose that girl when she was with me—everyone knew she was mine."

More silence. "How did you find me? It's Gracie, right?"

"Yes. Grace." She twisted her fingers together, her face pale with nerves. Nora stayed very still, trying not to disrupt them. "My grandmother—my *other* grandmother—told me what you did. That so-called scholarship you created."

"I asked her not to do that." Cathy's head shook back and forth. "You weren't supposed to know."

"I didn't believe Nana's story about some mystery scholarship I never applied for. I thought she'd cashed in her retirement savings, and I was furious. She finally told me the truth. She gave me this postcard." Grace held up a faded Gallant Lake postcard, and Cathy paled. "Why did you make her lie to me?"

"Paisley didn't want me in your life..."

Grace stood taller, walking to the center of the shop before stopping. She moved like Cathy, strong and sure.

"On the postcard, you say you're sorry, and you're doing better. Sorry for what? Better than what? Why have I never heard about you, or *from* you, all this time?" Her voice hardened as her mood shifted as quickly as only a teenage girl's could. "I was alone, you know. I was *five* when they died."

Cathy swallowed hard. Then she moved around the end of the counter, but no closer to Grace. She had a clear path, but she wasn't taking the first step. Nora willed her to do it, but both women were immobilized. Grace by anger. Cathy by fear.

Nora couldn't take it any longer. There was a flash of surprise in Grace's eyes when Nora walked over and took her hand.

"Honey, you're asking questions that can't be answered easily or quickly. But your grandmother didn't even know you existed until last year." Grace's eyes went wide. "And the minute she did learn about you, she sold the only thing she'd ever owned—this coffee shop—to help you."

The girl wasn't giving up her anger and hurt that easily. "She didn't come see me. She didn't call me. She just sent guilt money."

"No…" Cathy grimaced, trying to come up with the right words. "Well…yes. I have a lot to feel guilty about. Paisley had to put herself through school. I didn't want you to have to do that, Grace. Call it guilt money if you want, but I call it love money. From the moment I heard about you, I've loved you." Grace's eyes shone with unshed tears, and Nora suspected her own did, as well. "I know you have questions, and I promise to answer every single one."

Grace looked to Nora, then back to Cathy.

"Why did you name her Paisley?"

Nora and Cathy both laughed. "Oh, great, start with the *last* story I want to share with a teenager! Why don't we go back to my place and I'll tell you all about your mom, including how she got her name?"

She took a step forward. Grace recoiled, but she caught herself and met Cathy's gaze straight on. Cathy opened her arms, and Nora barely breathed as she watched mistrust and longing battling inside Grace. Finally the girl stepped into her grandmother's embrace. Nora quickly grabbed a pile of napkins from the counter, and all three women used them liberally to dry their tears.

Cathy took the next day off, not returning to the shop until after Grace caught her flight back to Seattle. Her smile was not only endless, it was contagious, and the shop still hummed with her positive energy. Even Asher noticed when he stopped in for his morning coffee. He glanced around and winked at Cathy.

"You sure you're only selling coffee in this place? It feels as though some herbal remedies are in use here today."

Cathy laughed. "Nothing but peace and love touching us here today, neighbor. Peace and love." She looked between him and Nora, who was at the cash register, and lowered her voice. "Peace and love for all of us, I think."

Nora blushed as Asher watched her intensely.

When she took his money, his fingers wrapped around hers and held on.

"I want to take you out to dinner tonight. Someplace special. And, yes, someplace out of town so no one will see us. Pick you up at six?" She nodded, feeling like a teenager invited to prom. They were going out somewhere nice. On a real date. Maybe it was time to tell him she was falling in love with him.

"Six is good. I'll be ready."

The noon rush was just winding down when Becky stopped in. Nora smiled, surprised to see her, but it faded quickly when she realized her daughter had been crying. Her cheeks were blotchy and red, and her eyes glistened with more tears to come.

"What is it, honey? What's happened?" Nora guided Becky to a corner table in the nearly empty café. "Are you sick? Is the baby okay?" Becky sat and shook her head. Cathy brought them two steaming mugs—coffee for Nora and herbal tea for Becky. Nora was just about to burst out of her skin when Becky began to wail.

"I'm so fat and ugly right now! I shouldn't even be surprised." She sniffed and wiped her tears away with the back of her hand. Nora had a hard time not smiling at her distraught daughter. This was a hormonal moment every pregnant woman experienced sooner or later.

"Honey, you're more beautiful than ever." It was true. Becky's skin glowed with health and her hair had grown longer than usual. "You're not fat, you're pregnant, and you wear it well. Now, tell me, what happened to upset you? Did Michael say something stupid?" Men could be such clods sometimes. He probably made a comment about her size that set her off.

Becky laughed, but there was no humor in it. "I don't know, Mom, why don't you ask the hot blonde he was talking to this morning? When he was supposed to be in New York listening to a lecture!"

Nora went very still. Pregnancy hormones could do a lot of things to a woman's self-esteem and judgment. And an eighteen-year-old was shaky in those departments anyway. But Nora had been married to an unfaithful man, and it was one thing she *never* wanted her daughter to deal with.

"Why don't you tell me exactly what happened?"

"Oh, my God, Mom! Don't you believe me?" More tears soaked Becky's face as she took a ragged breath.

"Honey, I just want to understand what happened."

"I decided to take a walk this morning, because it was such a nice day. I took that stupid shore walk, along the lake." The Gallant Lake business chamber had been planning on expanding the boardwalk for a while, connecting various docks and walkways behind the businesses along the water. They hoped to start the project in earnest that summer.

"That's when I saw them. Michael and some blonde. At first I thought I was wrong, that it just looked like him from behind, but he turned to face her and it was him. I ducked into one of the alleyways and watched, like I was on some horrible soap opera. She reached out and put her hand on him, and he *stood* there! He didn't shake her off, Mom. He stood there with her touching him."

"Then what happened?"

"I don't know. I couldn't stand to watch anymore. I came up the alley and walked around town for a while, then ended up here." Nora's heart ached. "You should have seen how pretty she was, Mom. Older, I think. Older than Michael. Tall and thin and classy. So put together, you know? Makeup, hair, clothes—the whole package. Everything I'm not. Why *wouldn't* he fall for a woman like that when I'm such a hot mess?"

"Okay. First, we don't know for sure he's done anything of the sort." A sour taste rose in Nora's mouth as she said the words. "She might be a classmate. Or an old friend. Maybe even a relative. You don't know."

But I'm sure as hell going to find out.

"Mom, he *lied* to me! He's supposed to be in class today." Becky sat back in her chair, dejected, then fixed a cold stare on Nora. "I know what happened. His dad got to him. The man you're sleeping with just broke off my engagement."

Nora blinked. "What are you talking about? Asher wouldn't do that."

"Really, Mom? Because your *lover* offered my fiancé a free ride to Stanford months ago if he'd leave me. He told Michael he'd pay him to move to California if he left me and the baby behind." The words were like a body blow to Nora's chest. Had Asher offered to pay Michael to abandon her pregnant daughter?

"Michael initially laughed it off, but his dad wouldn't quit. And I guess now he's finally convinced him to leave me. Maybe he even introduced Michael to this woman. I wouldn't put it past him."

Nora was silent. She couldn't deny how vehemently Asher opposed the wedding, and even the baby. In the beginning, he'd even hinted Becky should get an abortion.

But he'd changed lately. He'd mellowed about the baby and even admitted just a few nights ago that he was proud of Michael for manning up and accepting responsibility. Of course, he could be proud of his son's honorable intentions while still trying to change his mind. She pushed her suspicions aside, refusing to believe it of the man she'd given her heart to.

"I know Asher didn't want you and Michael getting married, but to be fair, honey, neither did I. And you're making a big leap from seeing Michael talking to some stranger to believing he's *leaving* you. You'll feel silly if this is all just a misunderstanding. Why don't you go home and talk to him? Remember what you told me about you two basing your relationship on trust and listening to each other?"

Becky was quiet for a moment, scowling at her coffee mug. Then she nodded, turning her head and grimacing as she rubbed her neck.

"Okay, I'll give him a chance to explain. One chance. And he'd better not lie to me again. But first I have a doctor's appointment." Nora sat forward and Becky shook her head. "Chill, Mother. It's just blood work. Then I'll go home, and you can bet Michael and I are going to talk." Becky frowned again. "She was just so pretty and thin…"

"Honey, when you're pregnant, *everyone* looks prettier and thinner to you. But not to the people who love you." She thought about the time she'd spent with Michael and Becky. "I really think Michael loves you."

Becky sounded fierce. "I *know* he loves me."

Another mercurial mood change. Becky had gone from accusing Michael of leaving her to defending his honor. Nora took Becky's hand.

"Then give him a chance to tell you the truth." They sat together while Becky composed herself. By the time she left for her appointment, her tears were dried and her complexion somewhat back to normal. Most important, her smile, while a bit tremulous, was back in place.

As soon as she left, Nora made sure Cathy was okay on her own, and she headed out the door. The Peyton men were pushing their luck with all this secrecy and nonsense. She was going to have a talk with both of them.

And first up was the guy next door.

ASHER POLISHED THE final coat of finish on the dresser top with a massive wad of cheesecloth. Layer after layer had been applied and sanded and polished, and now the cherrywood was gleaming. The drawers sat nearby, fronts up, waiting for the same treatment before he assembled the unit, added the hardware and returned the dresser to his client.

It was a good thing he was doing such mindless work today, because he couldn't stop thinking about what he'd seen that morning. His first stop after getting coffee and before opening his shop had been the hardware store across the street.

He'd run out of the tiny wood screws he needed to attach the back panel to the dresser, and he knew Nate would probably have them, since Nate always seemed to have everything. People joked that Nate was secretly a magician, since no matter what it was you needed, he'd manage to find it in the narrow aisles or dusty upstairs loft. And, sure enough, he found a single box of the exact wood screws Asher was looking for.

Nate had offered him coffee, and Asher surprised them both by accepting it. Nora's constant harping on his antisocial tendencies had gotten under his skin, and he wanted to prove to himself he was still capable of carrying on a friendly conversation with someone. Nate wasn't exactly a stranger, but they weren't close friends, either. Mainly because Asher had regularly rebuffed Nate's attempts to work together for the betterment of the downtown area. He'd never been much of a joiner.

But this morning, after already drinking a cup of Nora's espresso, he'd accepted a cup of coffee so thick it looked like tar and sat down with Nate in the back room of the hardware store, where a window looked out over the lake. In the distance, he could see Blake Randall's resort and golf course sprawled along the shoreline, and beyond that, the pink granite castle the Randalls called home. There really was quite a view on this side of the street, and he started paying attention when Nate said the same thing.

"I don't know what the town's founders were thinking, having the businesses on our side of the street face the road instead of the water. Sure, the fronts of the buildings look fine on Main Street. But if you walk the lakefront, you're looking at dingy old backs of dingy old buildings. Locked-up back doors instead of storefronts. Imagine the tourists we could bring downtown if they could walk and shop right along the water. If we complete the boardwalk, we can add gazebos and maybe get a couple restaurants to move down here. Think how nice it would be in the summer to dine outside and…"

Nate's enthusiasm was admirable, but Asher had lost track of the conversation when he saw a familiar figure standing on one of the few existing sections of wooden walkway. It was Michael. He wasn't alone. But he wasn't with Becky.

He was talking to a striking blonde who was wearing an expensive suit that fit her figure perfectly. The two were standing close, as if they didn't want anyone to overhear. She was older than Michael—maybe in her thirties. The woman reached out and touched his arm, and Michael left her hand there as the conversation continued. Eventually the blonde walked away, and his son turned and left in the opposite direction. Asher had politely extracted himself from Nate's sales pitch about the shore walk and gone back to his shop, half hoping he'd see Michael there, but no such luck.

Asher stood up from rubbing the dresser and stretched. The irony was that two months ago, he'd have been thrilled to see his son paying attention to a beautiful woman who wasn't trying to rope him into marriage. Michael stepping out on Becky would have solved a lot of problems. But now his stomach was sour and so was his mood.

Michael and Becky were good together. Sure, they were young and stupid, but they made a good little team. The idea that Michael might be cheating on her didn't sit well. First, that wasn't something Asher ever imagined his son would do—be unfaithful to someone. And since spending more time with Nora, Asher had gained a new appreciation for love and family. He'd known for a while that his offer to Michael was a mistake, but he hadn't done anything to correct it.

He tossed the polishing cloth on the workbench and poured a splash of whiskey into a shot glass. He needed something to dull the sharp pricks of guilt he was feeling like needles on the inside of his chest.

He'd be a hypocrite if he continued to let Michael think he wanted him to leave Becky. He should have talked to him before now. Told him he'd changed his mind. Told him he wanted him to stay with the girl he'd fallen in love with, because Asher was going to stay with the woman *he'd* fallen in love with. He set the glass on the workbench with a thud.

He was in love with Nora Bradford.

There was no sense denying it. She'd taken his heart away and he didn't even care, because without her he didn't need it. He reflected on that surprising revelation for a minute before remembering he might have ruined everything. If Michael did something stupid, like leave Becky, it would be Asher's fault. And Nora would never forgive him.

He grabbed his phone and dialed his son's number. If they met at the mountain house, they could have the conversation away from any curious eyes, like Nora or the pretty blonde stranger.

CHAPTER TWENTY-TWO

NORA WAS MOMENTARILY frustrated when she found Asher's shop closed, with a Be Back Soon sign hanging in the window. Fine. If she couldn't find one Peyton man, she'd find the other. She pulled her phone out right there on the sidewalk and called Michael. It took three rings, but he finally answered.

"Nora?" He was on speakerphone, and it sounded like he was in a vehicle.

"You and I need to talk, Michael. Right now."

"My dad just called and asked me to meet him up on the mountain. I'll stop by aft..."

"Your father can wait. I need to know what's going on with you and Becky."

Silence. "I don't know what you're talking about."

"No? Let's start with you having an intimate conversation in a public place with a beautiful woman this morning."

Michael's voice turned cold. "Who told you that?"

"Becky saw you, you idiot!"

"Oh, shit."

Nora didn't bother responding.

"It's not what you think, okay? I was trying to *protect* Becky. Look, I'm two minutes from town. I'll stall my dad and meet you at the café."

Nora shook her head. "Meet me upstairs. This is not a conversation I want to have in public."

"Nora, I didn't…"

"I'll see you in a few minutes." She hung up and stalked back into the café, waving off Cathy's curious look. She'd only been upstairs long enough to pour a glass of water when Michael knocked.

He was so pale his dark beard stood out even more than usual. His eyes had shadows under them, as if he hadn't slept.

Nora nodded to a barstool. "Sit. And start talking."

His chin lifted defiantly. "And you'll listen? Or have you already made up your mind and condemned me?"

"Save the pity party for later. I just spent an hour calming my hysterical daughter, who thinks you're leaving her, just like your father wanted you to. Is that true, by the way? Did Asher bribe you to leave Becky?"

She was supposed to be grilling him about the blonde. But she had to know the truth about Asher.

"I… He…sort of. I mean…he offered to pay for college if I went to California. But I *never* considered it, and that was months ago. He made the offer in *December*, for crying out loud." Michael's puppy-dog eyes almost made Nora soften. Almost.

"Did he ever rescind the offer?"

He looked down at the counter, unable to meet her eyes.

"No."

Nora gripped the counter tightly. Asher wanted his son to abandon her daughter. How could she have been so stupid as to fall in love with *another* man who couldn't be honest with her? She was so lost in her personal struggle that it took a moment for Michael's next words to sink in.

"That blonde was asking about Becky's dad."

Nora flashed from hot anger to cold fear. "The woman this morning? Asked about *Paul*?"

He nodded, staring first at his hands clenched tightly together on the counter in front of him, then up at Nora.

"Becky went to bed early last night. When her phone rang, I thought it was her girlfriend Taneishia from school. They were trying to hook up to go shopping this weekend, and Becky was expecting her call. I didn't want to wake her, so I grabbed it and answered in the other room." His expression hardened. "It was a woman named Daphne Tomlin."

She'd love to think it couldn't possibly be true, but Daphne was tall, elegant and blonde, just as Becky had described the mystery woman. Why would Daphne contact Becky? Wasn't it enough she'd chased Nora out of Atlanta? And what the hell was Daphne doing in Gallant Lake?

She didn't realize she'd spoken the last question out loud until Michael answered.

"Your brother-in-law's primary race is pretty tight, and Daphne is the new campaign manager for some guy named…"

"Tom Wilson," Nora said, finishing the sentence, her voice dull. So Daphne had moved from working on some obscure website to running Wilson's campaign. Nora had worked on enough of Paul's to know how ruthless things could get in a close race.

"Yeah. She said she flew here to speak with Becky and she wasn't going to give up until she did just that. So I told her I'd meet her this morning, figuring I'd get rid of her somehow." He looked up at Nora. "She had quite a story to tell about Becky's father."

Nora didn't answer.

"Nothing this woman told me matches what Becky says about her dad. Becky told me he was a great guy and a wonderful father. She makes it sound like you guys lived some perfect life when he was alive. She talks about what a great governor he would have been, and how hard he would have worked for the environment, just like I want to do. The guy sounded like a saint."

He looked hard at Nora, and when she didn't answer, he shook his head. "This Tomlin woman was telling the truth, wasn't she? Becky doesn't know anything about what her father was really like."

Nora walked around the counter and sat next to Michael. "Daphne was telling a version of the truth. But so was Becky. Paul *was* a loving father and Becky was his princess. Her memories aren't wrong. They're just incomplete."

"Why?"

Nora shrugged. "There was no need to tell a young girl that her late father had a gambling problem. Or that he'd slept around. Why tarnish her memories?"

"So, he really gambled away her college fund?"

"And then some. When he died, he left me with massive debts. I scrimped and saved to replenish some of her college money, and I made sure she never knew the truth about what happened."

"She told me once she hated being forced to leave her childhood home."

Nora gave a mirthless laugh. "She told me that

more than once, believe me. But telling her the truth wouldn't have made it any better."

They sat in silence, the only sound the muffled hum of cars going up and down Main Street below. Michael reached out and took her hands in his.

"You need to tell her, Nora. She deserves to hear it from you rather than some stranger. I'll tell her if you won't."

Nora had spent too much time and energy creating the Paul Bradford myth to walk away from it just yet.

"What did Daphne want, exactly?"

"She wants a big sensational story to derail Geoff Bradford's campaign. They've been spreading rumors about him and your husband, but rumors weren't enough. People lost interest. She wants confirmation from you or Becky that Paul and Geoff gambled everything away. Daphne said the story would kill Geoff's family values platform."

All those years of protecting her daughter were wasted if the story came out now. "What did you tell Daphne?"

"Well...I kind of fibbed, at Becky's expense. I told her Becky was sick, and if Daphne tried to reach her, it would look really bad." She could see the regret in his eyes. "I didn't mean to make it sound serious, but Daphne took it that way, and she was consoling me when she touched me this morning. It would have looked suspicious if I pushed her away, so I stood there and let her think I was grieving or whatever. Then she gave me her card. Said she'd give me money if I gave her a quote myself confirming the story. I didn't want her hanging around, so I acted like I wanted to do it, but said I needed a few days. She bought it and said she'd be in Georgia, waiting for my call."

When Michael didn't call her, Daphne would be back.

Nora had planned this all so carefully, but she'd never anticipated another Bradford family campaign. Geoff had to drop out of this race *before* Daphne took the story public. And Nora still had one way to compel him to do that, but if he called her bluff, she'd be forced to disclose the truth. And Becky would know everything about her father.

It was a chance Nora would have to take.

ASHER WAS IRRITATED when Michael called to say he couldn't meet him at the mountain house as they'd agreed just ten freaking minutes earlier. Something had come up that Michael had to take care of first. He tried to change Michael's mind, but no luck. His son sounded upset but wouldn't say anything more than he had to do this mysterious "something" right away. So Asher had turned his truck around and headed back to the shop.

He'd still be able to make things right. Michael promised to stop by later, and Asher would tell him to dump the blonde, stay with Becky and raise their child together. The offer to send Michael to California was off the table. The blonde would go away, Michael and Becky would be together, and Asher would finally be able to tell Nora he loved her. He started putting the hardware on the dresser drawer fronts, blowing out a long, calming breath. Yeah, this was all going to work out just fine.

Suddenly the door of his shop swung open with so much force the bell barely had a chance to ring. It just clicked. Nora stood in the doorway, dressed in black jeans and a gray sweater. Her hair was pulled back under a black headband. It all made her look serious.

No. It was the angry glint in her eye that made her look that way. Asher gave her a playful wink.

"Bad day?"

She didn't answer, and he set down the screwdriver. "Nora? Is everything okay?"

She shook her head slowly, and he was horrified when she spoke in a voice thick with tears.

"No, everything is definitely not okay."

He moved toward her, but she quickly held up both hands to warn him off. What the ever living *hell*?

"Is it Becky?" His heart thumped. "The baby?"

Her answering laugh was strangled and... furious.

"As if you give a *damn* about that baby."

"Come on, Nora, tell me what's got you so upset." A light sweat broke out on the back of his neck. He had a feeling he knew.

Another harsh laugh, and she turned to look out the window. Her body language screamed "stay away," so he did. He waited, afraid to do or say the wrong thing. Her voice dropped to a near whisper.

"I wanted to come in here and just tear you apart, Ash. I planned what I was going to say, and I was going to scream and yell and call you names and tell you how much I hate what you did...how much I hate you...but I can't do it." She turned to him, her face soaked with tears and her fists tightly clenched.

She knew. Somehow, she knew what he'd done. He closed his eyes to block her pain from his sight, but they snapped open again in surprise when she started to swear.

"Today has been such a *shitty* day, and you are such a *stupid* bastard, and I want so badly to tell you to go to hell. But...I also really need my friend right now, damn it. I don't know if I want to kiss you or kick you right in the ass."

He would have laughed except for the genuine hurt in her eyes.

"Nora, I can explain…"

But she didn't let him finish. She just flung herself at him and wrapped her arms tightly around his waist. He didn't hesitate to pull her in even closer, dropping his head to hers and not saying a word as she soaked his shirt with her tears. Every sob was like an ice pick stabbing his heart over and over. He'd done this. He'd hurt her. They stood there, right in his shop window, clinging to each other in a silence that was only interrupted by hiccups as she tried to control her crying.

Finally she lifted her head and looked up at him, as if trying to see who he really was. He wished he could tell her.

"I know what you did and I might even know why. But I need to know *how*. How could you?"

As much as he wanted to rush to defend himself, to blurt out that it was just a misunderstanding and he was going to fix everything, she deserved more than that. She deserved to be able to grill him about every step of every mistake he'd made. And he could give that control to her. Because he loved her. Which was something else he managed not to blurt out. Instead, he told her what she most needed to hear.

"I'm sorry." The tension lines eased around her eyes at those two words, so he said them again. "I screwed up and I'm *sorry*. Come upstairs and

I'll answer every question. Twice if I have to. Three times, even."

She didn't quite smile, but almost. And that was good enough to settle his heart rate. She nodded, heading to the back of the shop, while Asher hit the light switch and went to lock the front door. Before he could get there, it swung open, and Dan Adams walked in.

He was in full sheriff mode. Not just because he was in uniform, but because of his purposeful stride and grim expression. Apparently everyone was having a bad day today. As much as Asher wanted to help his friend, his priority was Nora.

"Not a good time, Dan. Nora and I were just..." He stopped when Dan looked across the room at Nora, and instead of smiling, his frown deepened.

"You *are* here, Nora. Good." There was nothing in Dan's tone that suggested he had anything approaching good news to deliver. In fact, those few words sent a chill down Asher's spine, and he didn't even know why. Nora must have felt the same shiver of dread, because her hand rose to her throat and she let out a soft sound of distress. Dan's face softened as he took a step toward her.

"There's no easy way to say this, Nora. There's been an accident. Becky's being airlifted to the hospital."

CHAPTER TWENTY-THREE

THE WAITING ROOM was cold. Nora couldn't understand why someone didn't turn up the heat. Why wasn't anyone else bundled up against the cold that had her shivering so hard she could barely think?

Asher and Michael stood by the doorway, silently staring off into space in their own private worlds—they didn't even have jackets on. Cathy was sitting in the corner, flipping through a magazine, her sweater folded over the chair. Her hands weren't shaking the way Nora's were. How could she not be shivering from the cold? Why wasn't she wearing her sweater?

Amanda came through the door with a cardboard tray of coffee for everyone. She was in short sleeves and seemed unconcerned, until she looked at Nora.

"Oh, honey, you're shaking like a leaf…" Her cousin handed the coffees to Cathy and hurried to Nora's side.

"Of course I'm shaking! It's colder than the ninth circle of Hell in here."

"No, sweetie, it's really not. You're just scared." Amanda grabbed Cathy's sweater and draped it over Nora's shoulders. "Everything's going to be fine."

Nora stared at her in horror, feeling hysteria bubbling up inside of her. "Don't say that! You don't know that! She's in surgery and she's *pregnant…*"

Cathy sat on Nora's other side. "Take a deep breath, Nora. And another one. You're having a panic attack. Breathe your way through it."

Nora closed her eyes and tried to do as she was told. But she felt so alone. She needed strong arms around her. She needed Asher's comfort, but he wasn't offering any. She looked up, and he quickly looked away from her. He had been almost totally silent since they got the news, tense and agitated.

She pulled away from Cathy's attempted embrace, channeling her fear into anger. Asher had never wanted the pregnancy to begin with. He'd tried to bribe Michael into leaving. That was why she'd been in his shop when Dan found them. He'd said he was going to explain, but how could he, really? And did it matter anymore, now that Becky was hurt and the doctors were trying to keep the baby safe and fix her badly broken arm at the same time?

Nora jumped to her feet and started pacing.

This anger felt stronger and more controllable than the shivering panic. And she was *so* angry. With God for allowing this to happen. With the texting teen who ran a stop sign and broadsided her daughter's car, then walked away without a scratch. With Michael for meeting with Daphne instead of driving Becky to the doctor. With Daphne for interrupting their lives. With her late husband for being such a flawed human being. With Asher for being such an idiot. With Cathy and Amanda for…well…she didn't have a reason to be mad at them, yet, but she'd think of something.

Amanda watched her, worry clouding her eyes. She started to recite the facts of the situation one more time, as if Nora cared. "The doctors said the surgery is safe. They're just setting her arm and putting a couple screws in her wrist, and then she'll be out. The broken ribs will heal on their own. She'll be okay. They're only keeping her overnight as a precaution."

Nora turned and glared at her cousin. "They're keeping her overnight because she had *contractions*. What if…?" She couldn't finish the sentence. Couldn't finish the thought. She felt completely isolated in her fear. Her daughter and grandson were in danger, and these people were just standing here, doing nothing.

No, that wasn't fair. She drew in a deep, shuddering breath, willing her tears back into their ducts, because she couldn't afford to cry. Michael stood against the wall, pale and grim, hands deep in his pockets, reminding her that she wasn't the only one with something to lose here. Amanda and Cathy loved her, and they loved Becky, too. And then there was Asher.

She stopped pacing, halting right in front of him and standing there until he couldn't ignore her any longer. He looked down, and the raw pain in his eyes almost made her stagger back. Then the dreaded shutters came down again, detaching him from the situation.

Her hand reached for his arm, and he flinched. Why hadn't she noticed before that he was like this? So brittle and ready to shatter?

"Asher." She whispered his name, and a flicker of emotion crossed his face before the mask fell again. She really needed him to be present right now. She squeezed his arm, but he stared out over her head. She didn't have the strength to delve into his emotions when her own were so overwhelming.

Amanda handed her a coffee and nudged her back to the sofa.

"I called Bree and Melanie. They're both ready to hop on a plane, but I told them to hold off until we know more." Nora nodded absently. "Blake's home with the kids, so I'll be here as long as you need me. He's been texting like crazy, worried about everyone and making calls to be sure all the best doctors are on the case. You know how he is—master of the universe."

Nora gave Amanda a thin smile, earning a wide one in return. "Blake does like to be the man in charge, doesn't he?" She glanced at Asher, still staring off into space. It stung that *he* wasn't stepping up and doing more than just standing there when she really needed him. When Michael needed his father.

The doctor appeared in the doorway, and the women jumped up and rushed at her. Michael was there, too, but Asher stepped back, sliding into the corner. Nora bit back her annoyance. She needed to hear about Becky and the baby before she dealt with him.

The doctor pulled off her flowered cloth cap and dark hair tumbled down her back. Her smile alone was enough for Nora to start breathing easier. Surely that smile meant something good. The doctor nodded to Nora.

"You're the mom, right? I'm Dr. Benson."

"Yes, Doctor. I'm Nora Bradford. How is…?"

"She's fine. She'll be in a cast for a while, but with any luck it'll come off before the baby arrives."

"And the baby?" Michael blurted out the question before Nora could.

"Her OB is with her now, but the contractions have stopped and the minor bleeding seems to have stopped, as well. We were worried about a placental abruption, where the placenta separates from the uterus. We'll monitor her closely, but right now things look okay. Are you Michael?"

He nodded, relief bringing some color back to his face.

"She's been asking for you. But be prepared, all of you. The airbags saved her, but they also left her with some facial abrasions. She looks worse than she is."

"How long will she be here?" Nora asked.

The doctor shrugged. "At least overnight. Possibly a few days if she develops any more symptoms of an abruption. That'll be up to Dr. Novak, her obstetrician." She smiled again. "I can only let one person at a time in Recovery. Do you want to see her?"

Nora nodded quickly, then turned to Michael. "I promise I just want to look at her and see for myself she's in one piece. Then you can go sit with her, okay?"

He dipped his head in quiet agreement, and she frowned. He was relieved, but he didn't exactly seem happy. She, on the other hand, was ready to dance across the ceiling in joy. Behind Michael, Asher leaned against the wall in stoic silence, with no apparent reaction at all to the news. She wasn't going to let the Peyton men bring her down. Her daughter and grandson were going to be okay.

The guys would catch up with the good news eventually and all would be well.

ASHER WAS RELIEVED when the waiting room finally emptied. Nora and Michael followed the doctor to Recovery. Cathy headed home after promising Nora she'd open the coffee shop in the morning. Amanda stepped out to call their cousins and grab a sandwich. And finally, *finally,* he was alone and able to breathe.

The past few hours had been surreal. Dan's arrival at the shop. The mad dash to the hospital. Nora's utter devastation. His son's frayed nerves. The tears, the prayers, the gathering of family and friends.

It was horrifyingly familiar.

How many times had he gotten a call and driven like a wild man to the hospital when Dylan took a bad turn? When the meds didn't work right. When the chemo only made him sicker. When the bone marrow transplant failed. When he died.

Asher had spent a lot of time in waiting rooms just like this one. People would mill around, trying to make each other feel better. Trying to cheer him up, as if he was supposed to be smiling while his son lay dying. The sad, knowing eyes of the hospital staff as they drifted in and out of Dylan's room and the waiting room and up and down the hallways. Everyone knew it was hopeless. But everyone kept trying to get Asher to feel *better* about it all.

He pushed off the wall with a dark curse and started pacing, much the way Nora had earlier. But it didn't work. The more he walked, the more the walls closed in on him. The more his hope evaporated. The more his doubts and fears clawed at the inside of his chest, screaming for release.

This. This was what happened when you loved someone. You gave them the power to fucking *destroy* you. Every breath they took could be their last, and where did that leave the people who loved them? It left them in ruin. That was where he was right now. In ruin.

He'd been a fool to think he had the strength to love again. He was no good at it. He'd used it all up on his son, and when Dylan died in his arms…when Dylan and God and everyone ignored Asher's pleas and ripped apart his world, his family, his life, his heart… Damn it, he had nothing left.

Nora had needed him, and he'd given her nothing. In the middle of her own pain, she'd reached out to comfort him, and he'd pulled away. His breathing was fast and shallow now, and something burned at the backs of his eyes. He'd pulled away from the woman he loved. He'd rejected her. Because he was *ruined*, and he'd eventually ruin her, too.

Asher spun and punched the wall, his fist leaving an indentation with the outline of his knuckles plainly visible. He had to get out of this place.

He was halfway down the hall when he heard Nora behind him.

"Asher! Wait up. Are you going to the cafeteria? I'm famished." He stopped but didn't turn around.

"Ash? What's wrong?" Her fingers on his arm felt like a branding iron, and he hissed as he yanked his arm free. She stepped in front of him and moved close enough that he couldn't avoid looking down into her amber eyes. She was killing him. The smell of her perfume. The temptation of her soft lips. The light of hope on her face after having seen her daughter.

She thought they were safe now. But he knew better. You were *never* safe.

"I'm leaving."

Her brows bunched in confusion. "Leaving? You mean, going home? Why not stay and we'll eat here together? I just saw Becky, and she's black-and-blue all over, but she..."

"I'm leaving, Nora."

"But you don't have to leave yet... Oh." Her

cheeks paled, then flamed bright red. "I see. You're leaving *me*. Is that what you're saying? You were just going to walk out and leave me without a word?"

His palms were sweating, and he rubbed them absently on his jeans. The fluorescent lights overhead lit the hallway in that cold hospital glow that made his skin crawl.

"I can't be here, Nora. Don't you get that? I can't be *here*. I'm no good for you. I'm not…" He wasn't whole. He'd only been kidding himself to think that he was. "I can't give you what you need. I was useless today, and you know it."

"Asher, you were *here*. I know it couldn't have been easy, but you were here. Please don't do this."

He moved to go around her. The door was right there, and he needed to be on the other side of it. The panic monster was clawing again, and his defenses were gone. She reached her hand out, but he grabbed her wrist roughly to stop her.

"Don't. I'm leaving. We both know it's the right thing. I'm not cut out for this." He gestured from her to the hospital humming around them. "I've done this once, and I failed then. I failed today. I've got to *go*."

"And what do I tell your son?" There was a cool edge to her voice, and he was glad. She should be angry. She should be chasing him away rather than trying to stop him.

"Tell him I can't do it." He released her hand. Instead of reaching out again, she let it fall to her side. "I can't do it, Nora. I can't."

He walked away, and she let him go. But not quietly.

"We're not done, Asher. We'll fix this."

He tossed his answer over his shoulder as he pushed the door open and left.

"Some things can't be fixed."

CHAPTER TWENTY-FOUR

NORA WALKED BACK to Becky's room in a cold rage. Not at Asher. Well, not completely. Her rage was primarily directed at the tragedy that left him thinking he had no choice but to leave. Dylan's death had left Asher frozen in a forever-grieving zone that convinced him he didn't deserve love or happiness.

She would have to do some thinking on this one and come up with a plan to help him find his way back into the light. She could do that. Despite his final words to her, she could fix this. Just like she could fix the Atlanta situation. Because a woman with a plan could fix anything, smiling or not.

She'd start with an email to Meredith on the Daphne Tomlin issue, with copies of a few of the receipts and records she'd kept that would prove Geoff's involvement with Paul's illegal gambling and, yes, even prostitutes. It should be enough to force Geoff to drop out of the governor's race. If not, Nora would give the proof to Daphne Tomlin herself and let the chips fall where they may. At least she'd be in control of the situation, instead of waiting for the inevitable. Either way, Geoff was finished. But if he dropped out now, the proof stayed buried and the reputation of the precious Bradfords would remain relatively untarnished.

And then she'd deal with Asher and knock some sense into him. She'd let him walk away today, but she wasn't letting him walk out of her life. This day wasn't going to be *that* disastrous. She wouldn't allow it.

Becky was finally moved to her own room around midnight. Michael and Nora both slept there on chairs, uncomfortable but unwilling to leave Becky alone. Her face was a bruised and swollen mess, her wrist had screws in it, there were monitors attached everywhere. But she was still her Becky. She was strong and beautiful, and she was a survivor.

Nora woke once during the night to find Michael standing near the bed, just staring at Becky with a strange expression. She whispered his name, and he started, then walked back to the chair by hers. He looked stricken.

"What's wrong?"

"God, Nora, she could have *died*," he whispered. "What would I have done? And the baby! What if something happens to the baby? What if Dad's right and I'm not ready for any of this?" Nora felt a fresh flare of anger at Asher. He'd planted those seeds of doubt in Michael's head based on his own fears.

"Michael, no one's ready for parenthood. But you'll figure it out."

He looked doubtful, but he nodded quietly and settled back in the chair, eventually falling asleep.

The doctors let Becky go home the following day, with strict orders for bed rest and careful monitoring of symptoms. Asher hadn't returned to the hospital, which was disappointing but not surprising.

But when Nora got back to Gallant Lake, she *was* surprised to see his shop closed and his truck nowhere in sight in the middle of the week. He didn't come back that night, either, and didn't respond to the handful of texts she sent him. She didn't want to become a stalker and text him endlessly, so she decided to wait him out.

It was Dan who disclosed Asher's whereabouts when he stopped at the shop for coffee the next morning.

"He said he was heading up to the cabin for a few days to 'think.'" Dan raised his fingers to make air quotes. "The hospital freaked him out, didn't it?"

Nora handed him his coffee. "Yes. I'm trying to give him space, but I don't know how much longer I can wait. He can't hide forever."

Dan sobered. "I don't know, Nora. Before you

got here, he'd been hiding in a bottle and in his work for years. He's pretty good at it."

She hadn't found time to come up with a plan for getting him back yet, having been too busy helping Becky and Michael. Things were tense in their little house. Michael was pulling an Asher act, all sullen and quiet. Which meant Nora's spare moments were filled with trying to keep Becky's spirits up.

In the meantime, her Atlanta plan had worked perfectly. Geoff had dropped out of the primary that morning, using some line about needing more family time. That conveniently left Tom Wilson without an opponent and guaranteed his primary win. Daphne could focus on destroying someone else's life now.

Nora was pretty sure she and Becky wouldn't be receiving any more invitations to holiday meals with the Bradfords, but that was fine with her. She'd just have to come up with some excuse to tell Becky.

She headed to Becky and Michael's house after the lunch crowd died down, with a basket full of sandwiches and sweets. Michael's Jeep was there when she pulled into the drive. She'd made sure to pack some of his favorite coconut macaroons, hoping they'd put a smile on *his* face, at last.

She heard Becky crying as soon as she walked through the door. She was curled up under a blanket on the sofa, with a mound of used tissues on the floor next to her.

"What's happened? Is the baby okay? Where's Michael?"

Nora fired off the questions as she rushed to Becky, checking her from head to toe.

"He left me, Mom."

"Who left?" She rested her hand on Becky's stomach. Much to her relief, she felt a strong kick against her hand.

"Michael. He's gone."

"No, honey. His Jeep is right outside."

Becky gave a harsh laugh. "Yeah, I know. He left it for me. He's on his way to his mom's house."

Nora wondered if Becky's medication might be causing delusions.

"But his mother lives in LA."

Becky nodded, blowing her nose loudly. California. Where Asher had wanted Michael to go in the first place.

"Tell me what happened, honey." Nora handed her fresh tissues from a box on the side table.

"He's been acting weird since the accident, pacing around and snapping at me whenever I asked what was wrong. Then, this morning, I saw him out back talking on his phone, and he came in and told me he was leaving. He said his father was right, that he wasn't ready to be a fa-

ther. The accident freaked him out, and he said
he couldn't deal with the thought of losing me or
the baby. He said we'd all be better off without
him *pretending* to be a father and a husband."

Becky's face crumpled. "That's what he said,
Mom. That he was pretending. That he didn't
want a family."

Nora sat on the edge of the sofa and pulled
Becky into her arms, letting her cry her heart out.

"I called him a coward and told him his dad
was a coward, too, and that they were both a couple of losers." She raised her head and looked up
at Nora, eyes full of pain. "I kicked him out! Oh,
my God, it's my fault he's gone."

"No, no, honey. It's not your fault at all. And
I'm sure he'll be back…"

"He *won't*. He showed me his ticket. His flight
leaves today. He's gone." Her eyes, even swollen and bruised, flashed with a healthy blaze of
anger. "But you're right, this isn't my fault. It's
your boyfriend's."

"No." But Nora knew it was true. After Asher's
meltdown at the hospital, he'd probably renewed
his efforts to convince his son to leave. And with
the fear Michael was feeling, he'd finally listened.

A dark maternal rage started to burn under
every inch of Nora's skin. Her daughter was now
pregnant and alone, just as Asher had wanted.
They'd had a chance at building a family, but

he'd betrayed her trust and ruined everything. She'd been a fool to give her heart to a man cold enough to do such a thing.

She eventually got Becky calmed down and fed, which helped her daughter's outlook somewhat. Amanda came over with little Maddie, providing a noisy, happy distraction. Once she saw a ghost of a smile on Becky's face and had Amanda's assurance that she'd stay as long as needed, Nora got in her car and drove up Gallant Mountain.

Her rage was all consuming. Michael had hurt her daughter. Because of Asher. Asher had left her in the hospital when she needed him most. Becky was going to be a single mother. Because of Asher. She almost missed the driveway to the mountain home and had to back up to make the turn. Her little car lurched and bumped up the road, and she didn't care. She was about to go apocalyptic on Asher Peyton.

HE WASN'T ALL that surprised to see Nora's silver car roaring up the drive. She wasn't the type to give up easily. He'd been adamant in the hospital, and at the time he was sure he'd been right to leave her. But his resolve had softened over the past couple of days, just enough that he was looking forward to seeing her. He'd still send her away, of course. He had to.

She was driving pretty fast considering she'd

never driven up here by herself. The little car bounced around, and he wondered why Nora wasn't hitting the brakes. But she managed to reach the top of the hill in one piece, bringing the car sliding to a halt that sent small stones flying.

He'd never realized she had such a lead foot. It was kind of hot. He shook that thought off and went out to meet her. Knowing Nora, she'd have a plan in place to win him back, and it would probably start with a kiss. He would stand strong, but he might let her get one kiss in. Just to have the memory.

She slammed the car door shut with surprising force. He bit back his smile, knowing she wouldn't like being laughed at. She walked toward him with purpose, her slender legs clad in tight jeans. A Gallant Brew T-shirt was pulled into a knot at her waist, hugging her curves just right. He was so busy admiring her swagger that he never saw the strike coming.

She slammed the heels of her hands hard into his chest, sending him staggering back and almost onto his ass. He caught himself with flailing arms, and she did it again, setting him back another step. By the time she moved in for hit number three, he was ready and grabbed her by the wrists, but she kicked out at him and connected with his shin.

"Ow! Damn it, Nora! What the hell is wrong with you?"

"You bastard! You finally got what you wanted, didn't you?" He didn't know what to do with her anger. He didn't know where it was coming from. Was she acting out because he'd left her? Had something else happened?

"Is Becky okay?"

Nora yanked away from him, her Southern accent deepening. "Don't you dare let her name come out of your mouth. Of *course* she's not okay! You've ruined everything, just as you planned all along."

His voice rose in frustration. "I don't know what the hell you're talking about!"

"Oh, my God, how could I ever have fallen in love with you?" He stepped toward her, but she held up her hands and shook her head, holding him back.

Nora's face paled, apparently realizing what she'd said.

"I'll get over it. Loving you. I'll get over it."

"No, don't say that. Tell me what happened."

"Are you seriously going to tell me you don't know Michael left?"

"Left? Left for where?"

"He's on his way to California, just like you wanted."

He turned to look out over the lake, unable to

meet her accusing glare. What had Michael done? What had *he* done? He turned back to her, holding out his hands in supplication.

"Come inside and tell me what happened. I swear I didn't know he was going to do this."

She walked sullenly into the house. When he closed the door and turned to face her, she was in the center of the great room, looking around at the unfinished space.

"You say you didn't know he'd do this, but isn't it exactly what you schemed? Didn't you bribe him to do it? And now he's finally listened to you. You must be so proud."

"I made that offer months ago, and he turned me down! He loved Becky so much, just like I…" He caught himself. This wasn't the time to be professing his love for her. Not when she was ready to throttle him. "Nora, that's what I was going to tell you the day of the accident. That I was going to make sure Michael knew I was withdrawing the offer. That I wanted him to stay with Becky and the baby." He ran his fingers through his hair, trying to make sense of everything. "Did he say he was leaving because of Stanford?" Guilt washed over him.

For the first time since she'd arrived, Nora hesitated. "No, not because of the offer specifically. But because of you. He told Becky you'd convinced him he wasn't ready to be a father or a husband. The accident scared him, and all he could think about was your shining example, Asher. The man afraid of love. And he ran. Like father, like son."

He stepped forward, but she shook her head. He wanted to hold her, but everything about her screamed "untouchable" right now.

"Becky said she called him a coward, and she was right. You're a coward, too." He flinched. The truth hurt. "Look around, Asher. This house. Your apartment. There's no family here. There's no love here. No warmth. Nothing soft. Nothing kind. No memories. No pictures on the walls. Do you even *have* any pictures of Michael and Dylan as children? If Dylan loved this place so much, why isn't there anything of him here? You've wiped away every shred of evidence that your family ever existed. How is Michael supposed to move on if you can't? You're so afraid of being hurt that you won't let yourself love."

"You're wrong."

Her head snapped back. "Really? When you left me, you said you 'couldn't do it.' You ran. Just like Michael is running. You convinced him he couldn't be a father, because *you* couldn't be a father. You convinced him he shouldn't be a husband, because *you* couldn't be one. And now I have a daughter who has to raise a child alone."

She shook her head. "No, not alone. She has

me. Because I'm not a coward. And we don't need either one of you." She walked past him without touching him. Her words shredded him. All he could do was breathe out her name. She turned when she reached the door.

"Don't call me. Don't come into my shop. Fix your own damned coffee. You told me you wanted no part of this baby, so you'll have no part of it. No part of me." She faltered on the last sentence. She shook her head sadly. "Except for the part I've already given you."

And she was gone. He stood there in the unfinished house and thought about the wreckage of his life. The shadows grew longer, and still he stood there. He didn't move until darkness had taken over, and even then all he did was light a fire and open a bottle of bourbon. He sat on the floor in front of the fireplace and drank.

He sat there the next day, too. And the next night. Just trying to kill the pain. Once in a while he'd pull something out of the freezer to eat, but the booze was killing his hunger. If only it would kill his pain. On the third day, or maybe the fourth, he was dimly aware of a door opening and closing somewhere.

"Nora?" His voice sounded like a croak. He hadn't spoken in a while.

"Christ, man. You're a mess."

Strong hands grabbed him under the arms and

Dan pulled him to his feet. "Come on, let's get some coffee and food into you. It's time to snap the hell out of it and get your head out of your freakin' ass."

THE FIRST THOUGHT Asher had as he walked up to his ex-wife's home was that her new life seemed to be going pretty well. The sprawling midcentury home sat high in the hills overlooking LA. On a sunny day like today, the Pacific was visible, blue and glittering in the distance. Michael had told him once that Amy's new husband was a producer or something.

She opened the door before he got to the front steps. She looked different—thinner, with shorter hair—but she was still the same Amy. Tall and tanned, she leaned against the door frame and folded her arms, probably ready for a fight, since that was all they'd done at the end of their marriage. But when she spoke, her voice brought back memories of times when her laughter, as she played with their boys in the yard, had been the most precious thing in his world.

"You came to take Michael back."

Asher stopped at the base of the steps.

"He's a grown man, Amy. I can't *take* him anywhere. But there's a girl in New York who needs him." It was too late to salvage his relationship with Nora, but he could at least save his son from making the same stupid mistake.

She nodded. "I figured. He won't say much about it, but he's miserable. What happened?"

"*I* happened. Michael followed my sterling example, and he ran. I have to make it right, Amy. He belongs with Becky and the baby."

"So you're into family reunions now, after all this time." The words were sharp, but her voice softened the blow. They'd loved each other once. Really loved each other. They just hadn't been able to love each other through the death of their son.

"You're happy here?"

She nodded. "It took some time, but yes."

"We gave up too easily, you and I." Her eyes went wide in surprise at his words. "We were tired and angry and sad and we just gave up on each other. We should have fought harder."

The only sound was the breeze pushing through the palms. Amy straightened and motioned for him to come inside.

"We should have. But we didn't. There's no going back, Asher."

"No. But we can help our boy learn how to fight instead of giving up like we did."

Michael was by the pool, fully dressed, sitting in a lounge chair and staring off into space. Asher watched him from the doorway and saw the tight set of his jaw beneath his beard. The hands that clenched and unclenched over and over. The eyes, sunken and dull.

"Holy shit, it's like looking in a mirror." He muttered the words softly, and Amy squeezed his shoulder.

"He's his father's son. Stubborn and proud."

He met her dark-eyed gaze. "You should see him with Becky, the way he loves her. He has your heart, Amy. Thank God, because my heart's not worth a damn." And he'd given it away to Nora.

"I appreciate that, Ash. But you were that guy when we met. You were our protector."

"I couldn't protect us from everything."

Her face was solemn. "No. And I shouldn't have expected you to. You're right—we gave up on each other too easily. But that's done, and we still have one son left. And as much as I love seeing him, he doesn't belong in LA." She gave him a sad smile. "Take him home."

Michael did a double take when he saw Asher walking toward him. In his worn jeans and plaid shirt, he was out of place on the elegant poolside patio, surrounded with palms and exotic flowers.

"Dad? What are you doing here?"

Asher sat at the tile-topped table nearby, gesturing for Michael to join him in the shade of the brightly striped umbrella. He started to protest, but Asher just pointed to the chair nearest him and arched a brow, daring his son to push his luck.

Michael moved to the table. Neither spoke, setting an undeclared challenge to see who'd break first. Asher finally shook his head. Age could easily defeat youth on this one, but that wasn't why he was here.

"I think the bigger question is—what are *you* doing here, son?"

Michael swallowed hard. "You know why I'm here. It was *your* idea."

"Damn it, Michael, I didn't want this. That's why I wanted to meet with you the day of the accident. I saw you with that blonde, and I knew I'd been steering you wrong. You fought *me* all this time to stay with Becky. Don't quit on her now."

"Did everyone in the whole damned town see me with her?"

"Who was she, anyway?"

"She was from Atlanta, trying to cause trouble in some political campaign down there."

"She was looking for dirt on Becky's father? His gambling? His cheating?"

"You *knew* about that? Oh, of course. Nora told you. Why did everyone assume I was cheating on Becky? I'd never do that!"

"And yet you had no problem walking out on her."

"No *problem*? You're kidding, right?" Suddenly Michael became Asher's little boy again, his voice dropping to a plea. "How is she, Dad?"

"She's okay. But she's unhappy, son. She doesn't understand your actions. No one does."

"You understand."

Asher sighed, staring at the ground while weighing his next words.

"You told her you left because of me."

"Not exactly. But I did tell her you were right about me not being ready. Dad, when I saw her in the hospital...when I realized we could have lost the baby...I couldn't take it. All I could hear was you telling me I didn't know what I was getting into. And you were *right*. I'm not ready. I can't be what she needs."

"Do you love her?"

Michael didn't hesitate. "More than anything."

"Do you love the baby?"

"So much it hurts."

"Does the thought of losing them terrify you?"

"It's a fucking nightmare."

Michael's face fell, and tears glistened in the corners of his eyes. Asher's heart was heavy. He'd led his son so far down the wrong path, sharing everything he'd learned from loss without sharing anything he'd learned from love.

"Do you wish you'd never had a brother?"

Michael bolted upright, his jaw rigid, eyes

blazing. "What a shitty thing to ask, Dad! I *loved* Dylan."

Asher nodded. "We all loved Dylan. And you and I have let him down."

"No. That's a lie."

"Michael, I've told a lot of lies, but that's not one of them. I've lied to myself. I've lied to you. I convinced myself the pain I felt was because I'd *loved*. There's some truth to that, but I carried it even further. I convinced myself I could avoid that pain by never loving again. And I tried to protect you by convincing you of the same thing. I lied when I said you weren't ready for love. We're born ready for love. It's how we're wired."

A warm gust of wind rustled through the palms above them. "Here's the thing, kid. Love is risky. But without it, we're just… We're nothing. We're empty. We're cowards who end up hurting people."

He looked up to the sky and choked back the emotion that suddenly clogged his throat. Where had those greeting-card words come from? Why was Nora's face the only thing he could see? And Dylan's voice the only thing he could hear? Was he losing his mind? No. Conviction settled over him. He was getting it back.

"We loved Dylan. Imagine how disappointed he must be watching the two of us scurrying away from love like it's some kind of monster."

Michael's brows came together as he worked through what Asher was saying. "So you tried to get me to leave Becky because of *Dylan*? You were afraid I'd lose her or the baby, because you lost *him*? But, Dad, you were right. It could happen, and I don't know if…"

"Can you live without them?"

He blew out a long breath. "I don't think so, Dad. It's killing me to be away from Becky."

"Then go back to her, Michael."

"But the risk…"

"Is worth it."

They sat in silence for a while before Michael spoke again.

"I'll go back. I don't know that I have a choice. I love her that much." He looked at Asher. "And what about you and Nora?"

His heart squeezed so tight he thought it might just stop. He tried to sound unconcerned.

"What about me and Nora?"

"Come on, Dad. I've seen the way you guys look at each other. Have you told her yet that you love her?"

"It doesn't matter. She left me."

Michael looked stricken. "Because of me? Because of what I said to Becky?"

Asher shrugged one shoulder. "She called me on all my bullshit. The unfinished house. My unfinished life. The way I tried to bribe you to abandon her pregnant daughter. She was pretty pissed off in general. And the whole coward thing came into play."

"But you love her."

"Yes."

"Then what the hell, Dad? Practice what you preach and fight for her."

He shook his head slowly. "It's too late."

"Really? Quitting again, Asher?" Amy walked up with a pitcher of lemonade and glasses on a tray. "So you're enlightened enough to recognize your mistakes but not enough to keep from making them again?"

"Amy, you don't understand."

She settled into a chair. "We let our love story die. If either one of us had bothered to fight for the marriage after Dylan died, we'd be together today. So if you've got a second chance at love, you'd better grab it."

"Just showing up won't be enough. She's had it. She's tired of my issues."

"Then fix your issues, Asher. Show her you know what went wrong and you're ready to change."

There's no family here. There's no love here. No warmth. Nothing soft. Nothing kind. No memories. No pictures on the walls.

He looked at Michael and smiled. "I may need some help, son."

"Whatever you need, Dad. It's what Dylan would want."

Nora wasn't the only Fixer in Gallant Lake. He could fix a few things, too, starting with himself.

CHAPTER TWENTY-FIVE

"NORA? ARE YOU trying to test the paint job on that thing?"

She flinched, snapping out of her scrambled, shadowy thoughts. Her hand was moving a cloth in small circles, wiping the espresso maker in the same spot over and over. Cathy stood at the doorway to the kitchen, shaking her head. It wasn't the first time Cathy had caught her completely zoned out this week. Between all the time she'd been spending with Becky trying to lift her daughter's spirits, running the café and missing Asher with every breath she took, she was exhausted.

Cathy had been annoyingly upbeat today, as if she could cheer Nora up just by being cheerful herself. She couldn't see that Nora's pain was soul deep. She'd given her heart to a man who'd turned his son against her daughter and ripped two relationships apart.

And she *missed* him. What was *wrong* with her?

"Who'd have thought I'd ever be lecturing you on cleaning?"

Nora gave Cathy a thin smile, trying to calculate how many hours were left in the day. This week had seemed endless.

"Yes, you've come a long way, Cathy." Nora tried to maintain the light tone, but she didn't have the heart for it, and her voice dropped an octave. "Or maybe I've just gone backward."

"Oh, sweetie, don't think like that." Cathy gave her a quick hug. "You're doing just fine. That idiot neighbor of yours has to come back sometime, and..."

Nora stepped back, shaking her head vehemently.

"I don't care if he comes back or not." *Liar.* "It makes no difference to me." *Liar.* "He's nothing to me." *Double liar.*

"Wow, you're, like, the worst liar in the world, cuz."

Amanda stood at the counter with Blake by her side, his arm casually draped over his wife's shoulders. That small act of affection was enough to prick Nora's heart, but it was just one of a million similar injuries that organ had received over the past week. Seeing couples together. Hearing some random love song. Seeing Asher's darkened furniture studio, or his back door locked up tight. Having someone order black coffee with raw sugar and a shot of espresso, the way Asher liked it.

"Jeez, she's even worse than you said, Cathy."

"Yeah, it's pretty sad to watch," Cathy agreed.

Blake's voice was solemn, but there was a glint of humor in his eyes. "Maybe we should come up with a plan."

Were her closest friends and family *mocking* her?

"I'm glad you all find this so terribly amusing!" She threw the cleaning cloth down on the counter and started to walk away, but Amanda ran around and caught her arm, pulling her in tight.

"Sorry, sorry! You know we all love you. But seriously, girl, you are a hot mess! Your skin looks like you're half zombie. Those dark bags under your eyes could hold my weekend wardrobe. Have you even changed your clothes this week? And your hair! Come on, we're going upstairs and putting you back together."

"First, thanks for the pep talk, which you suck at, by the way. Second, there is no 'putting me back together.'" Nora swallowed hard. "Look, I know you guys are trying to cheer me up or snap me out of it or whatever. I practically *invented* fixing things, remember? I'm the original 'smile and a plan' girl. But this is different. In my head I know time will make it hurt less and someday I'll look back on this and laugh…" She hiccuped as her throat filled. "Oh, God, Asher was right.

I *do* sound like a greeting card!" The tears that had been threatening all week finally overflowed.

Amanda chuckled. "That's pretty funny—you do sound like a greeting card a lot of the time."

Nora started to cry in earnest, sloppy and loud.

"Okay, let's get you upstairs and bring you back to the living, zombie princess."

Nora allowed herself to be led away, wiping her tears with the back of her hand, too tired and sad to argue.

AN HOUR LATER, she had to admit it *did* feel better to be freshly showered and wearing clean, pressed clothes from her closet. She'd been staying at Becky's place while they debated what to do, and she'd packed the bare minimum. Should Becky move here to the apartment, or should Nora move to the house and take over the lease there? She forced the question from her mind. She wasn't going to deal with any of that now. She was just going to sit here at the kitchen island and let her cousin take care of her.

Amanda seemed downright thrilled to be there, warming up some soup and grilling ham-and-cheese sandwiches. She kept humming to herself and sneaking glances at Nora, then smiling before turning back to the stove. She'd all but dressed Nora herself, insisting on skinny jeans and a dark gold sweater when Nora would have preferred sweats. But it was so nice being pampered that she hadn't argued.

When Amanda set the plate in front of her, Nora suddenly felt guilty. It wasn't easy for Becky to prepare anything with her arm in a cast.

"What are you fretting about now?" Amanda asked, sitting next to Nora with her own plate.

She took a bite of the sandwich. "This is great, but I'll have to run as soon as I eat. Becky needs dinner, too."

"Becky's being taken care of, so slow down and enjoy the meal." Amanda grinned at Nora's questioning look. "We're having a meal delivered to her from the resort."

Her cousin was practically bouncing in her seat. Something was going on, but Nora couldn't imagine what...

"Oh, my God, Amanda, are you *pregnant*?"

Amanda nearly choked on her soup, looking horrified.

"*Me?* Pregnant? Uh, no. Two kids are enough, thank you very much." She set her napkin back in her lap. "But rumor has it Bree may be expecting."

Nora nodded. "Yeah, but that's not what has you anxious as a long-tailed cat on a porch full of rocking chairs. You keep looking at the door like you're expecting someone. Is Blake coming up?" Amanda had prepared only two plates. They both took another bite of their sandwiches.

"No, Blake's headed back to Halcyon to meet Zach's bus. I'm just happy to see you relaxing. You've spent too much time being the caregiver, and not enough taking care of yourself."

"Becky needs me, Amanda. Her idiot fiancé left her alone and pregnant at eighteen. I'll probably end up having to move into the house with her and rent this apartment out, if you know of anyone looking for a place." She looked around, sad at the thought of leaving the home she'd just finished creating for herself.

"If I were you, I'd wait before making any plans."

The knock at the door made Nora jump, but Amanda didn't seem surprised at all. In fact, she seemed relieved. She swallowed the last piece of her sandwich and went to answer it. As she did, she gave Nora a serious look over her shoulder.

"Promise me you'll sit and listen, sweetie."

Before Nora could respond, the door opened and Michael stepped into the apartment. Nora jumped to her feet, ignoring Amanda's hand signal to stay put.

"Michael! What…"

"Nora, please. I know you're angry, and you have every right to be. I made a really stupid mistake. I'm so sorry."

Her maternal instinct wasn't ready to let down its guard. "I'm not the one you should be apologizing to." She glanced around. Amanda was nowhere to be seen. She must have slipped out when Michael came in. Nora frowned. She'd been set up.

"I've already apologized to Becky. In fact, I *groveled* to Becky for the past two hours. And she forgave me, thank God." He took another step. "I just left her at the house. I had to come talk to you."

She couldn't help being skeptical. "You came all the way home from California to apologize to her, and then you left her alone to come talk to me? Are you just on an apology tour and leaving again?"

He shook his head. For the first time, she noticed the dark circles under his eyes, and that he'd lost weight since she saw him last. She fought back the urge to offer him something to eat.

"I'll never leave Becky again. *Ever.* I made a huge mistake. But someone convinced me to fix it."

"Your mother."

He shook his head again.

"My father."

Nora sat down abruptly. Michael sat at her side and gave her a tentative smile.

"You're surprised." She nodded. "I was, too." He reached out and rested his hand lightly over

Nora's. It wasn't intimate, but more like he wanted to make sure she didn't run.

"He's changed, Nora. He never wanted me to leave Becky. I mean, he did want me to, in the beginning. But he changed. *You* changed him. That night at the hospital, everything was such a clusterfu... I mean...a mess. I saw Becky, all bruised and broken, then Dad freaked out and left, which freaked *me* out." He swallowed hard. "I thought of everything I had to lose, and I panicked. You were right when you told Dad he and I were cowards."

She cringed at the memory of throwing those words at Asher in the mountain house. She'd been so hurt and angry.

"Dad told me we were dishonoring Dylan's memory."

Nora squeezed her eyes shut, trying to hold back her emotions. Asher had talked to Michael about Dylan. That was a huge step.

"What did he mean by that?"

"He said he originally didn't want Becky and me to have the baby because he was afraid something would happen to the baby, and then I'd have to go through what he went through." Michael scrubbed hard at his beard. "He said he loved me so much that he didn't want *me* to love, which is messed up. But he *admitted* it was messed up. He said Dylan would kick our asses if we kept hiding from love." Michael's eyes met hers. "He told me love is a huge risk, but that it's always worth it. Love is worth fighting for. Love is worth anything."

Michael shifted on the seat uncomfortably. "I promised Becky I'll never run away again. And I'll never hide my feelings from her. I'll always be honest with her. I told her about that political worker, Nora. I told her everything."

"Michael, no!" All those years of keeping secrets, of building a legend around Paul's memory so his daughter would always love him. She'd given up her home and moved here to protect Becky. She'd forced Geoff to drop out of the race. And Michael had just brought it all crashing down.

"She *knew* already. She knew *everything*. She'd seen stuff on the internet and heard her uncles talking, and as she told me in no uncertain terms, she's not stupid." Michael squeezed her hand. "She still loves her dad, but she knows who he was and what he did. All this time you thought you were protecting her, and she was staying quiet to protect *you*."

Nora could barely breathe. She'd been an idiot to think her clever daughter wouldn't figure things out for herself. That she couldn't handle the truth.

"I need to talk to her." But Michael shook his head.

"Not today. I still have plenty of groveling left to do. And you have someone else you need to see."

She stared at him in confusion.

"You need to talk to my dad." She jumped up and backed away, shaking her head vehemently. "He knows he screwed up. But he *loves* you, Nora. He's on the mountain, and he needs you to give him a chance. Becky and I will be fine with you two being together—you guys belong together as much as she and I do, and screw what anyone else thinks. Please give him a chance…"

She held up her hands as if she could stop the words from piercing her heart. "I can't. He can't love me, Michael. Not the way I…" She stopped. She didn't know if she could handle being hurt by him again. It might be too big a risk.

Maybe she deserved better.

But she wanted Asher.

She grabbed her car keys.

CHAPTER TWENTY-SIX

THE FIRST THING Nora noticed as she drove up the private road to the log house was that the road had been graded and the holes filled. She was no longer at risk of cracking her head on the door as she maneuvered the winding route. The second thing she noticed were the solar lights that had been added all along the drive, making it much easier to follow.

When she rounded the final turn, she was amazed to find lights shining from every window in the house. It looked welcoming instead of vacant. And in some of the windows—were those *curtains*? She parked the car and walked to the door. There were four rocking chairs on the porch. And a swing at the far end. There was a doormat at the door, with little woodland animals on it.

She looked out over the lake, wondering for a minute if she was at the wrong place. She didn't see Asher's truck anywhere, but it could have been in the garage. The door was ajar, so she stepped inside, calling out his name. But her voice failed her as she took it all in.

The floors had been swept clean. The walls had been painted a warm beige. There were rugs down. And furniture. Lots of furniture. Big, over-stuffed chairs by the hearth. A sofa by the window. A desk in the corner. Lamps glowed softly throughout the room. The kitchen had cheery curtains at the window and bright towels hanging on the oven door. Something was cooking, and it smelled delicious. A round cherry dining table she knew Asher must have made was set for two. But where was he?

She walked up the spiral staircase in a daze, wondering how he could possibly have done all of this. She pushed open the door to the master suite. There was a massive wooden bed in the corner, facing the windows that looked out over the lake. It was flanked by two nightstands, both with lamps gleaming brightly. The walls were painted a mossy green that matched the pines outside. A huge oriental rug covered most of the plywood floor, and silk curtains framed the windows. A low-backed prairie-style loveseat was in front of the fireplace, and on one flat wooden arm were a bottle of cognac and two glasses. She walked to the hearth, where a fire was burning. That was when she saw them.

Pictures. The wall near the fireplace was cov-

JO McNALLY   371

ered with framed photographs of all sizes. There were pictures of Michael as a child with thick, dark hair like his father, and pictures of a laughing little sandy-haired boy. Dylan. The photos showed the boys at a theme park. Swimming in the lake. Playing computer games together in a hospital bed. Asher was in some of the photos, his smile so wide in the early ones that it made her heart ache all the more for everything he'd lost.

And there was a picture of Becky as a little girl, giggling in Nora's arms. Another of Becky riding in a horse show. Where did he get these? There was another, of Becky's graduation, with Nora smiling proudly at her side. There were photos of Michael and Becky together, hiking and snowboarding. And one of them standing on the lakeshore at sunset.

There was a large photo in the center of the collection. It was of her and Asher together. They were in profile, with Nora standing in front, leaning back against Asher's chest. They were on the veranda at Halcyon. She was smiling out at the lake, and he was smiling down at her. Amanda must have taken it. It was beautiful. The whole wall was beautiful. It was family.

She picked up a small framed photo from the mantel. She could hardly see it through her tears, but she knew what it was. It was Becky's sonogram. It was the next generation of this family. Of *their* family. She heard the door opening downstairs, and Asher calling her name. Before she could answer, his feet were taking the stairs two at a time. And then he was there in the doorway. His blue eyes lit up when he saw her holding the little picture.

Instead of a flowery declaration of love, he blurted out a flurry of nonsense.

"I thought I had dinner all planned, but I forgot dessert, so I called the resort and talked the chef into parting with some of his tiramisu, but it took me longer to get there than I thought it would, and I was scared to death that I'd miss you. Then I saw the truck was low on gas, and I didn't dare come back here without filling up, and I thought for sure you'd turn around and leave if you didn't see my truck here. I was going to call, but of course I left my damn phone here and..."

Her fingers on his lips brought the rush of words to an abrupt stop.

"Breathe, Asher. You didn't miss me. I didn't leave." She glanced around the room again in wonder. "How did you do all this?"

He covered her hand with his, kissing her palm. His eyes closed tightly during the kiss, then opened again as he continued to hold her hand, as if afraid to let her go.

"I've been back for three days. Michael was

here with me until today. Dan's pretty much been living here with a paintbrush in his hand. Blake and Amanda helped. Most of the furniture is borrowed." He grinned. "Your cousin has a friend who runs a showroom in White Plains. We loaded up a truck and even borrowed some of their display curtains. There's a lot of smoke and mirrors involved here, and a lot of it has to be returned, but I wanted you to see this as a home. I wanted you to see that I'm *ready* for it to be a home. I wanted you to see that I'm ready to be the man you deserve, Nora. That I'm..."

"Asher, stop talking." She started to laugh. She hadn't heard Asher string this many words together for as long as she'd known him. "You've convinced me. The furniture may be temporary, but that's not what's making this look like a home. It's love."

"God, I love you so much, Nora. I think I started falling for you the minute you sassed me in the grocery store when I was being such a curmudgeon. You were this tiny little thing with all that attitude topped off with a Southern accent, and I couldn't stop thinking about you." His smile faded. "I did my best to ruin things between us, but you wouldn't let me. And then, at the hospital..."

She held back the urge to rush in and reassure

him. It was important for him to say this. He cupped her face with his hands.

"I'm so damned sorry, Nora. I hurt you. I hurt Michael and Becky. I let my friends down. I let Dylan's memory down. But I love you, and no matter what happens in the future, I'll never run again. You're stuck with me, if you'll have me."

There was a beat of silence before Nora answered.

"I started falling for you the minute I heard you barking out all those swear words in the produce section, looking so lost and angry…and hot." The corner of his mouth lifted into a crooked grin. "You'll always be my Hot Produce Guy. And I will always love you."

Their lips came together, and there was no way to know who started what. It was a blazing kiss that quickly flamed into clothing landing on the floor and hands moving over bare skin. He nudged her toward the bed, but Nora dug in her heels.

"First, is dinner going to burn the house down anytime soon?"

"First? You mean, you have a list? While we're naked?"

She didn't move, and he finally relented, kissing her playfully on the nose. "I turned it to low when I came in just now, so it'll be fine. Although if we stand here and talk too long, it'll be mighty dry. What's second on this list of yours?"

She wrinkled her nose. "Is that a borrowed mattress?"

He laughed. "I bought the mattress and the bedding is new. But I'll build us a new bed, Nora. One that's just for this room. Just for us." She nodded. "Any more questions on that list?"

"Just one. Do you mind if we don't use the bed? Can we stay here by the fire, like the first time?"

He didn't answer, just turned and pulled her down to the floor with him. He grabbed some pillows from the loveseat, then turned to kiss her again, but she held her hand up to stop him.

"I hope you don't mind, but I have a new list."

He hesitated, then nodded, as if resigned to his fate.

"Whatever you need, babe. What's on this list?"

She kissed the base of his throat, making him groan softly.

"It's a list of all the things I want you to do to me tonight. Are you ready to get started?"

Asher laughed, low and soft, and Nora knew that she'd remember this moment, and that laugh, forever.

"I'm ready, Nora. Let's get started."

EPILOGUE

May 26

"YOU ARE SO BEAUTIFUL, BABY."

Nora smiled, her hand slowly sliding up Asher's arm to rest on his shoulder. The depth of emotion in those five simple words brought tears to her eyes. His voice was rough with it, his own eyes glistening with moisture. He swallowed hard before continuing.

"Your skin is so soft. You smell so good. And I love you so much."

She squeezed his shoulder gently, stepping closer to gaze at the tiny baby in his arms.

"He really is perfect, isn't he?"

Charles Dylan Peyton made a gurgling sound, scrunching his face and moving his hands, pushing the soft blue blanket aside. Nora couldn't resist reaching over to touch those little fingers.

Doctor Bartlett to Radiology. Doctor Bartlett to Radiology, please.

The monotone voice on the hospital's paging system was an abrupt reminder of where they were standing. She glanced up at Asher, and he smiled. He'd been smiling a lot lately, and nonstop this morning, even after a sleepless night in the hospital waiting room.

"Stop worrying about me every time that happens, Nora. There's no place on earth I'd rather be than in this hospital today." Charles fussed some more, his face turning bright pink. Asher started bouncing gently to quiet the baby. He was going to be an amazing grandfather. He had so much love to give, and now that they'd broken him free from the chains of his grief, he was so eager to give that love.

Michael came into the room and handed Becky a glass of juice. They both looked exhausted. He kissed her, then joined Nora and Asher. Like his father, Michael hadn't stopped smiling, tired or not.

"He sounds like he's getting hungry. I'll take him…" He reached for Charles, and Nora stepped away and pulled her phone out to take a picture of three generations of Peytons. There was a moment of silent communication between the two men that was so powerful she had to look away. It was far too personal to capture in a photo. Asher handed the baby to Michael, then clapped him on the shoulder in his version of a man hug.

"I don't know if I've said this yet, son, but I'm proud of you."

"Mom, you're leaking again." Becky was laughing, her voice husky after seven hours of labor last night. She still had a cast on her arm, but it would come off next week. Her hair was pulled up off her face, her skin still blotchy from the long night. She'd never looked more lovely.

"You're a mommy now, too, and trust me, you'll be leaking a lot in the years to come. I just hope your tears are from joy, like these are." Becky nodded and yawned. "You need some rest, sweetheart."

For once, her strong-willed daughter didn't argue. "I'm *so* tired. But first Charlie needs his midmorning snack."

Becky and Michael had chosen his name to honor both families—the Charles was for Nora's father. Michael helped Becky get the baby settled in for a meal. They might be young, but they were naturals at this. In just a few months, they'd be married—another Halcyon wedding.

Asher leaned into the corner by the window, watching his family. He winked at her and she went to join him, wiping her cheeks with the back of her hand. Asher pulled her close, locking his arms around her stomach. She rested back against him and he nuzzled his nose into her hair.

"You're leaking, Grandma."

"Happy leaks. Look at them, Ash. Look at our two beautiful children and their baby."

"That baby has done some pretty incredible things, and he's not even a day old yet."

She twisted to look up at him, not sure what he meant.

"Think about it. We would have been nothing more to each other than the memory of a brief encounter in the produce section. Without Charlie, I don't think you would have moved to Gallant Lake, scandal or not."

She nodded against his chest. The baby had been a major factor in her decision.

"You wouldn't own your own business. We wouldn't have fallen in love. I wouldn't have had the chance to be such a dumbass that you dumped me, which was the wake-up call I'd needed for years. I never would have finished the house we'll soon be living in."

"And not one of those things was scheduled in my planner."

"Well," he said, laughing softly, "a *little* planning is okay. In fact, I'm thinking you might want to start planning *two* weddings this year instead of just one."

Her heart jumped, and she turned her head to kiss him quickly on the cheek. But he caught her by the chin and kissed her back, sweet and tender, his mouth lingering on hers. She spoke against him.

"You're asking me to plan something? I thought it was all about the journey?"

It was only two weeks ago that she'd walked into the café to find Cathy's old poster hanging behind the register again, but in a fresh new custom-made frame.

Life is about the journey, not the destination.

"You're right, Nora. It's all about enjoying the journey. And I can't imagine a better traveling companion than you."

* * * * *

If you loved this story, be sure to check out Jo McNally's first book in
THE LOWERY WOMEN
Superromance miniseries

SHE'S FAR FROM HOLLYWOOD

*Available now from Superromance.
And look for more from Jo McNally in 2018!*

Get 2 Free Books,

Plus 2 Free Gifts—

just for trying the Reader Service!

HARLEQUIN *Romance*

Get 2 Free Books,
Plus 2 Free Gifts—
just for trying the Reader Service!

Get 2 Free Books,
Plus 2 Free Gifts—
just for trying the Reader Service!

♥ HARLEQUIN®

HEARTWARMING™

HW17R